THE SAGES
OF OAK PLACE

ISBN 978-1-62806-403-2 (print | paperback)
ISBN 978-1-62806-404-9 (ebook)

Library of Congress Control Number 2024904768

Published by Salt Water Media
29 Broad Street, Suite 104
Berlin, MD 21811
www.saltwatermedia.com

Cover artwork by Derek Lingle

THE SAGES
OF OAK PLACE

Carolyn Stegman

Cliff
To life!. Carolyn

To Annalise and Gwendolyn
May you grow old in a world filled with Oak Places

She shuffles, bent over, behind her walker,
remnants of last night's dinner on her blouse.
Her grandchildren are hesitant to touch her.
They do not know that it was she,
who cooked countless spaghetti dinners for causes,
knitted sweaters for the oppressed, and
said "yes, I will serve" over and over again.
In her own small way, without fanfare,
she humbly impacted lives.
Yet, much of who she was and what she did
—the quintessential unsung—
will very likely go to the grave with her.

CS

SPRING 2018

—

CHAPTER 1

Unscheduled and uninvited, two stern-looking men wearing dark suits entered Katherine's open-doored office, commanding her full attention. An anxious secretary, unable to stop them, trailed behind. Katherine, on the phone, looked up from her desk before aborting the call mid-sentence. "Ah—Gotta go!"

"I'm FBI Agent Walker. This is Agent Gultowski." They flashed identification robotically—first horizontally to show the badges, then vertically to display their photos—before abruptly snapping the wallets closed. "Are you in charge here?"

"Yes, I am." While Katherine replied in the calmest voice she could muster, she was unnerved by their intimidating introduction. She motioned for them to sit down. They remained standing. Katherine rose from her chair. If they weren't going to sit, she would stand as well.

"What's your full name and title, please?" Walker asked.

"Dr. Katherine Eich, CEO of Oak Place." Katherine's voice was steady as she approached them from behind her desk. She extended her hand. They made no move to shake it, intensifying the awkwardness. Just as well, she rationalized, as her palms were already beginning to sweat.

"We understand you have a patient here by the name of Stella Cordrey. We need to speak with her."

"We have a *resident* here by that name, and she lives in our assisted living complex. Ms. Cordrey just moved in a couple of weeks ago."

"We need to ask Ms. Cordrey some questions. Is she competent?"

"I believe so," said Katherine, knowing Stella was fully competent but suddenly feeling cautious about conveying any type of medical diagnosis. Despite the bullying first impression of these two thirty-something men, she asked, "Look, what's going on?"

"That's confidential."

Oh, come on, she thought. *Really?* "Then why are you here in the administrative offices? Why didn't you go directly to her apartment?"

"We don't know where that is. We need you to take us to her."

Katherine had recently spent some time with Stella, as she made a point of meeting all new residents, in groups or individually. Stella had fascinated her. At eighty-three, looking like a gray-haired Katherine Hepburn, she proudly displayed her rouged wrinkled cheeks, red lipstick, and matching nail polish. Ornate combs secured her long, still thick, curly hair close to the nape of her neck. She was charming and feisty, her confidence on display.

"I might be a bit disabled, but I'm not ready to sit in this chair and watch TV all day," Stella had told Katherine. "I've never been one to let life pass me by."

Indeed, Stella was still relishing life. And what a life she had lived: well-educated, extensively traveled, with an abundance of stories of lavish dinners with United Nations diplomats. Katherine got the impression that Stella, exercising flawless manners and grace, could converse intelligently with any head of state.

Unfortunately, a broken hip followed by post-surgical complications had seriously curtailed Stella's physical activities and turned her Manhattan apartment into an obstacle course. She knew she needed ongoing assistance but rejected hiring a paid caregiver "to loom over" her every move. "What I don't want is to be smothered!" she had proclaimed. "Assisted living in this fine place will suit me, at least for now."

Katherine directed her assistant to call Stella about the impending visit. But Agent Wilson intervened, demanding she not do that.

"She might not be home," Katherine told them. "Oak Place residents are free to come and go. And if you're worried about Ms. Cordrey escaping, she paces at about fifty yards per hour with her walker." She stared right into Wilson's eyes to assess if he understood the sarcasm, which, of course, he did.

Since no golf carts were available, Katherine decided to walk the agents to the assisted living complex through the expansive, botanical-like gardens nestled between the high-rise buildings of Oak Place. Despite the background sounds of Queens, New York—honking cars, shifting gears of trucks, and a lone siren—this oasis seemed to absorb them and lessen the daily invasive noises of city life. One enthusiastically chirping house wren boldly defied the racket that attempted to drown out its song. Whiffs of freshly spread mulch perfumed the spring air.

At first, the two agents walked several feet behind Katherine, as if to prevent any chance of conversation. Fully aware of this, she slowed her normally energetic pace. At sixty-five, she was both physically fit and savvy. Purposely, she briefly stopped the trio to acknowledge Mrs. Brimley—leg braces from childhood polio evident under her sky-blue polyester pants—sitting on a wheeled stool in a wide-brimmed sunhat, meticulously pruning the dead roses from a bush in one of the numerous raised bed plots, all proliferating with color and sustenance.

"Hi, Mrs. Brimley. Thank you for all your hard work. The garden looks so beautiful." From the corner of her eye, Katherine saw Gultowski glancing at his watch.

"Thank you for noticing," Mrs. Brimley replied in her low, gravelly voice, smiling from ear to ear, then adding with a wink, "and you're welcome."

As they walked the brick sidewalk through the grassy Commons area, Katherine became increasingly troubled. The agents were pretentious, using their status to flaunt power. She was already thinking about calling the Oak Place attorney.

They continued to walk, passing a few residents doing their own version of powerwalking along a wide path. "Hi, Katherine," one yelled out while exhaling. "We're on lap three!" Katherine knew better than to stop again, but used her slow pace to point out various Oak Place buildings within the vast campus, including the greenhouse, and Jake, the 22-year-old miniature pony who was resting on three legs inside his small pasture. "That building over there, the largest on campus, is our senior housing complex."

Neither Walker nor Gultowski said anything except, "Uh-huh," hardly disguising their irritation at slowing again, barely glancing in the direction Katherine was pointing. As they passed an elderly volunteer, John, readying a newly rescued yellow Labrador mix for therapy work, he called, "This dog will be perfect. He's so friendly and nothing seems to spook him, not even electric wheelchairs." Katherine gave him a thumbs up, smiling wide. No matter how many times she walked across the Commons, she always swelled with pride at the marvelous people who called Oak Place home, living testaments to aging with dignity.

"We believe aging is a process, not a disease," Katherine continued, momentarily not concerned about the stoic men's disinterest. She figured, unlike so many tours before, she wasn't going to evoke any curiosity. Still, she went on, quelling her uneasiness and daring them to hurry her. "Warehouses are a thing of the past. This is a place where seemingly ordinary, but actually extraordinary people can really live their last years. You know, over four thousand people live here. That building over there is our skilled nursing home."

Their continued silence spoke volumes. *Better not to test them anymore,* Katherine thought. She didn't know whether to be perturbed or anxious at their lack of engagement, settling on being both while studying Gultowski's still pimply face, also leading her to presume that this might be their first assignment. She was supposed to be somewhere else. She had initially felt an assistant could host this trek to Stella, but their attitude made her think it wise to take charge.

Entering the assisted living complex, they took an elevator to the eighth floor. Katherine directed them to Apartment 812 and knocked on the door.

"Come in. It's open," said a voice from inside.

Stella, dressed in casual pink sweats with matching sneakers and a coordinated paisley scarf, smiled from a comfortable chair as she closed her book. She looked almost ethereal as the morning light bathed her. "Oh, Katherine, good to see you again." Stella looked hesitantly at the two men.

"Stella, these men are from the FBI and want to talk with you."

As Stella's smile vanished, the agents went through the ritual of presenting their badges and introducing themselves. Then, in full power-wielding mode, they demanded that Katherine leave. Peering over the rim of her glasses, Katherine gave Stella a questioning look.

"I want her to stay," Stella said pleasantly, but firmly.

"Absolutely not," came the not-so-pleasant retort. "We have some very important questions to ask you in private. We can do this here or in custody if you refuse to cooperate."

Katherine's anxiety skyrocketed as she observed the two men towering over a frail lady. Why this demeanor? Why the FBI? Why not the NYPD whom she had worked with so well for decades? The cops had rescued many a lost and confused resident and arrested a few shady ones. Then Walker pulled his suit jacket back as he put his hand into his trouser pocket, a purposeful move that exposed the strap of his gun. For God's sake, who were these people? For an instant, Katherine considered leaving, but decided against it. She was staying. And she was livid.

Stella's friendly face transformed to a frown, eyes squinting. For a few seconds, she stared at Walker, as if gathering her thoughts and contemplating the confrontation. Then, whining like a preschooler, she yelled, "Oh, Daddy! You've come for me. I'm so sorry that Mommy is not here to witness this."

"Ma'am?" said Walker.

"Daddy, I tried to tell you. Mommy had a baby girl. Oh, you must meet her. I'm sure it is yours. Mom was ever so faithful, even when you left us for the war. Dear God, you weren't wounded, were you?"

"Is—your—name—Stella—Cordrey?" asked Walker, voice raised, speaking slowly as if to a child.

"Stella? No, it's Rose! Mommy named the baby girl Rose!" Stella began trembling, rocking back and forth.

"No, is—*your*—name—Stella?" Walker asked loudly again, clearly frustrated.

Katherine tensed up as she tried to assess if this sudden mental change might be the result of some acute health event. She listened intently, not taking her eyes off Stella, attempting to rule out a medical crisis rather than a well-acted fake.

"Katherine," Stella begged in an anxious voice, "please tell Daddy it's okay and I forgive him."

Stella started shedding real tears that quickly turned to sobs as she screamed, "Mommy loves you, Daddy! I know she does! Please come home!" She grabbed Walker's hand, then using that hand for stability, she slowly rose up in a hunched position. "Please! Please! Oh please! We miss you!"

With Stella's controlling handgrip, a stiff Walker gave a "What do I do now?" look in Katherine's direction, who immediately jumped into the drama. "Stella, it's alright. Why don't you sit back down? We'll have these men come back later."

As Stella returned to her chair, she mumbled, "When is this war going to be over? Please, be over."

"Gentlemen," Katherine said, "she's distressed. This interview is *not* going well. As a nursing professional, I cannot let you continue." Her voice demanded compliance. "Do you have a number where I can reach you?"

Walker stared at Stella, then Katherine, then Stella again, clearly conflicted as to what to say or do next. Seeing a frail old lady quivering, with rapid respirations and tears streaming down her face, clearly concerned him. So did Katherine, who by now had placed her body in front of a sitting Stella, her piercing eyes demanding he back off.

Katherine was alarmed. She needed to determine if the Medical

Crisis Team needed to be called in. And why, she wondered, were these agents being such creeps?

Walker presented his business card. "We need you to call us this afternoon, Ms. Ish."

"My name is Eich, pronounced with a long 'i' and a soft 'sh.' And, it's *Doctor* Eich."

"Yes, Dr. Eye-sssh," he said. Walker seemed not to be mocking her name but trying to get it right. His demure voice sounded relieved at being able to exit the apartment, thus leaving Katherine to deal with Stella.

Frowning and squinting, Katherine tucked her neck-length curly graying hair behind her ears, turning slowly from the exiting agents to Stella, who, upon hearing the front door close, had taken a deep, calming breath. As Stella raised her head to establish eye contact, she pursed her lips together, trying to contain a smirk. She couldn't gauge Katherine's anger at the incident but didn't want any of it directed toward her.

Jesus, Katherine thought, now confident this was not a medical event but disturbed at witnessing such a display of feigned dementia.

"Stella, what was that about? No one gets Alzheimer's in two minutes. Who is Rose? And, I might add, what a compelling performance!"

"Damn, Katherine! I needed a good cry. Besides, that Walker guy did remind me of my father; reminders that are not warm and fuzzy."

Arms out, palms up, shoulders raised, face grimacing, Katherine no longer held back her apprehensions. "But why?" she asked as her beeper buzzed, signaling her to be somewhere else.

"I promise. You'll get my story."

CHAPTER 2

If asked, Katherine could not precisely say when her passion for the elderly turned into her life's work. Many events—some small and some hugely significant—had prompted her activism. Familial experience was prominent in this evolution. Her loving grandmother, a widow who lived with the family while Katherine was growing up, had been increasingly incapacitated with Alzheimer's Disease (then called senility) and was finally moved to a nursing home after she accidently set the kitchen on fire while Katherine's parents were at work. Visiting her grandmother, Katherine observed conditions she didn't know existed: overcrowding, understaffing, and neglect. In a well-reputed nursing home packed with people, she saw her mute grandmother suffering profoundly from isolation.

One day, Katherine put her in a wheelchair and took her outside. Holding tight to the handles in front of her, she jogged through the parking lot and then across the lawns. Her grandmother laughed out loud, stretching her arms up, face skyward. Katherine tipped the wheelchair back, small wheels elevated, running and turning, her grandmother giddy with laughter, the jubilation only ending when Katherine was finally out of breath. She sat under a tree and they stroked each other gently like they used to, until a rigid nun in full habit came outside to berate Katherine for "stealing" her grandmother from the "safe" confines of her room. "You will not be allowed to do this again. She could get pneumonia!"

I hope so, Katherine thought, *instead of this cruel fate you have subjected her to. May death spare her this indignation.* She felt tremendous guilt having to leave her grandmother that day as she returned to college.

The next time she saw her grandmother, who had now been

declared an escape risk, she was moaning gibberish and trying desperately to maneuver the waist restraint that secured her to the bed. Katherine cried at the sight and became sick to her stomach. She wanted to scream at someone on the staff: *Don't you know that if you touch her or sing to her, she calms? How can you treat her like this?*

This was the grandmother she cherished: the immigrant, the sweatshop alumna, the one whose back had paved the way for a better life for her children and her children's children.

After college, Katherine plunged into research, ever more drawn to the elderly and the memory of her grandmother, the nostalgia of love and family, yet plagued by those last cruel years. She amassed reams of information on nursing home conditions in the New York metro area, as well as across the country. By the time she was in grad school, some of the conditions she uncovered—rampant bedsores, unjustified restraints, patients lying in filth—were reported to the authorities, leading to arrests and trials. One nursing home was closed. Katherine's work was getting attention.

During that time, Katherine met Peter, also a graduate student. Already an investigative reporter for *The New York Times*, Peter was pursuing his doctorate in journalism in preparation for the next leg of his career: academia. Their courtship lasted three years, mostly because he was always off somewhere in the world on assignment, which included multiple trips for long periods to conflict zones, including the fall of Saigon. The pace of his life made even an ambitious Katherine tired. She gave him his first article on burnout, and since PTSD was not yet an official diagnosis, he immediately labeled himself a burnt-out casualty. "You cannot maintain weeks of insomnia and see untold human suffering without emotional consequences," she told him.

Katherine had fallen in love with him almost at once. He was dark-haired, bearded, and handsome. Soft-spoken and intelligent, he was driven to make the world better by exposing information and political posturing that seemed to start or drag out wars and raise death tolls. Prior to meeting Katherine, he had been under immense pressure as he followed through on one of his journalistic missions; reporting on the Vietnam war and its aftermath.

Activism in their respective areas, while worlds apart, was each other's catalysts as they uncovered and exposed abysmal situations. In time, Katherine was driven to proceed further; namely, to do something about it. In her case, it would be to create a place for older Americans that could be a utopia, a place that would not just meet standards, but set the bar. Furthermore, matured past idealistic dreaming and now well-credentialed, she believed it was possible.

An article published in the early 1980s in *The New York Times* about her vision vividly described what was possible and elicited a phone call from an interested reader, who had asked for permission to call her.

"My name is Theodore Oak. I read your article. Do you have a few minutes to talk?"

Katherine, still beading sweat after a jog, was in her small studio apartment on the Upper East Side surrounded by reams of papers piled high, the culmination of ongoing research. She relished the break. "Tell me how I can help you."

"I had a bachelor uncle, childless, my father's cousin, whose name was Samuel Oak. He was a successful businessman and worth millions, but he progressively descended into dementia, which became overtly apparent when he courted a woman sixty years younger than he, a woman who dressed in scant negligées, most likely bought out of a back-street porn shop. She isolated my uncle from his few friends still living."

"I'm sorry, Mr. Oak." Katherine was well aware of many painful stories like this, too many to count.

"Please, call me Theo."

"Okay, Theo, and call me Katherine." *I wish we were having this conversation in person,* she thought, *so much more personable.* "Tell me more."

"My father, having not known Uncle Samuel well since childhood, but being his only living relative, intervened long distance after one of those worried friends called him. Attorneys were hired. That made the new trophy girlfriend nervous. Ultimately, she decided grappling for Uncle's money wasn't worth it and she disappeared, albeit much richer for the experience."

"Unfortunately, your story is not unusual. Financial exploitation of the elderly is too common. And it's especially hard when loved ones don't live nearby."

"You can say that again. And get this! Then he got scammed by a neighbor and God knows who else. He was spending money like there was no tomorrow. Eventually, the attorneys, under my father's authority, were able to deem him incompetent by the courts. But, to add to the horror, some of those same attorneys charged outrageous, over-the-top fees and even tried to convince my father that they could handle his money wisely, all the while embezzling large chunks of it."

"The lawyers also! Dear God, just when your uncle needed them most." Again, this was not new to Katherine. Exorbitant fees from attorney charlatans. She'd heard it all before. "What did they do?"

"One charged $50,000 for a brief court appearance. Meanwhile, Uncle Samuel was evicted from his apartment and was residing in a ramshackle hotel room, living in squalor, malnourished, and getting bedsores while being charged thousands a week for nursing care."

"Why didn't they put him in a nursing home?"

"They said he had refused and was better off with private nurses, but they didn't give a fuck about him, only his money. Excuse me. I'm sorry I used harsh language. This is a hard story to tell."

"This is a hard story to listen to. I understand."

"Our family lived six hundred miles away and my dad, who had been named executor of his estate after one of the attorneys finally found the will, knew he couldn't handle things over the phone any longer. He came East and aggressively intervened, going so far as to report the lawyers to the District Attorney's office. My uncle died shortly thereafter, and by the time my dad recouped all the extravagant billings, which included suing two attorneys, he uncovered an estate worth well over $500 million, which he subsequently used to establish a foundation benefiting the elderly."

"I'm so sorry your uncle suffered so. And your dad? How painful it must have been for him."

"He was grief-stricken, angry that people could do this, sickened by the greed."

Katherine could hear his sniffling nose and shaky voice. "How long ago did this happen?"

"Just two years ago, and we're still working to establish a board of directors and implement some sort of strategic planning. In the meantime, my father, who did all the work, just recently died—under much more loving circumstances, I might add."

"I'm sorry about your dad. He must have been a very special person. Not many people would inherit all that money and want to use it for public good."

"How serious are you about creating this principled place where the elderly can live out their lives with dignity? A place where my uncle could have gone and been cared for. A place where he would not have been taken advantage of."

"I *am* absolutely serious. Like you, I've a sad personal story that drives my quest." Katherine told him about her grandmother. "Since her death, I've come to view many nursing homes as warehouses. And not just the abhorrent ones concealing outrageous abuse, but others, the majority actually, which are mediocre at best."

"Where do you live and when can I meet you?" asked Theo.

"Why don't you send me your mission statement and goals first and I'll review them."

Katherine didn't want to jump in too quickly. Better to take this slowly. Still, she was trying to temper her elation. *Did he really say $500 million?*

"Well, we still don't have that done. Please, can you help us? I feel we might be on the same page, wanting to create a place above all others. But I don't know where to start."

"I *cannot* help if it's only for wealthy people such as your uncle. It must serve all incomes, with subsidies available." The last thing Katherine wanted to do was create a ritzy place for the rich and famous.

"I agree wholeheartedly. I'm a high school teacher. I've seen what poverty does to kids. I can only imagine what it does to seniors."

And so began a long and satisfying relationship with Theodore Oak. Katherine joined the fledging board of directors—refusing a salary at first—and invited others, including geriatrician Dr. Jeff Titus, who later became medical director at Oak Place. All enthusiastically adopted a mission of creating a progressive nationwide philosophy of eldercare, as well as a local refuge for the elderly.

Within five years, the Samuel Oak Foundation had a credible reputation and many more millions, enough so that the board for the Borough of Queens, New York, offered eighteen acres of land for the creation of Oak Place. Eventually, Katherine drew a wage consistent with other well-known nonprofits of similar size. She remained ethical almost to the extreme, embracing public service rather than personal gain.

During Katherine's tenure on the foundation, she had convinced several nursing homes to change, at least partially, from a mindset of antiquated caregiving to something considered radical at the time; creating places to live, not die. Some were lured into compliance with grant money, others by being threatened with media exposure or loss of licensure. Whatever their incentive, follow-up academic studies showed improvements. This was the proof that the Queens Borough Board needed to justify their land agreement. Federal monies became available as well. Oak Place, a nonprofit experimental haven for older adults at all levels of care needs, was born.

By the time it was created but before the first brick was laid, Peter and Katherine married. At the age of thirty-five, Katherine was pregnant. Those were exciting years for them. Peter had a more workable schedule of studying while still maintaining contractual projects at *The Times*. When he completed his doctorate, he was offered a full-time path to a professorship at Columbia University. Katherine worked part-time with architects in the planning of Oak Place. It would be the first time in five years that they had a stable income and could pay off some of their college tuition debts.

By the time their daughter, Jill, was two, the twenty-story senior living complex, extending the entire length of the campus, was completed and rapidly filled to its capacity of three thousand residents. Construction of both the multi-storied assisted living and skilled nursing home buildings followed on the other side of the campus. In the middle, the Oak Place Gardens took shape. In honor of Samuel Oak, one stately, mature white oak tree in the center of the complex was preserved. Smaller oaks were planted.

Despite her capability, Katherine was at first torn about taking such a demanding position and implementing the mission she had nurtured. The responsibilities, as well as the expectations—including her own—were enormous. As the token woman, she felt tremendous pressure to prove herself. Yet she would have to spend long hours away from Jill, her precious toddler, as well as Peter. Both would feel the strain in their marriage.

That was more than thirty years ago. Katherine, now at the pinnacle of her career, had become an internationally known figure in the field of aging.

CHAPTER 3

What could Stella have done that warranted a personal FBI visit, prompting her to stage a convincing psychodrama? The question consumed Katherine's thoughts as she walked hurriedly across the rain-soaked courtyard on her way to meet out-of-town professional visitors who were waiting in her office. She had phoned her senior VP to start without her.

The sound of, "Hi, friend," brought Katherine back to her surroundings. She quickly backtracked to embrace Shirlee Jonas, one of her oldest friends and director of education at Oak Place.

As they hugged, Katherine asked, "How are you? Can we walk and chat?"

"Looks like we're heading in the same direction."

"I just escorted the FBI to a new resident in assisted living."

Shirlee stopped to face Katherine; her eyes riveted. "What was that about?"

"Don't know yet." They started walking again. "She's a classy lady who's been around—apparently a lot. The United Nations was like her second home. But something's going on. She actually pretended to be confused, as if she had sudden-onset dementia."

"Don't tell me you're going to get involved in some international scandal?" Shirlee rolled her eyes.

"God, I hope not." Katherine shook her head and cracked a fake smile while thinking, *The idea of a frail Stella being involved with something illegal does seem a bit preposterous. Most old people just don't fit the criminal stereotype.* "Shirlee, they even threatened to take her into custody!"

"FBI? Hmm? Espionage? Spy? Smuggling? Maybe she has a dicey past?"

"Shirlee, I hope it's none of those." They walked arm-in-arm quietly for a few seconds as it began to rain. Shirlee opened her umbrella to shield them. Katherine stared off, listening to the rain hit the umbrella, clearly focused on what had just happened in Stella's apartment.

"Katherine, you really do seem rattled."

"I am." Katherine had no hesitation admitting that to her trusted friend. "In all my years here, I've never dealt with the FBI. And these agents were rude and arrogant. They knew nothing about how to speak to an elderly person. Or to me, for that matter."

Katherine stopped by a raised bed next to the brick sidewalk to study some proliferating roses. "Look at these pastel orange petals." She took a deep breath as she sniffed. "Beautiful. Are residents cross-pollinating them in the greenhouse?"

"Yes, there's some sort of contest going on. And it sounds like those FBI guys need a course in *Dealing With Little Old Ladies 101*."

Shirlee and Katherine had known each other for almost forty years. They met while teaching at a school of nursing in the Hell's Kitchen area of Manhattan in the late 1970s. Katherine was a naïve transplant from small-town New Jersey. Shirlee, also from New Jersey, was anything but naïve. She had integrated the Girl Scouts in a Trenton suburb. As a young girl, proud of her oversized Afro and the heritage it represented, she had lifted her arm to grab her father's strong hand as they marched with Martin Luther King, Jr. She was a passionate woman, someone Katherine instantly admired and emulated. During their first months of teaching together, they formed a powerful bond that has remained to this day.

Eventually, they applied for graduate school at the City University of New York and took every class together. Katherine continued as a doctoral candidate, while Shirlee stepped off the advanced academic track to care for her husband, a New York City police officer who had been diagnosed with muscular dystrophy and was progressively becoming disabled. Years later, having earned national recognition for her progressive work in aging, Katherine hired Shirlee as the educational director for both staff and residents at Oak Place.

Ironically, they didn't see each other very much because both were busy with their respective responsibilities. So, it was always special when their paths crossed spontaneously.

"By the way, when can we have lunch or dinner again? Seems like it's been weeks."

"Dinner sounds good," said Shirlee, smiling. "You know, even though we work in neighboring buildings, it sometimes seems like we're miles apart. We've both said this before; friendship is work—and we've gotten lazy again."

Just then, Hal approached them. He was homeless but often slept in Jake's stall in the small brown barn with dark green shutters, which was right in the middle of the Oak Place campus next to the largest of the oak trees. Hal's long, straight, thinning hair was haphazardly pulled back into at least a week-old braided ponytail. Somehow, even in his slouched position, his slim body, now decades neglected, hinted of a once robust and fit person. He was covered in straw and reeked; Katherine and Shirlee instinctively stepped back.

Shirlee, in her commanding bass voice, cut right to the point. "Where's your jacket, Hal? You'll catch cold in this damp weather. Have you been taking your medications? And when was the last time you had a shower at the shelter?"

"Not *that* long ago," said Hal with a hint of sarcasm, but not enough to piss Shirlee off, which he knew from experience was better not to do.

The homeless shelter was six blocks down the street, and Shirlee made sure it was always stocked with extra clothes bequeathed from deceased residents. She also coordinated with the Oak Place chefs to send certain leftover food to the shelter instead of wasting it.

"Well, you need a shower! Today! And please, get some clean clothes, then come to my office. I have some work for you if you're interested. Also, would you brush Jake? The kids have been cooped up with this rainy weather and been neglecting him. Oh, and there's lunch for you in my office," Shirlee added with a wink.

Hal loved Jake, and he also loved Shirlee despite her authoritarian demeanor, which he knew he needed. Plus, the staff at Oak Place had come to know and trust him. As a Vietnam veteran, Hal, now in his seventies, had a Purple Heart, along with other commendations, but he had never integrated into society after his tours. Years ago, they had actively tried to get Hal mental health intervention, but he never followed through with appointments or medication.

"Thank you, Ms. Jonas. I appreciate that. Jake will get brushed right after lunch. Have a blessed day. You too, Dr. Eich."

"Oh, I wish I could get to that man," Shirlee said as they continued their walk.

"It's not for lack of trying."

"Clean clothes, shower, today's lunch—all short-term fixes to much bigger problems. Jesus, Katherine, we've been trying to combat homelessness since our days in graduate school."

Katherine chuckled. "Yeah, that's one problem we haven't solved yet."

They walked a few more steps before Katherine stepped out from under the umbrella. The rain had turned to drizzle. "Sorry, gotta hurry. I'm meeting with a new rotation of medical and nursing students. There's also a group who've flown in from Texas. They want to start an Oak Place near Houston."

"Hey, friend," Shirlee grabbed her arm and looked at Katherine, "I bet you're itching to get more of Stella's story. But be careful. Just because she's cute and frail doesn't mean she has a Betty Crocker past."

"Yeah, yeah, *Mother*. I know." Katherine forced a laugh.

"Don't get sarcastic on me. I'm serious." Shirlee gave Katherine a stern parental look to convey her concern.

"I hear you. Really, I do. Look, when I left Stella's apartment only minutes after the agents, I told her I'd be back later. Because of their overbearing approach, I feel some obligation to advocate for her. Plus, you're right. I'm curious as hell about what's going on."

CHAPTER 4

Already late afternoon and seriously behind on her day's goals, Katherine was ruminating about working with the Houston visitors as she walked back to Stella's apartment. She had tried Stella's cell. No answer. *Why is it that old people never carry their cellphones,* thought Katherine. She would have to call the FBI newbies soon but felt compelled to get more information first.

"I think Stella is in the art room, painting," said a nursing aide as she pushed a resident in a wheelchair down the hall near Stella's apartment.

"She was here, but I think she's walking now," said a fellow resident in the art room, who didn't even look up from her painting to see who had asked the question.

Feeling increasingly frustrated at having to track her down, Katherine decided to call the FBI, as they had demanded, without more information about Stella. The incident kept rumbling through her head: *arrogant and over-the-top FBI agents, feigned senility, staged tears from Stella.* The more Katherine thought about it, the more her concerns intensified. Besides, she would have to level with the FBI about the fake dementia. She wondered again if she should inform the Oak Place attorney, but again decided to hold off.

Dialing the agent's phone as she walked outside, she spotted Stella on a bench in a therapeutic garden and cancelled the call. Katherine stopped for a few seconds, thinking how lovely Stella looked in the shadowy light of the cloudy sky, her posture relaxed as if she was meditating. Loose strands of her hair danced in the gentle breeze. A multi-colored pastel shawl provided warmth.

Katherine thought of her own beloved grandmother, who Stella reminded her of, before quickly reflecting on Shirlee's words: "Frail and old does not mean a Betty Crocker life." She wanted to trust Stella, but her own past was dotted by incidences of trusting too quickly, too fully, and being burned. She approached Stella with caution.

"Lovely day, isn't it?" said Stella. "The rain has made things smell so fresh. And look at all those birds gathered around the feeders. The cardinals are brilliant, as are the goldfinches."

"I never get tired of looking at the birds," Katherine replied, using her hand to brush away the tiny puddles of water on the bench before sitting down. "They brighten even the most dismal day. See the Baltimore oriole getting his share of the seeds?"

"You know, Katherine, I'm still trying to find my way around this place. Yesterday, I discovered yet another dining room, and oh, the theater is magnificent! Also, that state-of-the-art gym! Wow! What a great place to continue my physical therapy."

"Have you been to the lounge yet?" Katherine asked with a twinkle in her eye. "At night, you can enjoy entertainment while sipping a glass of wine or cappuccino."

"Not yet. Need to put it on my almost empty calendar. You know, this place is so different, so alive. Today, I joined the Grandmothers for #MeToo Club. I might even join the Poetry Club. There are so many clubs! Would you believe my neighbor belongs to the Recovering Catholics Club? Wonder how that one has grown since all these priest scandals?"

"Sometimes the number and variety of clubs even surprises me. They give people a chance to connect."

"Oh, and a biracial lesbian couple who drove me around in a golf cart told me about the active Gay Alliance. You know, Katherine, some of my contemporaries, gay and straight, grew up in the dark ages when it comes to homosexuality."

"Yeah, I know. A decade ago that same couple started a book club, where racially diverse members discuss books on race, then break bread together at potlucks with ethnic foods. In fact, Stella, when you're up for it, check out the continuing educational program. You can take a class in anything from analyzing climate change to basket weaving to how to read poetry."

"I've seen the schedule. Next semester, I want to take the Shakespeare course. Tell me something, Katherine. I see so many young children. What're they doing here?"

"We have a preschool, actually an Upward Bound Program. Many of our residents volunteer there, especially retired teachers. By the way, have you heard about Jake, our horse?"

"Sure have. Never seen such a small horse. A beauty."

"Well, the kids think he's *their* horse. They beg to bring him in the classroom, and the teachers often oblige."

"Is he housetrained?"

Katherine laughed. "No! But not for lack of trying."

The birds chirping ramped up as they fluttered about, tussling for their spot at the feeders. Katherine and Stella watched in silence, while Katherine patiently waited for Stella to bring up what had happened in her apartment that morning.

"So, I suppose you want me to explain what happened today," Stella said, eyes closed while facing the sun that had temporarily peeped through some clouds, her fingers tightly intertwined on her lap as if anticipating an unsympathetic response.

"It was pretty intense." Katherine spoke gently, aware of Stella's nervousness. "It's obvious you don't have dementia."

"You're right. I don't." Stella pursed her lips.

Katherine thought Stella might be at a crossroads, perhaps wondering if she could trust her. "Then why the show?" A group of walkers passed close by, one shouting out, "Hi, Katherine!" She quickly acknowledged them, not wanting to take her eyes off Stella.

"I don't have a very trusting history with police." Stella twirled her thumbs as if she knew what Katherine's next question would be.

"How come?"

"I've been a victim of bad policing more than once. Not always, of course."

The two stared intensely at one another, both searching for the silent clues.

"Did those FBI agents remind you of that kind of policing?"

"Arrogant shits! Moral pontificates! Speaking to me like I'm a four-year-old." Stella put a hand over her mouth as if to control her anger. It began drizzling again, but neither noticed.

"Pretty strong language. Is that why you pretended?"

"Absolutely! I'm not telling them a thing. I'd rather go to jail."

"Jail?" Katherine's gut was feeling trouble.

"No, not really," Stella said quietly. She bowed her head as if ashamed.

The two sat silently for a while. The on and off drizzle brought still more residents to the courtyard, people who had been cooped up by heavy rains for many days. Both were relieved their bench was off the beaten path, and they remained undisturbed. Katherine marveled at the sight of such picturesque gardens, most within raised beds so resident volunteers could more comfortably tend them. She never lost her sense of pride at being the founder of such a magnificent place.

"Stella, you should have a lawyer."

"Don't need one. Don't want one. Besides, I think I know what they want. Come to think of it, I wonder why it took them so long to contact me? Anyway, it's the story of a compassionate man who worked to end apartheid in South Africa."

"That's special. How did you know him?" asked Katherine, feeling calmer upon hearing about a man trying to end apartheid and remembering a time when she demonstrated against apartheid in front of the United Nations. Hopefully, this information lessened the possibility of Stella being on a *Most Wanted* list.

"Kevin Finchley and I were lovers. In fact, he was the only man I ever loved. It's been a long time since I've said his name out loud, or revealed my love for him."

"Where is he now?"

"Dead! Murdered! Assassinated! Probably tortured." Stella's eyes welled with tears. She lowered her head as she began to cry. Her hands, now in fists, covered her face, her anger and grief exploding like a cork blown off a bottle of champagne. Years of stoic emotions were now out of control. Barely able to speak, she said, "I'm not faking, Katherine."

"I know. I'm so sorry," said Katherine, increasingly intrigued but still wondering if she really wanted to get pulled into this.

"A friend told me I should be over his death by now. Easier said than done."

"Stella, we never get over a loved one's death. We get over the flu, not a death." Katherine hated it when people made assumptions about when someone should be "over" a death.

"Never heard it said that way. So true."

Katherine handed her a tissue from her leather shoulder pouch before saying, "When did this happen?"

"Thirty years ago." Stella paused and blew her nose. "I know you're going to ask me how his death is relevant now."

"For you personally, it's still relevant. For the FBI, that was a long time ago."

"Katherine, I want to tell this story. Kevin deserves the truth. He was not a criminal! I'm not a criminal either. Yeah, we did some un-conventional things. Will you hear me out?" Stella looked at Katherine pleadingly, tears still streaming down her cheeks.

Katherine was itching to hear more but remained hesitant. *'Unconventional things,'* she thought, *covered a lot of territory; this could turn into a time-consuming mess.* She peered over her glasses. "Unconventional things? Look, Stella, I may not be the right person to share this with."

"I trust you. Please grant a dying lady this wish."

"Are you dying?" Katherine asked matter-of-factly.

"I'm eighty-three, almost eighty-four. I've had hip surgery with complications, plus heart issues." Then Stella smiled. "Do you need an exact time frame?"

"Okay, so you could live a long time." Katherine chuckled,

understanding the manipulation but not turned off by it. "Stella, what do you want from me?"

"I want you to stay with me while I tell my story to these FBI newbies. I can't fake dementia forever."

"I'm not going to lie to the FBI," said Katherine firmly.

"I know. And I don't want you to. But I need support; someone I can trust. They're going to ask a lot of questions, starting with how Kevin and I met."

Katherine still considered backing off. Now would be the time. Get a social worker or one of Oak Place's attorneys. But she was drawn to Stella and couldn't do it. *I'll just ask a few more questions and then decide,* she thought.

"How you met?"

"Sounds like a pretty innocuous question, doesn't it?"

"So, how did you meet?"

Stella stared straight at Katherine. "Katherine, I spent most of my life as a prostitute."

Katherine's eyes opened wide. "I wasn't expecting that!" *So much for Betty Crocker,* Katherine thought to herself. *Plus, what an unexpected oxymoron: a long-living prostitute.*

"Don't worry. I'm retired now."

Guess so, thought Katherine. *Don't see many prostitutes using walkers.*

"I make no excuses. I came from a highly dysfunctional family where I was both physically and sexually abused."

"That must have been torturous," said Katherine, wanting to say more but at a loss for words.

"I managed to get out when I was sixteen. Ran away. Far away."

"To the streets of New York."

"Walked some of the city's most dangerous streets dressed like your stereotypical floozy: scantily clothed, hair teased, heavily made up, boobs all but exposed. I can't believe I survived."

"Is that where you encountered the good and bad cops?"

"Cops different as night and day. Some as abusive as my father. I thought about them as soon as those FBI agents opened their mouths."

Katherine's mind was flooded with thoughts. What a story! She was hooked. Here sat a sweet little old lady who could pose for the grandmother in an Andrew Wyeth painting. "How long have you been retired?"

Stella laughed out loud. "Ha! Guess you don't know many old prostitutes. Trust me, there aren't many of us. She continued laughing as if to release some of her tension. "Retired a decade ago. Don't have a pension, though. Actually, I was lucky, extremely lucky."

"How so?"

"Some of my clients were rich drunks who weren't even sure what they paid me. Eventually, I had enough money to afford my own East Side apartment and look decent, more sophisticated. That's when I met my first United Nations client. And word spread. Soon after, I became a *Madam*." Stella looked at Katherine, her eyes swelling with pride.

"So, you brought people together?" Katherine found herself sitting on the edge of the bench, fascinated, wanting more information. This was one story she'd never heard before.

"The UN is a big place with lots of lonely people and families far away."

"I believe that."

"Once word spread that I was discreet, my phone kept ringing. Had a thick black book with lots of names, some of them powerful people. I hired more girls. And two men. Made millions."

"Think that black book might be what they are after?"

"Doubt it. Besides, I burned it a few years back."

"Stella, I never knew a Madam before. You're my first. Still, it sounds like a hard life."

"Some glamour, more than a few pigs." Stella paused as if contemplating rising above the small talk. "Katherine, I was a wounded woman. The scars of my past were horrific. But something very significant happened. I began seeing a compassionate therapist who helped me understand the circumstances of my life and actions, and could see that I was actually intelligent. She gave me books to read and sent me to the library, then back to school to get my GED. I grew up in her office, in essence hiring my very own surrogate mother, which I needed desperately."

"I admire your courage to confront your demons," said Katherine. "I remember one psychologist who used a metaphor to compare emotional wounds to broken objects. When we break something, like porcelain, we can throw it away or sloppily glue it back together—neither restoring its original potential. But an ancient Japanese tradition called Kintsugi carefully mends broken objects with a special lacquer from the Urushi tree, then paints the cracks with gold, thus making them stronger and more beautiful than before they were broken."

"Wow. Great metaphor. My cracks were probably like fissures, long and deep. I needed a lot of gold."

"Stella, it took guts to do what you did."

"Thanks, Katherine. Is that a sign you might stick around for the rest of my story?"

Katherine smiled.

CHAPTER 5

The drizzle had turned to steady rain and Stella invited Katherine back to her apartment. Stella swayed back and forth on the bench before getting enough momentum to rise slowly to her walker. She looked tired. The morning had been stressful. Katherine walked close beside her.

"Why's that tall fence over there?" asked Stella.

"That's the memory care section. The fence prevents confused patients from wandering off. Behind it is their own enclosed village and gardens, where they are free to roam. It even has a no-money-exchanged grocery store and its own coffeehouse, often filled with music and singing." Katherine told her it was unofficially called Maria's Place in memory of her grandmother, who, after her Alzheimer's diagnosis, never had any freedom to roam.

"I'm sure it's a nice place, but I hope I never have to go there."

"Me too. But if I do, I know I'll be treated with dignity and respect."

Once back in her apartment, Stella's fatigue became more evident as she sat in her chair, head resting on the back. Her rescued gray, white-pawed tabby cat meowed from its elaborate perch, constructed two feet from the ceiling, before coming down to nestle in Stella's lap.

"That's some cat shelf and staircase," Katherine said. There was a twelve-inch-wide carpeted shelf that extended around the room of Stella's cozy, welcoming one-bedroom home; a home that wasn't flashy but it was impeccably decorated in warm colors and designed for efficiency. The paintings on the walls and sculptures throughout the room were most definitely pricey.

"Shay loves looking down from her safe haven," said Stella. "I promised her that after we moved, I'd make things right for her. I hope she's forgiven me for the unwelcome uprooting. Cats hate change, you know."

"Lucky cat."

"I found her on the streets one night, wet, cold, meowing. Couldn't just leave her there. Katherine, I don't want you to leave for fear you won't come back, but I need to rest. I'm sorry."

"I understand," Katherine said as she checked her beeping phone. The text message was shocking: *Suicide just happened in senior housing.* "Stella, don't worry. I'll be back. Right now, I have an emergency."

⁂ ⁂ ⁂

Katherine was upset seeing eighty-year-old Mr. Riggins lying dead in a pool of blood on the concrete in the stairwell between the fifth and sixth floors, with his wife wailing, "Why? Oh God, why?" An initial survey of the scene indicated he had put the gun in his mouth, pointed it upward and pulled the trigger, thus guaranteeing a mortal wound.

Dr. Jeff Titus, Oak Place's medical director, and nationally recognized for his work with the elderly, was already there, holding Mrs. Riggins tightly as she wept, but not attempting to remove her from the scene. There were really no words to be said. The staff shook their heads in silence, unable to comprehend the tragedy. One security guard removed the gun with gloved hands and asked people to vacate the area, while another put a blanket over the body, not covering the bloodied face as Jeff requested.

Jeff, Katherine, and Mrs. Riggins eventually sat on the concrete steps, looking at the body. "I could see that he was in pain from his spreading cancer," Mrs. Riggins said. "But if he had said something! Anything! I'm sure we could have helped."

"Perhaps he wanted to spare himself the suffering," said Jeff. "Or perhaps spare you from his misery."

"Just this morning, he seemed happy, and we had a delightful lunch only an hour ago. He told me how much he loved me and thanked me for fifty-two wonderful years."

"Maybe he already knew what he was going to do and was saying goodbye," said Katherine as her eyes teared, becoming increasingly grief-stricken herself. She had known Samuel Riggins for over a decade. Most staff called him Mr. Riggins, just as people had done at the high school where he had taught his whole career. Katherine never saw him without a tie and hat, a formality he retained from his Southern roots.

"Now that I think about it, that's probably true," Mrs. Riggins acknowledged. "These last few days, he seemed to be getting everything in order, right down to putting together a notebook of all our financial statements. He also kept calling the kids. In fact, he was calling them every day."

With her hand on her forehead, she sobbed, "Oh, Sam, why didn't you say something? Why go out like this? I just don't understand." She paused, anger emerging. "I'd just called hospice. Why didn't he give them a chance to help?"

"Mrs. Riggins, there is so much we don't understand about why people choose to end their lives, what they were thinking. Being angry about what he did is normal."

"I am mad! So very mad! I have to tell our children that he killed himself. How could he do this to me? He hated guns! When did he go out and buy this gun? Jesus, he was such a gentle man. Why a damn gun? Couldn't he have just swallowed pills?"

Mrs. Riggins got up and sat on another step closer to the body, lovingly touching his blood-spattered face. "You foolish man. I forgive you. Always have. Goodbye, my love."

The stairwell door opened forcefully, hitting the back wall hard. Her son, who had coincidently been on his way to visit, entered. "Oh my God! No! Oh my God!" He turned to his mother and hugged her tightly before looking at his bloodied father and dropping to his knees, limp like a dish rag, nose dripping. He started sobbing so uncontrollably that Mrs. Riggins began comforting him.

"He's at peace now," she said, unable to get on her knees but bending over as she tightly gripped her son's shoulders to steady herself. "We were blessed to have him for these many years. He was a good and kind man."

For a few minutes, no one spoke, the silence broken only with sniffling and the pulsating breathing that accompanies tears of intense grief. "Come," Katherine coaxed after a while, "Let's go back to your apartment. Is there anybody else we can call?"

A staff person led them back up the stairs to the hallway already filled with visibly grieving neighbors, all who knew him, most of whom considered him a friend. They surrounded Mrs. Riggins and her son, touching them lovingly as they passed. "Oh Betty! Oh Dwayne! Margo!" cried Mrs. Riggins as she embraced those most intimate, blood from the mortal wound noticeable on her long sleeves. Most could not, did not talk, as if knowing there was nothing they could say to lessen the overwhelming shock she was experiencing.

Katherine and Jeff sat silent again after they left. "Too many older adults are doing this, especially white men in their eighties," Jeff finally said. "I just saw him last week in the clinic. The cancer was aggressive. We talked about calling hospice to treat the pain. I gave him his first narcotics to get him through the next couple of days. I wouldn't have guessed he'd do this. But then again, most don't divulge their plans to their doctor."

"There'll be a lot of people upset by this," said Katherine. "He was such an energetic resident: head of the choir, active in the grandchildren program. There will be many questions asked. I'll call Shirlee to get some social workers over here to offer grief counseling."

"I'm already here," said Shirlee upon entering the stairwell, followed by a NYPD officer. Shaking her head, she said, "My, my, this is going to be hard for everyone." Fixing her eyes on Mr. Riggins, she said, "You dear, sweet man. I will always remember you. Nobody will ever sing "Summertime" like you did."

With that, everyone got down to business, examining the scene and providing information to the police investigator. The physical therapist who had heard the gunshot and discovered Mr. Riggins was still visibly shaken when he was summoned back to the scene for his statement. Within the hour, the body was removed.

ॐ ॐ ॐ

B efore going back to his office, Jeff visited a new patient in the nursing home. The staff told him she was confused much of the time. Upon entering the room, she seemed amazingly lucid.

"Mrs. Wainright, do you know what year it is?"

She answered correctly, "2018."

"And who is our president?"

"The guy with the orange hair: Trump."

"How old are you?"

"Be eighty-nine next week."

She answered every one of his questions quickly and accurately. He completed his exam while she chatted about her kids and growing up on a farm, as well as her move to Oak Place. He wondered why the staff would say she was confused.

After twenty minutes, he said goodbye and turned to leave.

"So, doctor, when is my baby due?"

With his back to the patient, Jeff's chuckle expanded into full-blown laughter. After he composed himself, he turned around to ask her why she thought she was pregnant. But he started laughing again, so much so that he had to bolt out of the room. A passing nurse asked him what was so funny, but he couldn't stop laughing. Standing outside her room, leaning on the wall, he must have laughed for five full minutes before tears of grief for Mr. Riggins started streaming down his face.

"Been a stressful day," he finally said at the nurse's station, still laughing and crying intermittently. "Getting my emotions mixed up. I guess I'll never completely understand dementia—or suicide."

Jeff knew, of course, what was going on, diagnosing himself as having a post-traumatic anxiety attack; that is, when a highly stressful event causes one to sometimes react with the opposite of appropriate emotions, such as laughing instead of crying, and being triggered by something as seemingly inconsequential as, "When is my baby due?" The laughter displaced his deep grief.

For him, the sustained crying and self-imposed recriminations came later in the privacy of his office; "If only I had asked him…"

CHAPTER 6

Before Katherine left for the day, she dropped in on a group of seniors who were rehearsing for a play, *Camelot Revisited,* an interpretation of the original Broadway hit, except all the characters had aged fifty years, making King Arthur eighty-plus-years-old and hard of hearing. There were outbursts of sidesplitting laughter as they tried to master their lines or belt out a tune.

A resident seamstress had designed and tailored one woman's costume, which raised the actress's seventy-eight-year-old breasts while simultaneously squishing them tightly, resulting in a remarkable bosom popping out of the top. Being the good sport that she was, the woman paraded in front of a man in tights—in character, of course. Together, they were singing, "Tonight, tonight, won't be just any night…." The director, a man with a Mel Brooks type of humor, was intent on lampooning the concept of a youthful *Camelot* while having fun. Considering his own age of ninety, he wasn't about to make a mockery of aging, instead choosing to find the fun in its challenges. The new words to the Bernstein masterpiece included STD prevention, condoms, and lubricant.

"I thought that was from *West Side Story*," Katherine said, laughing after they finished.

"Yes, but *Camelot* should own it for a while. Besides, it fits so well," said the bosomy grandmother.

The spoof continued as they sang "I Could Have Danced All Night" from *My Fair Lady,* inserting "and if I take my meds, could still—have asked—for more." Next, from *South Pacific,* "I'm Gonna Wash That Man Right Outa My Hair," came the new words, "I'm going to wear my wrinkles as badges of life." Somehow, as Katherine watched, it all came together remarkably well. Their version of *Camelot* was told the way they wanted.

Her pinging cell showed a text from Peter, "It's 7:00 pm. I've made a mighty salmon bake. When are you coming home?"

"Leaving now," she texted. She left with a smile on her face, a positive end to a long, trying day.

As she walked outside, she smelled marijuana as she did regularly, because it had been decriminalized in New York for medical use. Two baby boomer gentlemen, both graduates of Woodstock, one with a ponytail, puffed away, already in la-la land. Katherine knew they had the appropriate prescriptions due to age-related arthritis and joint pain. In fact, after all these years, a good many seventy-somethings were delighting in getting their dope legally.

Too tired to take her usual subway train back to Manhattan, Katherine called Omar, her friendly independent cab driver whose mother had lived at Oak Place. Within minutes, she was relaxed, head back, in his rickety cab. Twenty minutes later, she hugged Peter extra-long. His arms were always welcoming.

"Long day?"

"Well, it started with two FBI agents flashing badges in my face and ended with me at a play rehearsal. In between, there was a suicide and a visit with a sweet old lady who just happened to have been a prostitute all her life. Maybe I'm getting too old for this."

"Come here. Want a backrub? Hungry?"

"Yes and yes! Heard from daughter Jill? Are we having dinner with her tomorrow?"

"Also, yes and yes! By the way, Jill wants to know if Aunt Shirlee is free."

"I don't know. Remind me to call her tonight. Oh, this backrub feels soooo good. Don't ever stop."

Peter continued rubbing her back, then put his hands in her hair and messaged her head. Her neck-long wavy hair still had remnants of its original auburn color, but gray was more prominent now. She had colored the gray once, but regretted it. Katherine's journey into aging would not include coloring or enhancing, nor did it need to.

Furthermore, she liked the maturity of her face, lines and all. She still looked trim and fit, walking a couple of miles daily to and from Oak Place buildings, and usually climbing a few flights of stairs before switching to an elevator.

Her aged appearance and manner exuded professionalism. She was easygoing but not one to be toyed with. If need be, she could play hardball with any of the 'big boys.' Katherine advocated for older Americans with unparalleled determination.

For Katherine, living with Peter had always been easy—minimal drama on both their parts. They meshed well. While not always successful, they had tried to balance their professional lives with their marriage and parenting. His university schedule was more flexible than Katherine's and he had more time off, especially in the summer. But she had worked hard to build a skilled administrative staff so that when she took time off, Oak Place was in capable hands.

"Jeff and I found Mr. Riggins, a dear man admired by all of the residents, lying in a stairwell in a pool of blood after he shot himself through the mouth," Katherine said later as they ate dinner by candlelight. "He had just been to Jeff's office requesting help with his terminal cancer. I know Jeff will agonize over what he could have done differently."

Katherine paused, fiddling with her food for a couple of minutes. "Peter, remember a few years back when I did some soul searching about becoming a recovering workaholic?"

"Yeah, I remember it well. About the same time, I felt I was single-handedly struggling with the antics of a rebellious pre-teen while you were off giving speeches or working ten hours a day. Didn't I call it an intervention?"

"Oh, yeah. One of the many challenges of our marriage. I remember you saying you weren't thrilled being married to someone you never saw." Katherine chuckled, then got serious, "Peter, I'm tired, and if truth be known, I think Jeff and Shirlee are also. Jeff is sixty-eight, Shirlee's almost seventy, and I'm soon sixty-six. We've all grown gray together. We're almost as old as many of the people we serve. In the not-too-distant future, we'll be the age of the majority of them. Maybe it's time to pass the torch to a new generation."

"Are you thinking the 'R' word? Retirement?"

"Maybe."

"And what would you do with your newfound time?"

"Not retire completely. That's for sure. Not ready to play shuffle-board or string beads. I could still work at Oak Place—maybe—in a reduced capacity. Or as a consultant to other budding Oak Places. I could write a book, plant a garden on our terrace, and if Jill ever gets pregnant, become a doting grandmother."

"I always wondered if the three of you were going to retire only if they wheeled you into the nursing home. Have Jeff or Shirlee said anything?"

"Not yet. And I just started thinking about it today. But since I'm stressed, not a good idea to dwell on it. Tomorrow is a new day."

"Even if you don't retire for a while, we still need to continue planning."

"What about you, Peter?"

"Retirement? I could be lured away from the stereotypical twenty-two-year-old student and finish that last book I never started. Every year, my students are the same age and I'm one year older. That age gap is approaching five decades. I'm old enough to be a grandfather to most of them. But it'll be two years before I'm eligible for my pension. And tonight, I still have a boatload of papers to grade. I doubt I'll make it to bed until after midnight or beyond. And by tomorrow afternoon, I'll be craving a nap, which I fully intend to take. Retirement sounds tempting."

"Since I have no hope of an afternoon nap, I'd better get to bed and leave you to your grading. It's almost ten. Time to read myself to sleep."

Rather than read, Katherine ended up talking on the phone with Shirlee for half an hour, mostly processing Mr. Riggins's death, then turned on the TV to watch Trevor Noah on *The Daily Show,* someone guaranteed to make her laugh, even at life's absurdities.

CHAPTER 7

At home, Jeff was still recovering emotionally from Mr. Riggins's death when unbeknownst to him, a hook and ladder fire engine was barreling toward the senior living building, sirens blaring. Smoke was evident on the third floor, specifically in Mrs. Garner's apartment, who had forgotten the potatoes boiling on her stove. When the water dissipated, the pot started cooking itself, the smoke triggering the fire alarm. So embarrassed was Mrs. Garner that she tried to put out the potential fire herself, grabbing the pot with her bare hand while trying to get it to the sink. She dropped the intensely hot pot, first burning her hand, then, as it crashed to the floor, large chunks of burnt steaming potatoes dislodged and attached themselves to her shoeless foot. By the time the staff arrived, she was painfully screaming for her cat, Ernie, who had made a beeline for safety.

Fire department visits to Oak Place were common, mostly to kitchens to retrieve the forgotten cookies in the oven or something on the stove. The sensitive fire and smoke alarm systems always caught a potential fire before the blaze started, staff having to mostly deal with the putrid smell of smoke, plus a panicked and embarrassed resident who was apologizing profusely. On his night off, Jeff was beckoned to assess the injuries to Mrs. Garner, who consented to go to the infirmary only after they found Ernie safely huddled under the bed.

As medical director, Dr. Jeff Titus was brainy Ivy League all the way, but his unorthodox feminine attire of silk shirts and pierced ears had most strangers doing double takes. His naturally curly, graying, dirty blond hair almost reached his shoulders and had the windblown appearance of someone who'd just gotten off a sailboat. Most residents described him as beautiful rather than handsome.

He loved working with the elderly and had dedicated most of his professional life to Oak Place. Now, in the waning years of his career, he looked back on the many fruits of his labor: the residency program rotations, his nationally recognized research, a stellar reputation among the staff and patients, and his progressive ideas that had made Oak Place a model for elder care. Katherine thought he was brilliant.

On this night, Jeff was hastily replacing the doctor on call, who was sick with the flu.

"What happened, Mrs. Garner?" Jeff asked.

"Oh, Dr. Jeff, I was so foolish. I was so totally absorbed in an episode of Downton Abbey that I forgot I was making potato salad for the luncheon tomorrow. But I'll be okay. Don't make a fuss. By the way, that's lovely lipstick. The color is just right for you."

"Damn! I forgot to take off my costume makeup!"

"Gotta gig coming up?"

"This Saturday, complete with new dress. Gonna sing "Bridge Over Troubled Water." Tough song to get right."

Jeff had hastily changed clothes when he received the emergency call. What Mrs. Garner didn't see was the long-sleeved, black silk clingy dress with a plunging V-neck that was draped over his prosthetic breasts, and hemmed just below the knees. The sashed waist had streaming tiny black beads. Jeff had also removed the black stockings and silver-beaded black heels.

"I wish you hadn't taken off the dress. Do you have a photo?"

"Of course." Jeff pulled out his phone. He always took photos to help him visualize the complete transformation.

"It's beautiful. Love the beads."

"Why, thank you. My wife picked it out. I put it on tonight to figure out how to accessorize when I wear it on stage. I'm thinking pearls. Do you think the dress makes me look fat?"

During the day, Jeff wore pants and loafers. But on some nights, the macho apparel was closeted and Jeff transformed into a beautiful woman. He wouldn't describe himself as a transvestite, queen, or a cross-dresser, preferring instead to be known as a drag artist. He didn't lord his alternate lifestyle over others, but he didn't hide it either. On occasions such as this, when he was not really prepared to be on call, patients could sometimes catch a glimpse of the beautiful Jessica.

Jessica was a performer, singing in nightclubs and drag clubs all over the city. His wife, Amy, often accompanied him when she wasn't working as a reputable Broadway stage set designer. She was accustomed to the flamboyance of the theater. Some three-plus decades ago, before their marriage, her shock meter barely registered a quiver when he introduced her to the beautiful Jessica.

Jessica's wardrobe was packed with hair extensions, wigs, enough costume jewelry to start a small store, and, of course, dresses—mostly gowns or cocktail attire appropriate for the stage. On any given night, she could be flashy, glitzy, sexy, refined, outrageous, or any combination thereof. She was quite stunning, a lady that women emulated not just for her looks, but her utter delight in being a woman. Jessica epitomized female pride and was a dedicated feminist.

When Jeff's children were young, they had bought him jewelry and highly decorated hairpins, which Jessica loved wearing. They thought "Jessica" days were dress rehearsals for Halloween. That all changed during their teenage years when they became grossed out, insisting on "Please don't tell anybody, Dad" assurances. Now, as adults, they again seized the opportunity to dress Jessica.

Occasionally, a resident at Oak Place, usually a man, would rant: "Who are you, some sort of homosexual?" Jeff would turn it into a teachable moment: "Actually, even though most drag queens are gay, some are not, including me. I dress this way to enhance my feminine self. It actually helps me relieve stress."

The staff had long ago accepted *him* becoming *her,* almost like the *M.A.S.H.* cast had accepted Klinger's cross-dressing. They also realized that Jeff, unlike Klinger, wasn't doing it for ulterior motives. In fact, the staff so admired Jeff that they would go out of their way to defend him to those few who cast aspersions. It was considered out of bounds to mock him, and that included any new resident at Oak Place.

"He's the most loving and skilled doctor I've ever known," said one highly religious aide. "It's not for me to judge, nor *you* either. He saves lives and makes old age almost glorious. That's how God will see him when he ascends the stairs to Heaven."

Katherine, in particular, doggedly defended him. When someone called him a "faggot," she rather curtly told him he was free to leave, and thank you for not using that word again as Oak Place was a prejudice-free zone, as noted in the signed leases. When he persisted in his threatening and scary diatribes about homosexuals, and used the N-word with equal animosity, Katherine did just that.

"I'm revoking your lease. You have until the end of the month to leave," she had said with an armed security guard by her side. His family, who seemingly had inherited his prejudiced ways, rebelled to no avail. "No one, nooooo one threatens my staff in this manner! Your father is of sound mind, and I consider his words verbal violence, as well as a hate crime."

They took her to court and when it was apparent Katherine and her team of like-minded lawyers would win, he apologized and begged to stay. She accepted his apology and made him sign a contract stating he would treat all staff with dignity and respect, or move out immediately. After that episode, he became a model client, a reformed Archie Bunker so to speak—at least in public.

Katherine always believed you could most definitely teach an old dog new tricks or at least make them stop their public outcries. "Be a racist in your apartment by yourself if you must," she would say. "But when you step out the door, leave your bigoted rants behind."

At Oak Place community events in recent years, both staff and residents would beg Jeff to perform, either as himself or as Jessica. His voice was so extraordinary that he brought many to tears with his alto renditions of "Summertime," or "What a Wonderful World," (made famous by Louis Armstrong) and yes, even "Somewhere Over the Rainbow." Sometimes, he even did a duet or two with wife Amy, whose soprano voice was equally melodic.

Once, a woman on her death bed, barely able to talk, whispered a final request: "Please have Dr. Jeff sing "Amazing Grace" to me." She died peacefully during the third verse with a smile on her face.

Jeff believed in music therapy and there were instruments all over the place, as well as choirs and Sweet Adeline Quartets. Even if someone hadn't played the piano in fifty years, they could reinvigorate their urge to hit the ivories. The same applied to trumpets or marimbas, violins or flutes. Since the beginning, Oak Place had its own stellar orchestra, jazz and rock 'n' roll bands, folk and harmonizing groups, two choirs, and one hip-swaying, eighty-year-old Elvis impersonator. If someone didn't qualify, they could practice for another year and audition again. Many did. It was an honor to finally take a coveted chair with instrument in hand. And if they didn't qualify, well, they could always take part by finding a jug or kazoo.

Musicians or singers in the surrounding communities, including professionals from Manhattan theaters, regularly contributed their talents to the bands or orchestra. The place was often hopping with music, including big band renditions of songs such as "Boogie Woogie Bugle Boy of Company C." With Jeff and Amy harmonizing, people danced—even in wheelchairs—into the night, which for most elders meant eight or nine o'clock.

Jeff's musical therapy extended to debilitated patients, mostly those in the nursing home. With earphones over patients' heads, perhaps playing the upbeat tunes of Cab Calloway, one could see demented eyes open, stilled fingers begin to tap on the tray table, and feet stomp. Some who were previously slumped over began to posture upright.

Music opened the doors to a decaying brain scarred with plaque. Often, one could hear staff singing out loud to patients as they dressed them or helped them eat. Somehow, in some way, it was calming, flushed out memories, brought a smile, and seemingly some relief from the living death of apathy. It was a sight to behold.

A music therapist taught other musicians, all volunteers, how to use music to bring patients back from their secluded inner world, perhaps to relive the days when they sang and danced. Families and caregivers were encouraged to attend and learn how to use music creatively. This often triggered their own stories of the past, when vibrance ruled and their loved ones were more engaged.

As a physician, Jeff treated the whole person and was often the catalyst for helping physical bodies, even decrepit ones, rediscover their souls.

CHAPTER 8

Already awake before dawn, Katherine laid in bed as the garbage truck invaded her quiet, tree-lined street of brownstones on the Upper West Side. She had spent the whole of yesterday going from one crisis to another, daily challenges she'd encountered a thousand times. Recently, though, she felt overtaxed and drained. She got a call in the middle of the night about a real kitchen fire at Oak Place. Then, this FBI situation and the agents' arrogance. *What did they really want from Stella?*

Katherine tucked a section of her hair behind her ear, then pulled the comforter up to her chin. She would much rather be the visionary creator, the one who built Oak Place and converted people to progressive thinking about eldercare. *Maybe I have been at this too long,* she thought. *Maybe it is time to pass the baton. Maybe Jill will get pregnant and I can be a grandmother.* She focused on the hanging collage of black and white framed photos of family, current and past, on the wall beside her. Light was beginning to invade the cozy, earth-colored room. She didn't want to get out of bed.

The garbage truck stopped below the window, picking up and tipping another load of bins before loudly gulping the contents into its belly. Peter stirred and opened his eyes.

"You awake?" he asked.

"Yeah, just trying to get my brain organized before another day begins."

She reached over to touch him and the two embraced, her head on his muscular shoulder, pressed against his gray beard, legs intermingled.

"Sleep well?" she asked.

He stroked her hair. "Not long enough."

Hugging Peter was comforting and secure, even after four decades.

It hadn't been all bliss; both having struggled with the vicissitudes of life. The low points tested them, especially raising a daughter while managing equally demanding careers, thankfully leaving resilience in its aftermath. The high points sustained them, strengthening their resolve to move forward together. Till death do us part? Somewhere along their journey, neither remembering exactly when and probably not doing so simultaneously, they had both decided that it would be death that ended their now solid marriage.

"What's your day look like?" Peter asked.

"Flying out at nine, speech at one in Boston, six o'clock flight home."

"Oh, I forgot. Thought that was last week."

"No, last week was Philadelphia. Or was it Chicago? Hell, I don't remember."

"And so, my wise old sage, another few hundred people will absorb your words and go forth?"

Katherine smiled, knowing he was her biggest advocate. "Hope so. Maybe. Besides, you know how I like being that wise old sage. How about your day?"

"And a sexy sage too." Peter kissed her forehead. "As for me, two classes, one graduate seminar, papers to grade, student advising. Guess I won't see you till late tonight…again. Some kind of life we lead."

"Wasn't this treadmill supposed to stop after our midlife crises?" asked Katherine. They both laughed.

The automatic coffee maker's fresh aroma wafted into their bedroom. They stopped talking and hugged tighter, making love with their clothes on. In their younger years, they might have progressed to sex. But that spontaneity—and talent for quickies—was no more. It was time for both of them to kick into high gear.

ꙮ ꙮ ꙮ

Katherine was led by a conference host to a private area, something she always requested for the hour before keynote speeches.

"Will you be needing anything else?" the host asked.

"No, this is fine. Thanks," she said, acknowledging the pitcher of water brimming with ice cubes on a silver tray.

Katherine surveyed the boardroom, smiling as she thought how Hilton-esque it was. The massive mahogany boardroom table atop lush, cedar-green carpeting was wax-shined and matched the waist-high wainscoting. On the walls were modern oil paintings of Boston Harbor. She envisioned the powerful decision-makers who might have surrounded this table, then put her briefcase down near the fresh-scented flowers, wondering if they'd been ordered on her behalf.

For a moment, she stared out the room-length sliding doors that overlooked the empty puddled courtyard, listening to the trickles of rain dripping from the overhang directly outside. She thought the beautiful oriental maples amidst camellias and rhododendrons, with water rhythmically falling off budding leaves, seemed like a country setting. She opened the double thick drapes to expose the full view and turned down the overhead lighting, leaving the room cozily lit with porcelain table lamps.

Throughout the decades, her private pre-speech rooms offered un-spoken information about the audience she would soon face. Since *knowing* her audience was vital to her preparation, she routinely re-quested a list of participants. In this case, it was CEOs, CFOs, presi-dents, medical directors, all from for-profit corporations where nurs-ing homes were their business empires. Just minutes before, she had peeked into the large ballroom with its crystal chandeliers and linen covered tables, where mostly Brooks Brothers-suited, cufflinked men sat.

She was aware of the contrast between where she was now and the numerous nonprofit Holiday Inn-type conferences where she had spoken in the past. There, in those private rooms, she would have found no paneling in a windowless, Cloroxed space, a laminate table on industrial carpeting—perhaps with a stain or two—mass-produced watercolors, plastic plants and the infamous styrofoam cups wrapped in cellophane. The audience would have been the budget insecure: nurses, social workers, and activities directors in a ballroom with florescent dimmer switches.

Outside, flashes of heat lightning followed by rumbles of thunder reminded her of the morning's turbulent flight and the resulting coffee spill on her blazer. Katherine took a cloth napkin, dipped it in the water and wiped it clean. She smiled again as it became invisible and took it off to hang properly on a chair so she wouldn't get too hot in the warm room. Her no-wrinkle, washable wool navy blazer was her costume for day business trips. She thought she could have slept in the gutter and woke up looking like the consummate professional. Hundreds of thousands of travel miles had taught her this. Her initial appearance was to project her own power. She hated frumpy, so from head to toe, makeup to hair, nails to classy, glitz-free jewelry, and often wearing hand-me-downs from upscale consignment shops, she exuded that power.

Katherine sat in the comfy tilt chair with armrests to do a final dress rehearsal for her talk. While there was fresh coffee surrounded by fine china on an ornate credenza, she poured herself a glass of water instead, safer than coffee for not initiating urgencies, another sign of her aging.

She talked out loud, practicing several punchlines. Before long, her phone alarm beeped 12:45. Fifteen minutes to curtain. She started taking deep breaths and ritually reflected on her grandmother. Katherine stood up and once again looked out at the courtyard, as if to see her younger self with Grandma in tow, like that day some forty years ago when she had put her in a wheelchair and took her outside.

Katherine stroked her grandmother's faux ruby brooch on her blazer. "Okay, Grandma, welcome to the Hilton. Let's do this." Armed with that memory, Katherine was prepared for her speech as if for a performance, using education as theater, her anecdotal stories impeccably rehearsed, thus making years of research and hours of organizing work seem effortless. She checked herself in the mirror, using her handy lint roller to evict some hairs from her clothing. Then, right on cue: "Ladies and Gentlemen, Dr. Katherine Eich, founder of the internationally renowned Oak Place."

She strolled out to face the audience, wired for sound, away from the crutch of a lectern, pumped up, ready to rock and roll, an evangelist armed with science. For an hour, she spoke without notes about nursing homes, using gripping slides as backdrop, hoping some would find value in lessening profit and learning about the possibilities of compassionate care.

CHAPTER 9

Katherine had called the FBI duo and left a message before leaving for Boston. They responded by text that they would not be available again until the end of the week. *Great*, she thought. *Gives me more time with Stella.*

The next day, Katherine took her lunch to Stella's. She was itching to hear more, and Stella was waiting for her.

"Come in," said Stella. "I'm so glad to see you again. Thanks for not getting cold feet."

"I still think you should get a lawyer." Katherine, while intrigued, remained nervous, and she wanted to establish boundaries. "And if I start feeling uncomfortable, catch you lying, or am asked to keep secret any criminal behavior, I'm gone." Her tone was firm but not rude, because she actually wanted to hear the whole story and was hoping Stella wouldn't disappoint by being deceitful.

"Fair enough. I *am* keeping the lawyer option open. Most importantly, I'm grateful you're here to listen to the story of an old whore."

"The last word I would use to describe you is *whore.*"

"Thank you for that."

"You know, not having met many prostitutes and never any madams, I find it heartening that you sought therapy and found yourself a surrogate mother. I keep thinking about that. As I said before, I admire you for that kind of courage."

"Hundreds of hours in her office, thousands of hours reading psychology books. Did a lot of crying and venting. My dad had been raping me for years, and my mother, so beaten down and abused, couldn't protect me. In the early 1950s at the ripe old age of sixteen, I got out after some middle-aged, drunken slob, who was supposedly a friend of the family, offered me a hundred dollars if I would suck his dick. After doing that for all of two minutes, I decided that this could be my ticket to escape an oppressive life. I took that hundred dollars and ran away, far away, and never looked back. Well, once I did, but we'll save the sob story of my disastrous visit back home for another conversation."

"Stella, you don't have to explain. I'm not going to judge you." Katherine wondered why Stella was giving her much more information than necessary. Perhaps she felt compelled to justify or rationalize her life. Maybe she just decided to be up front and describe her life uncensored, warts exposed. Furthermore, the use of the word "dick" most definitely didn't fit the sweet old lady type. Katherine was convinced that this woman had, in fact, been around, and she was on guard, tense, figuring that this story was *not* heading in the direction of 'happily ever after.'

"I do need to explain. Please forgive the rambling confessions of an old woman. I want you to trust me. That is, if you still can after that disastrous FBI meeting."

Stella didn't wait for Katherine's response and continued her story. "Once I was able to permanently avoid the pimps and stay off the streets, my phone rang often. And are you ready for this? I started counseling runaway girls and getting them off the streets, while never recruiting one of them into my own—well, let's call it *profession*. Can you believe some thought I was a social worker?"

Katherine smiled as Stella talked about counseling and rescuing young girls. Until now, she thought she'd heard it all. Stella reached for her hand.

"I was a prostitute trying to help other prostitutes, especially those who were vulnerable to abuse by pimps: the young ones, those barely into puberty. I handed out condoms every chance I got. I'd like to think I saved some lives. I convinced more than a few to finish their education and go back home. That is, if their homes were civilized, of course, not like mine. Paid for their bus fares too."

"Dear God, Stella. What guts." Katherine really wanted to convey her validation. She knew prostitution, especially of young girls, was tragic. Now, an old lady sitting in front of her—hopefully telling the truth—had managed to live through it.

"Katherine, see that framed photo over there on the wall?" Stella took a deep breath, her voice dropping almost to a whisper. "That's Jenny. I sat at her hospital bedside after she hemorrhaged from a botched, back-alley abortion that her pimp had arranged before it was legalized. She was seventeen, died in my arms." Stella's eyes welled. "Jenny was so beautiful and had so much to live for. Her father was her first rapist, just like mine: the fucking, goddamn shits!"

"I'm so sorry, Stella. Dear God, I can only imagine how torturous that must have been." Katherine had heard many elder stories of pain and suffering, including from Holocaust survivors. But she never got used to them. They never got easier to hear and always left her drained.

Katherine took a bite of her sandwich before walking over to the framed photo and looking into the eyes of the teenager, innocence captured, who should have been an athlete or academic or class officer, anything. Instead, she went from a classroom to a casket.

"I'm glad you were there to hug and love her."

"I reported the pimp to the police, but he found out who I was and ordered a hit on me. However, he had burned a lot of bridges and made enemies. Last I heard, another pimp shot him full of bullets."

"Jesus, Stella! How did you handle a bounty on your head?"

"Well, as a matter of fact, I went to college. By the mid-sixties, I was a college graduate. I majored in world history and political science, of course."

"So you could carry on conversations with your newfound United Nations clients?"

"Absolutely. For many, I was more than a tryst. That's how I got invited to lavish dinners and learned how to navigate seven pieces of silver."

Katherine glanced around at the apartment. The photos were in expensive frames, ebony-carved African wildlife were dispersed throughout the room, small ones on tables, a three-foot giraffe on the floor. The walls were filled with oils and watercolors. The warm atmosphere was elegant, yet surprisingly simple and uncrowded. Extraneous furniture had been eliminated so as not to obstruct a walker.

"Your apartment tells me you've been around the world."

"You should see what I didn't bring, what I put in storage. But I'm happy. It's all just stuff. Someday, an auctioneer will reap a hefty commission and the profits will go to charity."

"So, Stella, how long were you on the streets before the UN presented its upward mobility opportunities?"

"Upward mobility opportunities. I like that. On the streets? Probably three or four years, long enough to get repeatedly arrested, raped, robbed, mugged, and otherwise encountering death-threatening situations. Then, my lucky break."

"What was that?"

"A drunk, rich guy in town for a week. He emptied his wallet every day, wads of cash. By the time he left, I could afford a decent apartment and bought myself a classy wardrobe. Everything changed, including clientele. Still mostly creeps, just rich creeps."

For a few minutes, the two sat quietly, hands touching, both comfortable with the silence. Stella was lost in revisiting her past. Katherine was trying to digest what she had heard. She was captivated.

Then Katherine asked gently, "Stella, where does Kevin fit into this picture?"

Stella perked up. "Kevin Finchley was a UN envoy whom I met in the late sixties at a large cocktail party. He was alone and my client was focused on a business deal with someone else. We started talking. He called me the next day and the next after that, at first on a professional basis. While he was from South Africa and his affluent family were major shareholders in the country's diamond mines, he was adamantly opposed to apartheid, that repulsive system formally sanctioned in the fifties."

"Repulsive for sure. The whole world was watching." Katherine glanced again at the ebony African animal figures and surmised a strong connection to Kevin's homeland.

"Well, we fell in love. And Katherine, as I said before, he's the only man I ever loved. While we were together, he worked tirelessly to end apartheid, earning him ugly alienation from his family, who convinced the South African government that he was treasonous."

"How so?" Upon hearing the word treason and starting to connect the dots, Katherine began to understand why the FBI might be involved. She wondered if the CIA had also been involved.

"He became a special envoy for human rights at the United Nations, not representing the South Africa government, of course. In fact, he was shunned by many of his own countrymen, who, along with his family, were far from ready to relinquish their form of enslavement. Kevin talked endlessly about his shame over the Nationalist Party of white Afrikaners who had slowly enacted apartheid into law. Even their Dutch Reformed Church, believing themselves to be ordained by God, while Blacks were 'inferior,' proclaimed to be the protectors of Blacks, whatever that means." Stella raised her voice, the floodgates of her anger opening. "Talk about hypocrisy in religion. I mean, how is oppressing a whole race protecting them? And invoking God to justify their actions? Go figure."

"One of my professors in grad school called apartheid Jim Crow on steroids,'" said Katherine. She recalled many conversations with Shirlee about racism. Katherine had learned from her friend what white privilege really meant. It had been painful for her.

"Jim Crow on steroids," Stella repeated. "Accurate description. Anyway, I can remember Kevin bursting into tears about this. I'd never seen such kindheartedness and sensitivity in a man. Or anybody, for that matter."

"I remember the Race Classification Act that labeled people as white, Black, or Asian. And mixed races were considered colored," said Katherine. "And I recall the Immorality Act, which made it illegal for whites to have sex with non-whites. I suppose that was to preserve their warped belief in a master race."

"And Katherine, let's not forget the strictly enforced law that defined for each group where they could live. What a sham! Black people needed passes to get into white areas. Can you imagine? Kevin even told me that people, including him, were spied on by the police. Why? Because he was mortified by those laws and had no problem speaking his mind!"

Katherine sensed Stella's desire to convince her of Kevin's honorable intentions by telling her about the life of the man she once loved. What Stella didn't realize was that Katherine was already hooked. She was totally mesmerized by Stella's story.

"I remember those years when it was all over the press. Thankfully, that's over now."

Katherine and Stella talked more about apartheid. Then Katherine asked, "Why was Kevin killed?"

"You mean murdered? Probably not even a proper grave for a man who did so much!" Stella began crying. "I can't believe I'm crying as I retell his story after all these years. Jesus, I must have repressed a lot. Wish my shrink was still alive."

Watching Stella cry, Katherine thought, *Thirty years dead? Why now for an FBI visit? Maybe something else. But what?* After a few minutes, Stella said, "How can a man who did so much for human rights be relegated to an existence that isn't worth remembering?" Then she was silent.

Katherine thought about Stella's poignant words, so indicative of the fate of countless elders: being relegated to an existence that isn't worth remembering.

Stella had tapped into one of the many reasons Katherine had started Oak Place.

CHAPTER 10

That afternoon, Katherine learned that a celebration of life had been planned at Oak Place for Mr. Riggins. Since Jeff had worked closely with him over the years to develop and enhance music therapy programs, Mrs. Riggins wanted him to give the eulogy. "Hi Jeff," said Katherine over the phone. "Just called to check in. We haven't talked since Mr. Riggins's death. Saw you're going to speak at his memorial. You doing okay?"

"We've both seen hundreds of elderly people die over the years. We both know death does not get easier with practice. But this one's been particularly hard. You know, I considered him a friend. That's part of my grief."

"I believe you. Besides, this very special person took his own life." She figured Jeff might feel guilty and wanted to test her theory.

"Are you thinking 'what-if' and 'if-only' like I am?"

"Jeff, are you blaming yourself? Do I need to remind you his suicide was not your fault?"

"Technically, I know you're right. And, he'd have died of cancer in a few weeks."

"I hear a 'but' coming."

"But, he was in physical pain and couldn't see any quality in the undeniably reduced time left in his life. Maybe I could've given him that. I gave him a low dose of narcotics, probably too low.

"You're a good man, Jeff. I'm truly sorry this is so hard for you."

☙ ☙ ☙

Katherine and Jeff had worked together for over three decades since the inception of Oak Place. They cared passionately about the elderly, cringing in tandem at what had become standard warehouse elder care and attitudes. For them, society was not age-friendly but rather age-phobic.

"We sort of abandon them," Katherine had said frequently. "Once you outlive your usefulness, you get relegated to a form of purgatory—neither dead nor truly alive."

Jeff had felt the same way. "Society will be judged in part by how we care for our elders. And our judgment day isn't looking so good."

Both had seen too much dumping of the elderly, more than their share of abuse cases, and too many elders curling up to die and be done with it.

Katherine and Jeff were professional soulmates of sorts. When presented with problems or challenges, each instinctively knew what the other was thinking. They met regularly to share groundbreaking data and test progressive ideas out on each other. Between the two of them, they had coauthored numerous articles and were in demand at professional conferences.

Their attitudes and philosophy were on the same page, their missions in sync. And so was something else. There had also been a heightening sexual chemistry between them, producing strong desires. But they had decided years ago—in the mid-nineties—that this impending affair would absolutely not be allowed to happen.

It had started simply enough; time spent together in a professional manner. But then the looks between them became more sustained, and there was more touching. They became aware that many of their face-to-face meetings could have been handled by phone. Finally, there was the hug that neither could let go of. With these escalations, both realized almost simultaneously that they were on a calamitous trajectory. They knew they needed to have the talk.

"If I followed my impulsive desires, I'd be taking you to a fabulous hotel and making love all afternoon," Jeff had said in a coffee shop in downtown Manhattan.

"And if I followed my impulsive desires, I would be enjoying every second," Katherine had responded. "But afterward, I'd be plagued by shame." She paused. "Jeff, we're married to two terrific people and have beautiful children. I cannot, under any circumstances, justify our running off into a nightmare of our own creation."

Jeff responded, laughing, "Well, like Dr. Zhivago and Lara, how about if we're amid the Russian Revolution and trapped in a frozen house in the middle of nowhere. Could you do it then?"

"And we're low on firewood, it's minus thirty-five degrees, and all we have are fur blankets and each other. Would we want to do it? Could we even do it?" Both laughed nervously at the unrealistic scenario. "Let's change the location to the Bahamas after a nuclear war and we're on the beach, waiting for the aftereffects to take us away."

"That's better," said Jeff. "I think I'd rather sweat than shiver." The forced laughter continued but couldn't rescue them from their intense distress. They stared off into space, avoiding eye contact. Katherine fidgeted with her phone.

Jeff clumsily cleared his throat. "The world is filled with those who have acted on impulsive yearning and fleeting passion; lovers who were driven by their hormones rather than their minds. I don't want to be that statistic. It's not fucking worth it."

"You mean when lust becomes the drug you need?" Katherine's thumb traced the lip of her coffee cup, eyes down.

"Yeah, I guess. You know, I loathe affairs and quite frankly, I despise that behavior in people who capitulate. I promised Amy honesty and I intend to keep that promise. But I just don't know how to make my feelings for you go away."

Katherine looked into his eyes, realizing that her career and personal life—as well as Jeff's—were on the line. "This is a train wreck waiting to happen."

"Katherine, divorce courts are filled with people yearning to change partners midlife, those who have reinvigorated tryst hormones, searching for ways out of boredom, not necessarily marrying a new and improved spouse, just a different one."

"I know what you mean. Peter has a friend who ended one marriage for another and later regretted it, saying he wished he had stuck it out, worked harder to jump start the plaguing mediocrity. The pain was just not worth it, and the second spouse—as it turns out—while nice enough, was not the wished-for panacea."

"You can say that again! New partners come with their own baggage, often not discovered until after a divorce and remarriage."

"Of course, neither of us have any *baggage*."

"Of course not." They both laughed.

"Jeff, I don't think either of us could live with the remorse of hurting people, namely, our innocent spouses. And, would the children ever forgive us?"

"Our romantic, free-spirited love would probably last a couple of months before guilt reared its ugly head. We'd never be free of it."

"Jesus, Jeff, I'm an emotional mess right now! I feel like I'm standing at the edge of a cliff with a fire I started right behind me. No, I'm not going to destroy my family—and, for that matter, myself. It's not that either of us is miserable. Yet I seem to be chasing an elusive happiness instead of working on the happiness I already have."

"If we had met before I married Amy and you married Peter, we probably could have had a great marriage."

"Jeff, I don't doubt it. *But* we didn't. In fact, what's really happening is that Oak Place has consumed my energy so that when I get home, there's little left. Some days, I'm home so late that my little girl is already asleep." Katherine started crying. "And I have very little reserve for Peter. God, he's such a good man. You know, I hate myself right now."

"Like you, Katherine, the sacrifices I've made for Oak Place include my marriage. You and I have elevated each other's creativity to national recognition. In doing so, we've ignored the people we love. So, we sit here today, trying to untangle a potential disaster."

"Jesus, we should've talked sooner. Why didn't we?"

"Fear?"

"Duh, you think?" Katherine's hands were shaking as she took another sip of coffee.

"I'm scared as hell right now! Can we still work together effectively? Should I leave?" Jeff asked, his eyes watering.

Has it really come to this, thought Katherine. "Have we really gotten to the point of either-or? Maybe I should be the one to leave."

"Can't we save both our marriages and our careers?"

"I'm willing to try. Look at the fucking alternatives."

"Me too. I'm calling my therapist. Got lots of work to do."

"Mine retired, but not a bad idea. You know, we get an A+ for our professional work together. Let's flunk the lust part. If we don't get off this powder keg, we risk so much misery."

Since then, Katherine and Jeff never had another conversation about their mutual chemistry. Each had made the same decision not to act, and each knew the costs of wavering. Certainly, it was difficult at first. They tended to go out of their way to avoid each other, fearful of their weaknesses. No more articles were written together for two years. Joint travel was kept to a bare minimum. In-person meetings became sporadic and only if absolutely necessary.

It wasn't easy. Both had difficulty purging their fantasies. Occasionally, in difficult periods of their respective marriages, the 'what-ifs,' like hibernating demons, would reemerge. This was particularly true for Jeff, who at one point almost separated from Amy. The easy way out would have been to seek love elsewhere. Instead, they worked on the marriage, not only saving it, but strengthening their bonds. Katherine and Peter likewise concentrated on their own marriage and child-rearing. Mainly, Katherine rejected the workaholic treadmill, at least most of the time. "Oak Place will survive and thrive even if I don't put in a sixty-hour week," Katherine had told her therapist.

Neither shared their emotional turbulence with respective spouses. Katherine's close friend, Shirlee, who had just started working at Oak Place, never knew. Eventually, over the years, their yearnings subsided. Both seemed to have made it through the storm. Their relationship was born out of mutual respect and admiration. They knew they had made the right decision. The affair that never was instead became a nationally recognized professional partnership and friendship. The work they did for the elderly resolutely trumped any intimate desires they had had for each other.

CHAPTER 11

"Look, what's the deal? I thought you said Stella Cordrey was competent," FBI Agent Gultowski said to Katherine over the phone.

His tone was condescending, reminding Katherine why she was so angry after their first visit with Stella. *What an asshole,* she thought. Trying to sound professional, Katherine said, "I hadn't seen her behave like that. I think she was scared. Most octogenarians don't get a formal visit from the FBI. Plus, she just moved here after being immobilized by hip surgery and having complications. A lot of changes are taking place in her life."

"Well, we need to talk to her. *And* get some questions answered."

"Perhaps you can tell me what this is about. Maybe I can help," She hoped her offer was acceptable.

"This is official government business and classified."

Katherine raised her voice a little. "Look, if you want answers, I may be able to help you get them. And it won't hurt if you establish some trust. Unless, of course, she's wanted for a serious crime." She was more than vaguely interested in whether Stella had a criminal past.

"We can take her into custody."

"Oh really? Do you think that will make her cooperate? If you ask me, that's what will make her get a lawyer. And I've already suggested she do just that."

There was a long pause. Finally, the agent said, "She's not wanted for a crime—yet. However, information solicited from her might make her an accessory."

"Accessory to what?"

"Can't tell you. Classified."

"Look, you're dealing with an old lady who can no longer live by herself without assistance. I'm willing to help you get what you need.

And quite frankly, I think she wants to cooperate. She started talking about a man named Kevin Finchley. Are you looking for information about him?"

"Confidential."

"Ms. Cordrey has told me she wants me present when you visit her again. At first, I was hesitant to agree, but maybe it'll help you if I *am* there. And, you're going to have to present yourself in a gentler manner or you run the risk of her clamming up again."

There was another pause. Katherine thought the thirtyish Gultowski might be trying to figure out if a different tactic was warranted.

"You must keep these communications entirely confidential. What is your social security number?"

"What?!" Katherine thought Gultowski might be nervous. Asking for her social security number showed his need for control and a lack of experience.

"We'll need to run a background check."

"My fingerprints are on file. Also, you can find any information about my professional life all over the internet. I've testified and lobbied before Congress. I've been a member of the White House Council on Aging. All that information is freely available. I do not give my social security number out over the phone. If you still want it when you visit next, I'll make it available. And by the way, how do I make sure you're legitimate?" Katherine hated playing tit for tat, but she was irritated.

"You can check our credentials by calling the FBI or having your attorney do a background check. It'll be very easy for you to confirm our status." Then Gultowski gave Katherine his and Walker's badge numbers.

"When would you want to schedule your next visit?"

"How about tomorrow morning at ten?"

"If you don't hear back from me, it means she's available at that time. I'll meet you in the lobby by the fish tank. Oh, and by the way, she's well-educated and is not hard of hearing. So don't treat her like a child."

CHAPTER 12

At 9:30 the next morning, Katherine made her way to the assisted living complex. Stella would be expecting her, and Katherine wondered how the FBI interview—or more likely, interrogation—would proceed. As she passed Jake's stall, she noticed Hal was busy cleaning it. The straw on his clothes and in his hair indicated he'd once again spent the night with Jake. Katherine knew Jake liked to lie down at night on his side with all four legs outstretched. Many times before when she had arrived early, she had seen Hal snuggled next to Jake, with his arm draped over the horse's shoulder, elbow bent so his fingers were wrapped around Jake's ear, as if he had been stroking him before they succumbed to sleep. It seemed both horse and human had found symbiotic comfort with each other.

Her initial thoughts of intervening had dissipated long ago. Besides, Hal's presence hadn't encouraged other homeless people to descend on Oak Place. Letting him sleep with a horse he loved so much seemed the least she could do for the sacrifices he'd made for his country. One of the residents had provided Hal with a blanket to cover the side of him that was not pressed against the warmth of Jake's body.

A small commotion interrupted Katherine's thoughts. She walked over to the gathering people to find a resident, Otto, shuffling about naked except for briefs. This wasn't the first time.

"I forgot to pick up my clothes from the dry cleaner," he said. "I have an office full of patients waiting."

Katherine knew Otto, a long-retired medical doctor who was a couple of years into his Alzheimer's diagnosis. His wife, who had been looking for him—beside herself with worry—finally appeared to rescue him. Katherine called security to have someone come on a golf cart with a blanket and take them home. In the meantime, another resident took off his sweater and put it over Otto's shoulders to protect him from the cool temperature.

"I was in the shower and he just walked out," his wife said, tears streaming down her face. "I dread the day I have to put him in the dementia unit. I've already lost him mentally. I can't imagine losing him physically, but now I'm scared. We've been married fifty-five years."

Katherine knew this agony: a beloved person, cognition diminishing, forcing the family to make painful decisions about full-time care or institutionalization. She surveyed the small group surrounding him, pity in their eyes. She knew what they were thinking; *Could this be me someday?*

Now late, Katherine almost jogged to assisted living. Gultowski and Walker, whose credentials had been verified by the Oak Place attorney, were waiting in the lobby, both seemingly captivated by the massive round aquarium stocked with colorful fish.

"Good morning," said Katherine with a smile.

"Ma'am," both Walker and Gultowski said simultaneously. Walker then said, "I've never seen an aquarium so big and so beautiful except in a museum. Is it saltwater?"

Katherine responded to the small talk, feeling it might just help everyone relax. "Yes, a patient's family donated this tank a decade ago. Their father, who lived here for years, had been an oceanographer. It's twelve feet high, holds thousands of gallons of water and hundreds of fish, drawing people to this lobby as if to an oasis. Residents and their families often gather here. The fish and the sounds of cascading water are mesmerizing. As a matter of fact, to maintain a tranquil effect, no cellphones are allowed in this part of the lobby."

Walker and Gultowski continued looking at the aquarium, so Katherine kept talking. "Students from a school of oceanography help maintain it. We only use fish that breed in captivity. We no longer remove fish from the ocean. That's also why the reefs are artificial."

Katherine pointed to the other notable features in the lobby.

"Volunteers nurture all the beautiful plants and potted trees throughout the atrium. The preschool is down that hall and the children, who consider this *their* fish tank, have named most every fish. That seahorse swimming by now is Dexter, I think. Or is it Chloe?"

Both Walker and Gultowski grinned. "Doesn't look like a Chloe to me," said Gultowski.

Katherine waited a few more minutes, hoping the calming effect would prevail, before guiding them to the elevator and Stella's apartment.

"Come in," Stella yelled upon hearing the knock. She was in the kitchen retrieving the cream and sugar, and had already placed coffee and her freshly baked, still warm blueberry muffins on the dining table, the aroma filling the apartment. "Please make yourselves comfortable."

Stella shuffled slowly out of the kitchen using her walker. "Well, what do you want in your coffee?" When both Gultowski and Walker quickly turned her down, she got sassy. "Look, let's break bread together. I'm not a criminal, this isn't poison, and you need to lighten up and let a little old lady serve you. Jesus, I've been up since seven baking. And it's not easy when you have to navigate a walker and carry filled cupcake tins between the counter and an oven."

"I'll take some cream and sugar—and the muffins smell so nice," said Katherine as she got up to help herself. "Thanks."

Walker and Gultowski relented, clearly uncomfortable breaking protocol.

"Okay," said Stella, taking charge, "let's talk about the other day. The doctor said I had an ischemic brain attack, causing temporary confusion. I get them when I'm stressed."

Katherine knew she was lying through her teeth but understood. It just might work on the agents. She didn't plan on intervening unless it happened again.

"What are your first names?" asked Stella.

"Ma'am?"

"I am not going to sit here for however long and call you Agent Gultowski and Agent Walker, so what are your first names?"

"I'm Jeb Walker, this is Brian Gultowski. Did you know a Mr. Kevin Finchley?"

"Sure did. For many years."

"What was your relationship with him?"

"Companion, listener, dinner date, debater of Shakespeare's tragedies, particularly King Lear, which we saw together five times. Oh, did I mention lover? That was the best part. Oh, excuse me! Is that too much information?" Stella gave them a huge smile. She even winked at Walker.

"Uh, ah, how long did you know him?" asked Walker a bit nervously.

"On and off over twenty years."

"On and off?" asked Gultowski, taking another bite of his muffin.

"He traveled back to South Africa a lot. He'd be gone months at a time, once almost a year."

"Did you know he was married?"

"Yes."

"And that didn't bother you?"

With a titanic change in tone, Stella said sternly, "What are you, the fucking morality police? I suggest you get off your sanctimonious judgmental asses until you know the full story!"

Katherine knew a little old lady saying "fuck" would draw attention. It certainly qualified as a "wow" factor. Such a common word, yet it most often came from the mouths of the young. People generally expect grandmothers to act more matronly, more prim and proper, as if they were cuss-virgins. That was not Stella.

Walker looked embarrassed, enough so that he was mute for a few seconds, as if regathering his thoughts or perhaps wondering if another 'ischemic attack' was forthcoming. Katherine hoped he might apologize but he didn't.

"When was the last time you saw him?"

Stella glared at him as if she wanted to slap him. "Apartheid started collapsing in 1990," she said curtly. Then, in a calmer voice, "I saw him twice before that. Once in 1989 and then in early 1990."

"Did you expect to see him again?"

"He had been rebuffed by his government for standing up against apartheid. His passport was revoked, and he was sent home. After that, I traveled twice to South Africa to see him. I missed him terribly. Sadly, he had changed. He looked older than his years: haggard, solemn, hesitant, always looking over his shoulder like the life had been sucked out of him. At that time, he was focused on the release of Nelson Mandela." Stella sighed loudly and looked down. "Yes, I wanted to see him again, but deep down, I was afraid for him, for us."

"Do you know that he is dead?" asked Walker gently, which was surprising.

"Died in 1990, not long after the release of Nelson Mandela," Stella murmured without looking up as a single tear, following the path of a wrinkle, slowly trickled down her cheek. "He was murdered, probably tortured. He didn't live to see a democratic South Africa."

Neither Walker nor Gultowski said anything, instead giving Stella time to regain her composure.

After a couple of minutes, Stella continued. "What a waste. Such a tender, loving man. I never realized the happiness we found together would be his last. He'd been shunned by his family and friends for speaking out against apartheid. His wife was the worst. I never met her, but she was by his account a flaming bigot—abhorrent—a rich, white bitch."

"Did you know he was going to go on trial for stealing millions from his family's fortune?" asked Walker.

"Yes, I knew," she said, once again looking straight into Walker's eyes.

"And that he was aiding rebel factions in other parts of Africa?" Walker asked, his voice raised.

"Stop! Enough! No Way!" Stella started crying. "He never did that! Never!"

"Ma'am, we need more information," Walker shouted, not a bit of empathy in his voice. "He was accused of stealing diamonds to give to rebels and subvert the South African government."

"Listen to me! He never gave one penny to rebels! Not one!" Stella continued to cry but tried to make herself stop; she was angry and wanted to clearly express that feeling. "Who told you that? His family? Those bastards!" Stella's hands were shaking, and her lips quivered. Katherine knew this wasn't for show.

Even after a few minutes of silence, Stella couldn't get herself together. Her breathing was rapid. "I'm feeling lightheaded. I don't think I can go on today. Can you please come back tomorrow?" She began to cry again.

Gultowski and Walker were still thinking about the other day. "You're not going to get confused on us again, are you?" Walker was blatantly sarcastic.

"No, I am not confused, but I will not put up with your goddamn attitudes!" Trembling, Stella shouted at them while gasping for air. "Where in the hell did you learn your interview skills? Either talk with me properly or I'm going to get an attorney and you'll need subpoenas to get your asses in my door again! For what it's worth, gentlemen, I am willing to cooperate, mostly to save the name and reputation of a dear man of honor. But I'm not going to have some naïve FBI novices turn this into a 'gotcha' road show. Is that understood?"

There was silence. The Madam had spoken. This sweet little old lady was undoubtedly street-smart beyond anyone in the room. Old age wasn't hampering her ability to take care of herself or the rights she knew she had.

Walker and Gultowski reluctantly obliged, especially after Katherine, by now equally as angry as Stella, swung her head toward the door as a cue that they had best leave. They knew they had blown it. Portraying themselves as hard-nosed, in-control authorities had backfired—again.

After they left, Katherine turned to Stella. "I'm so sorry. He must've been so very special to you." They hugged for a while as Stella cried.

"This is no act," Stella said. "Katherine, besides my hip, I also have congestive heart failure. Seems every time I get emotional, I can't catch my breath."

"I know this was no act. Do you want me to stay with you for a while?"

"I prefer crying alone, and I feel better now. You know, Katherine, I've never, ever been able to share this story. Even though he's been dead almost thirty years, I guess my grief is still just below the surface."

"Like I said a couple of days ago—while one can move on, you never get over a loved one's death. Besides, sometimes old emotions resurface, making it seem like his death was just yesterday."

"Katherine, he treated me so tenderly." Stella was silent for a moment, reminiscing. "Tenderly," she repeated. "What a beautiful concept. Before Kevin, that was just a yearning for me. He let me feel it. I learned tenderness from him. Oh, what Kevin and I could've had if we'd been able to grow old together!"

After a pause, Stella whispered, "Katherine, will you come back before they come again? I have something I want to share with you privately."

CHAPTER 13

L ater, Katherine walked to the senior living complex for her class, Writing Your Story. She loved teaching, or as she called it, facilitating the learning of others. While she sometimes groaned about the extensive preparation, when it came time to deliver, she was always pumped up.

Over the decades, she had been fervently dedicated to motivating people to write their stories. Everybody had a past, some of it up front, readily shared, perhaps even bragged about. This was particularly true for the elderly, who might seek to divulge their life experiences, exposing worthy or not so worthy accomplishments to those, mostly family, who might want to know about them.

At the same time, Katherine disliked resume-style memoirs that listed important dates, awards, or career promotions. Katherine publicly called these boast books. Privately, she called them justify-your-life books. She found them boring, like so many obituaries that tell a reader what a person did—in chronological order, of course—with nary a hint of the truly meaningful experiences in their lives or how they felt about them. Katherine had read too many lengthy memoirs without gaining any insight as to who the person really was. "Don't just tell me you were born in a log cabin without electricity or a bathroom." she would say. "Tell me what it meant to you. How it shaped you."

Katherine was so intrigued by life stories that she had started autobiography writing classes for residents at Oak Place years ago. Interestingly, at first only a few came—timidly—after holding back dams of thought, wanting to tell, share, justify, explain, or merely let someone know they existed and were worthy of their story being told. Those first few participants spurred on many more as word spread, and she was delighted to see the classes filling up. Their words became simple books, assembled using a copy machine and interspersed with photos, turning into precious gifts to families on holidays as the authors swelled with pride. Some, on the other hand, were apprehensive about the response from family members to exposing what might be perceived as family secrets.

Sketchy, fill in the blank type books were eventually replaced with a yearning to get out the "real" story. Hurt and pain told. Bitterness exposed along with the resolved and unresolved. Katherine was very honest in telling them that writing some things down could cause anguish for them or their families, and would ask if they wanted to do that. Her thought-provoking questions made some change their minds, while others went full-steam ahead.

One woman, who had inflicted much emotional scarring on her children, wrote of her own pathetic childhood. She ended her story by writing that she hoped her children, two of whom refused to speak to her, wouldn't pass on this harmful legacy, and she apologized for being a "bad" mother. One of her estranged children came to visit the day after receiving the autobiography. The crying and tears ended with forgiveness, and later with visits from preteen grandchildren she'd never met. Other touching experiences took place repeatedly as more and more autobiographies were written.

Not all life stories were put to paper. Many went to their graves with their secrets, embarrassments, or regrets. Katherine's initial impression of Stella Cordrey was of a society lady who would impress with her worldly stories. It would have stayed that way except for the events of the past few days, which, like an archeological dig, now revealed a much more complicated existence. Katherine wondered how much Stella would expose.

"My story is not that important in the scheme of things," a woman in the back of the room said meekly.

It was just the sort of comment Katherine had hoped for. "Why do you say that?"

"I was a wife, mother, went back to teaching third grade after my kids were older, and now I'm an involved grandmother. I don't have a room full of awards. I'm just an ordinary person."

"You mean you *didn't* get a Nobel Prize or go to the moon?" asked Katherine. Everyone laughed.

"I was Classroom Volunteer of the Year once back in the sixties," the woman replied with a chuckle.

"I made lots of mistakes," one man shouted. "They will go to my grave with me. Why would I want to burden my children with my screw-ups when even I don't want to remember them?"

Katherine had heard this many times before, often involving secret affairs or something to do with money, lies of various magnitudes, or hateful words that had severed relationships. It was her policy to never push anyone to expose things they preferred kept to themselves.

"My mother survived the Holocaust," said a woman in the first row. "My kids know this, but not all of it. She was scarred, paranoid, and so wrought with anxiety that she was never a loving mother."

Another man stood up slowly, using his walker to steady himself, "I lost my son in the Vietnam War, needlessly I might add, because of the stupid pride of politicians. His wife was pregnant with my first grandchild. That was forty-eight years ago. I'm ninety-four years old now, and I am still angry!"

The participants began sitting upright and leaning forward, as if ready to expose raw emotions. Katherine didn't attempt to stop this catharsis.

From the back, a man started talking but didn't stand up. "Well, I'm a Vietnam vet, drafted as soon as I graduated college in 1968. I hated the war that destroyed so many lives. And for what? I was assigned to a unit smack in the war zone. I was ordered to patrol regularly, deep into the surrounding jungle, to flush out the Viet Cong and shoot them before they shot us. Well, we went out alright, just outside the barbed wire perimeter of our fort, and sat down all day out of our superior officer's sight. On some days, I read whole books. No way was I going to get shot or step on a land mine for a country that lied to us, while shameful politicians directed death from the cozy confines of their offices. My whole unit of twelve men never divulged our secret combat refusal. A few months later, we all came home safe without one iota of guilt or feelings of cowardice."

The room went so silent you could've heard a pin drop as they digested yet another war story that perhaps had never been told before. Blatant disobedience of orders. Not willing to die for political reasons.

Katherine was speechless for a moment, then said, "Thank you for sharing. I know that wasn't easy." She knew that speaking his truth could trigger intense reactions from some in the audience.

Another participant spoke. "At the funeral of my mother, one of her colleagues talked about how my mom courageously volunteered to be the first white teacher in an all-Black school during the turbulent desegregation process in Florida in the 1960s. Sure, I knew some superficial details, but I found out at her funeral how gutsy it really was and the bravery it took. Afterward, I longed to learn more, but most of her friends and colleagues were already gone. If only she had shared more about significant events in her professional life. If only I had asked! I still wonder what else I don't know about this unsung heroine, my mother."

"Well, my mother *cried* when I was born," said another, "because I was a girl, not the coveted son. In fact, I spent my life trying to show my parents I was worthy. In my fantasies, I was famous, very famous, so famous that my parents were impressed at last. In real life, as I became more educated, my parents, instead of admiring my accomplishments, worried about me becoming an old maid. I was wounded, craving some of the attention that my brothers already had. But, what I did was never enough to squelch the profoundly antiquated misogyny of not having a penis!"

Some in the audience gasped. The woman continued, "How's that for unresolved anger? Should I write *that* down?"

"Perhaps writing it will help you dissect your feelings," said Katherine. "Remember, you can always throw it away later." Katherine secretly hoped she would find the courage to tell her children and grandchildren so they might better understand the history of women's struggles.

Katherine then asked the participants, "So, what makes a meaningful life? What makes *your* life worth sharing? What's the difference between the autobiography of a celebrity and yours? Are you impressed by red carpets, fame and fortune, or the touching stories of, let's say, *On The Road with Charles Kuralt*? Remember him?" Most nodded. "Does the overworked social worker who placed hundreds of foster kids deserve some semblance of acknowledgement and gratitude? Is their story worth being told?

"The famous in a society have left a paper trail of biographies, often memoirs that were like a soap opera, and never made it to a second printing. Celebrities might figure their lives warrant a place on the immortality bookshelf. In fact, they refer to each other as icons. Really? Considering the extreme overuse of that word, it's misleading.

"One only need talk to people like you, looking back and looking inward, to see a fascinating life, absent the narcissism, yet one that most likely would never be preserved in print or on film. You're the most captivating. Ask yourselves, 'Do you want input on how you'll be remembered?'"

Katherine paused to look around and get a feel for her audience's reaction.

"I feel like my kids and grandkids treat me like a child," a white-haired man said, hands on his walker. "They choose to see me as cute, sitting in a rocking chair with a loving, wrinkled smile, savoring my grandparent and great-grandparent status, fussed over as I celebrate another birthday complete with photos snapped of multiple generations, preserving what might be the last photo of me. I know that's what they're thinking. Sometimes, I want to scream! They really don't know me. And yet, I realize some of that is my own fault."

After the class, the man who had lost his son in Vietnam walked over to the vet who had defied orders, first shaking his hand, then tearfully embracing him while saying, "I'm glad you lived. I wish my son had been in your unit."

❧ ❧ ❧

Those first participants spread the word about the class. The next one had to be split into two, and there was still a waiting list. One woman who never learned to read or write privately approached one of the teachers. "No problem, Mrs. Jones," said the teacher. "We can record your story on tape. I'll help you do it." In future sessions, more than a few recorded their stories, some with video cameras.

The autobiography philosophy was extended to grandparent/ grandchildren gatherings. Adolescent grandchildren were given questions to ask their grandparents. They ranged from the simple (What was your first car? What did you do on dates? How did the Great Depression affect your parents?) to the complex (What accomplishments are you most proud of? What were your biggest regrets?). The answers almost always strengthened intergenerational understanding and bonds.

Katherine, knowing most teenagers were plugged into electronic devices, also encouraged grandchildren to watch movies like *The Notebook*. While not a great movie in her view, its flashbacks of an older couple in their youthful romantic and incredibly steamy relationship proved that grandparents were once young and—yes—sexual. The kids loved the story, inviting many to visualize younger versions of their grandparents and consequently ask more questions.

Katherine always ended her class with the words, "The death of an elder is like the burning of a library."

CHAPTER 14

Katherine's fast-paced walk in the brisk air slowed almost to a stop as she passed several children from the primary school taking turns with Jake's lead rope as they led the miniature horse around the complex. Two residents were assisting, and many others were watching as they sat on nearby benches. The children were thrilled, their faces beaming at being given the responsibility. They were handed apple slices, and they took turns holding out their palms, carefully so that Jake couldn't grab a finger. They giggled as Jake's lips tickled against their hands to munch the special treat. After the walk, the children took turns brushing Jake. Jake loved all the attention, especially the brushing.

Mr. Jenkins, considered the resident horse expert because he had owned a pony seventy years ago as a child, cautioned them to keep their voices low and not make sudden movements that might startle Jake. They followed his advice, and Katherine smiled at the sight. Sometimes with an index finger pressed to their lips, she could hear one child shushing another if they got too excited.

It had been several years since a resident had approached Katherine with the possibility of bringing this miniature horse to the complex. After all, the price was right. Jake would be donated in honor of the years of accounting services the resident had given to their horse farm. Hesitant at first, Katherine had weighed the liability and costs of having a horse in the middle of Oak Place. Also, Oak Place was in New York City, not the rolling hills of rural America. And Jake would take up precious space. She had spoken with local zoning officials, neighborhood veterinarians (most of whom had experience with cats and dogs but not horses) and, of course, the residents.

Katherine, along with many residents, was drawn to horses, having ridden as a teenager. A *Bring Jake to Oak Place* committee was formed, which eventually came up with the funds needed to build a stable and small pasture. Many signed up for 'Jake care,' as they called it. They even secured money for a scholarship to train a vet in miniature horse care. Most were not interested, but Katherine convinced one veterinarian's mother, who was an Oak Place resident, to appeal to her son. "I never thought you would conspire with my mother to get me into this," he had jokingly told Katherine. "My, my, you sure know how to make things happen."

So, with all in place, everyone celebrated when the large horse trailer pulled up and out trotted this tiny, magnificent black horse about the height of a Great Dane. At first, Jake was not happy. Who would be, with hundreds of daily gawkers, many of whom had never seen a miniature horse? Plus, there were the sounds of the city that he wasn't familiar with. Sirens were especially frightening for the tiny horse, and he reared up and ran around his pasture every time they sounded, which was often.

On the third day in his new home, he managed to unhook the fence—or someone failed to secure the latch—to his pasture. Jake escaped and was enjoying the lettuce and carrot leaves in one of the therapeutic gardens. What he didn't eat, he trampled. When one little old lady with blue hair tried to shoo him out by poking him with her walker, he spooked. Immediately, several residents tried to capture him, realizing too late that Jake, mane flowing in the wind, could outrun any human, especially older ones. He ended up galloping into the street, his panic intensifying as horns blasted and brakes screamed.

"Am I crazy?" asked a fireman sitting next to a coworker while taking a break from polishing a fire engine. "Or did I just see a little horse run past the station followed by a group of fast-walking, gray-haired old people waving their hands in the air?"

"What did you drink last night?" the coworker joked.

The fire station was two blocks from Oak Place on a street bustling with small businesses. The entire neighborhood surrounding

Oak Place had always catered to the needs of residents, and businesses didn't last long if word spread that they were not old-age-friendly. Many residents regularly traversed the city blocks, often stopping to chat with local firefighters or police, shopkeepers, or merchants. They also knew the pharmacists, veterinarians and doctors, as well as the ministers, rabbis and priests, some of whom conducted services on Oak Place's vast campus. In fact, more than a few residents supplemented their incomes by working in the neighborhood, and some residents owned businesses.

It was there, in the middle of a busy boulevard, that Jake met homeless veteran, Hal, for the first time. "Whoa, boy. Easy now," said Hal in a calm, trusting voice while his hands stroked Jake's neck. "It's going to be okay. Whoa. Whoa. Easy." Hal's voice elicited Jake's almost instant trust and a 'please get me out of here' look.

The old people, now breathing heavily, finally caught up. "Jesus," one said, "that horse is fast! Can't believe he didn't get run over!"

"Well, I almost did!" said a woman, panting. "Wait till I tell my grandchildren that their grandma chased a horse through Queens. They really will think I have Alzheimer's!"

"It *was* a horse!" said the first fireman as he saw the motley crowd of old people gathering. "Get out the oxygen. Half the people out there have their hands on their knees trying to catch their breaths."

"Never seen a horse that size," said the other fireman. "I wonder if Oak Place has added this to their animal menagerie. Wouldn't be surprised."

Despite being safely rescued after his escape, Jake became sick, and struggled to walk toward the end of his first week at Oak Place. Foundering, they called it, a painful hoof condition; the consequence of eating too much of certain foods—in Jake's case, junk food. Seems everybody was feeding him. They would gather apples and carrots, and in some instances, cat food, glazed donuts, and uneaten Reuben sandwiches. Jake never turned anything down.

The vet was called. Katherine became particularly worried when she observed him with his *Caring for a Miniature Horse* manual open, his mother helping him thumb through the pages as he attempted to diagnose poor Jake, all the while mumbling, "See what you got me into, Mom."

He called a horse specialist colleague in Kentucky whom he hadn't seen since vet school. He had also canceled his other scheduled non-emergency four-legged patients, and Katherine recalled envisioning the specter of exorbitant vet bills in her head. The vet, at the guilt-inducing urging of his mother, tried to be gracious by only charging five hundred dollars for the three-hour visit. Jake perked up after a day of fasting and some medication, which had to be retrieved from upstate Connecticut. Thereafter, a sign was placed on his fence: DO NOT FEED THE HORSE.

After all the preliminary work, they became aware of a significant oversight; a horse's hooves need regular manicuring. Farriers are rare in Queens, but one was found on Long Island. Farrier Dewey was eighty-two but remembered his days on the racetracks filing hooves and crafting horseshoes. Of course, Dewey's current back pain made it especially hard to bend to this horse's level, so a very hesitant Jake was led onto a two-foot platform, allowing Dewey to work in a more upright position. Jake, however, decided he wasn't happy with this arrangement and kicked Dewey in the ribs to demonstrate his displeasure, after which four older men and two women stepped in to help contain the two-hundred-pound horse. Naturally, at that very time, the fire alarms blasted piercingly, resulting in two more helpers getting kicked, while the only one wearing sandals was stepped on after Jake reared up and jumped off the platform. Jake may have been a small horse, but he was strong and not inclined to let a bunch of gray-haired humans try to control him.

After a couple of months, Jake's entourage of caretakers got the hang of it. Jake calmed down, and the vet didn't need to be summoned for another acute crisis. Dewey had a broken rib, but Jeff took extra special care of him for free in the hopes he wouldn't sue. In fact,

Dewey liked Oak Place so much that he and his wife signed up to live there, which they happily did until he died. During his time at Oak Place, anticipating that he would become more limited as he aged, Dewey trained Hal and another resident in the care of Jake's hooves.

Hal started showing up daily to check on Jake and eventually found his stall a perfect place to sleep. Katherine balked at first. Being homeless and unkempt, with knotted hair down to his shoulders, Hal was not a model senior, especially when covered with straw. He also scared some of the residents, not by *being* threatening, but *appearing* threatening. That's when Shirlee took charge with military precision. "If you're going to help care for this horse, you need to look better. First, let's go to the shelter and get you some clothes, and then a haircut."

Then, with a blazing burst of authority, drawing Hal to immediate attention, Shirlee yelled, "Now!" By day's end, few recognized the new and improved Hal.

Hal was then taken to Jeff for a full physical and mental evaluation. Between Katherine, Shirlee, and Jeff, the rehabilitation of this homeless Vietnam veteran began. It was not as successful as they hoped, but Hal was happier than he had been in years, in part due to the antidepressant Jeff gave him. While not outwardly scared of Shirlee, he tried to avoid her and would often hide from her in the bushes. Upon finding him, she would more often than not march him to the showers or to Jeff's office to get his blood pressure checked.

"You're *not* my mother," he would tell her while laughing. One time, she retorted with motherly, though nonetheless threatening words delivered in a superior tone, "Don't you mess with a post-menopausal woman!"

Hal instinctively realized that Shirlee, under the façade of an uncompromising power woman, had a heart of gold. But he figured she had her limits, and he wasn't inclined to test them.

"I wonder how many senior resident facilities in the U.S. have a homeless man living in their midst?" Katherine had remarked. "Please, when the hospital accreditors come, let's take Hal to the homeless shelter for the day."

Despite a rocky start, Jake was a wonderful addition to Oak Place and brought joy to children and residents alike. In the winter, to keep the chill out, he was warmed by a homemade bright pink wool sweater that fit tightly around his abdomen. He looked ridiculous, but nobody had the heart to tell the ninety-two-year-old woman who had made it. However, after finding out Jake was male, she gladly reconfigured the sweater to leave an opening for his often dangling, sizeable penis.

Now at twenty-two and in the twilight of his years, Jake was arthritic but still quite healthy. He loved attention, and he and Hal became inseparable. Jake also loved attention from the children and residents who stopped by daily. When families visited their elder relatives, the kids begged to see Jake. On a beautiful Sunday, it was not uncommon to see several multigenerational families hanging out by the pasture, now surrounded by benches.

Nursing home patients who were less mobile often asked for someone to bring Jake to their bedsides—a request rarely turned down—even though Jake was known to pee or poop anywhere at any time. The clickity-clack of his hooves on the floor outside the nurse's station, plus Jake's frequent and vocal neighing, was enough to perk up even the most withdrawn residents.

Even though Jake's pasture wasn't that large, he never lacked for exercise. He truly became a working therapy animal—loved and adored, stroked by a thousand hands and touching everyone's hearts. While probably the most popular, and certainly enjoying the most celebrity, Jake was only one animal of the pets who called Oak Place home. Every floor had impeccably behaved therapy dogs, often trained professionally. Master dog trainers and their students spent significant volunteer time teaching these canines everything from not being freaked by wheelchairs to eliminating untoward behaviors like crotch sniffing. They also taught residents how to reinforce the animals' training.

Cats, mostly untrainable and with pompous attitudes, were also present on almost every floor of the nursing home and assisted living buildings. They could be seen parading through the hallways, jumping on a bed, particularly when it was drenched in sunlight, or snuggling on a patient's lap. Certain areas were designated cat free to accommodate those with allergies.

Most of the animals, and only those with the appropriate temperaments, were selected from the various city humane societies' collections of castoff pets. In many cases, their owners had died, leaving older pets—no longer the cute, sought-after kittens or puppies, and unwanted by the surviving family members—doomed for euthanasia. The staff who rescued them found their plight not all that dissimilar to what many of the nation's elderly had experienced. Lucky was the cat or dog who got chosen to live out their life with loving attention at Oak Place.

The healthier residents walked, groomed, combed, and loved them. A long, rectangular fenced dog area was created to exercise and play with the animals. Cat duty, of course, included changing kitty litter. The pets required a lot of attention, but it was all worth it. The staff regularly witnessed wet nuzzles gently forcing open a closed hand, or a cat perched on the back of a comfy chair purring into an ear, resulting in relaxed smiles and constant stroking. It was a mutual exchange of affection that all, whether animal or human, enjoyed.

The Oak Place live-in pet population was in addition to the residents' privately owned pets, which were required to be under thirty pounds unless they were trained, licensed therapy animals. In fact, one woman who had waited two years to become a resident, tearfully said she couldn't live at Oak Place if it meant she had to give up her ten-year-old, overweight lab mix, Bruno. Instead of turning her away, Katherine's staff, knowing animals were like family to many—and kept them from feeling isolated—helped get her dog trained as a therapy animal after she agreed to put him on a diet and regularly take Bruno to the nursing home for patient visits. The dog was reenergized by exercise and less snacking, and the woman faithfully complied until Bruno died.

Over the years, only a few problems had occurred. One three-year-old child tried to ride an older therapy dog. A two-year-old attempted to give a cat a bath—in a toilet. In both cases, the animals rebelled against the innocent bullying, resulting in a screaming kid bolting into a teacher's or parent's arms, the dog's teeth marks not penetrating, the cat causing only minor scratching, and the children definitely learning a lesson.

CHAPTER 15

The nursing home, which included the hospice and palliative care unit, was the most professionally staffed building due to the increased care needs of the patients. Devoid of the usual carpeted rooms and hallways, it was challenging to make it look homey. Hallways needed handrails, which meant less furniture. Rooms were equipped with hospital beds and oxygen outlets. Wheelchairs and walkers were everywhere. Patients could, of course, bring personal belongings like cherished photos of loved ones, a treasured afghan, or needlepoint pillows and stools.

Outside each resident's room, hanging near the entrance, was a collage of photos spanning lifetimes, as well as a brief history of the patient, there to remind even the family that their loved one was once young. Often, family and friends added stories to this memory board—snippets of a life, memories of a past.

A typical story: *Joe coached girls softball for many years, making sure these young women knew they had athletic potential, especially with practice. They admired and respected him. Once, he took these fourteen-year-olds, his daughter included, all the way to a state tournament, placing third.*

Next to this short bio was a photo of Joe with his team, celebrating and holding their trophy proudly. Another photo showed a smiling Joe frying fish in an iron skillet over a bonfire next to the words: *Joe was an avid fisherman who loved taking his children and later, his grandchildren. He cleaned and cooked the trout he caught, then invited family and friends for an evening of sustenance and fish stories.*

Upon entering a nursing home unit for a staff meeting, Katherine could hear shouting coming from down the hall and around the corner.

"Look at her!" a man shouted to a frightened nurse's aide, who was nervously looking around for someone to help rescue her. "She's like a zombie! Is that urine on the bed? Her room stinks! When was the last time she had a bath? What a despicable place!"

Jim Barclay, with wife Johanna in tow, had come from his ritzy Connecticut suburb to see his ninety-two-year-old mother, who had suffered dementia-inducing strokes. Visitation records showed that the last time he'd been there, some six months ago, the same thing had taken place: scream, threaten, leave.

Little did he know that if he sat quietly and stroked her hair, she smiled and looked you straight in the eyes, perhaps triggering a long-ago memory.

Katherine was accustomed to the Jim Barclays of the world, the families who presented themselves every so often, laden with their own guilt and directing it at the staff. She approached him.

"Mr. Barclay, I'm Dr. Eich, the administrator here. Let's go see your mother together."

"I'm calling my lawyer!" he shouted so everyone could hear.

Ignoring his statement, Katherine walked into his mother's room. "Hi, Mrs. Barclay. I'm Katherine," she said as she gently stroked the patient's arm.

Mrs. Barclay looked up and smiled at her. "Your son, Jim, is here to visit and so is Johanna. They came here from their home in Connecticut. I bet your grandchildren are so grown up."

Mrs. Barclay smiled again, probably not really understanding, but just reacting to a soft voice.

Jim Barclay paced the room, not even looking at his mother, as Johanna nervously spoke, "Don't you look nice in that silk nightgown we bought you. Love that color on you. Here, I also brought you some talcum powder and perfume."

"Yeah, she really needs that perfume the way this place smells." Jim Barclay was shouting again, his contempt apparent. "Where'd you get your staff, Ms. Administrator? The streets?"

"Mr. Barclay, may I see you outside?" Katherine asked, her own voice raised slightly as she walked out of the room.

Pointing his finger at the floor, Barclay yelled, "No! Let's talk here. I do not take orders from you!"

Katherine kept walking until Barclay realized she was leaving, and that if he wanted to continue to shout, he had to follow her. He hesitated and then followed her, his desire to berate her seemingly outweighing his stubborn unwillingness to appear submissive. Katherine led him to a nearby conference room and closed the door loudly behind her.

Standing and making piercing eye contact, Katherine spoke in a clear and commanding voice. "Look, Mr. Barclay, I understand these visits must be hard for you, seeing your once vibrant mother like this, and knowing she is nearing the end of her life. And if you'd like to call your lawyer, then that is your prerogative. But I would think about it before you do. Your mother has been here for two years, five if we count her time in assisted living. She's alive today because of the care she's received, and she has been treated with dignity and respect, which we will continue to do."

Katherine wanted to add, *And how many times have you been here in these last five years?* But she resisted the urge, not wanting to exacerbate the already volatile situation. Besides, she knew the answer because the staff had shared this after his last complaint.

Katherine was now angry. "But if you insist on making an ugly scene every time you come, then I will have to ask you to stay away."

"You can't do that!"

"Oh, yes I can, and I am. Nothing we've ever done for your mother is enough for you. Yet she is clean, free of bedsores, gets out of bed three or four times a day, is taken outside, is visited and read to by volunteers, has a minister who visits regularly, and has a physical therapist exercising her body daily. We cannot help that we cannot save her, make her better, or reverse the strokes she's had."

"Well, just let me say something…"

"I'm not done yet!" declared Katherine, further raising her voice as she moved closer to him. Now in his personal space, less than two feet from his face, she said, "I have had it with your accusations, threats, and insults that upset other patients and my staff. Your mother is incontinent and has to wear protective diapers, which she is constantly trying to take off. When she wets the bed, we change her sheets. What would you have us do? Tie her down?" Barclay didn't respond.

"If you have constructive criticism, I'll listen. But if you're going to rant and shout, then get out! Do I make myself clear? And you *will* need your lawyer when I obtain a court order forbidding you to enter these premises."

"Uh…"

"I'm still not done, Mr. Barclay!" After pausing and changing her tone, Katherine said, "Your mother must have been a special person. She has old friends who still visit and tell me what a classy lady she was, that she volunteered for so many causes. They miss playing bridge with her, and they miss all those knitting groups where she helped knit hundreds of caps for newborns at area hospitals. And, they still talk about her signature chocolate pound cake.

"I wish you could come more often to see how people treat her. They remember her from before these vascular strokes when she lived in assisted living, and they talk to her about the past and her amazing long life."

Barclay was silent for a long time, perhaps contemplating what Katherine had said; more likely wondering if she was finished yet. Katherine thought he might be calculating his next move.

"My mother and this place are a far cry from the dignified life she once had," he said sarcastically.

"It is hard to watch someone you love as their body betrays them. But she's not suffering, and she's not in pain. And soon enough, she will leave us. Until then, we touch her and love her. She really responds to touch." Katherine, still staring at Barclay, waited a few seconds to see if her words had any impact. He stood silently, not looking at her.

"Come, let's go back to your mother," Katherine said as she headed for the door, holding it open for Barclay.

Then, signaling for a nurse, Katherine asked if Hester was available. Within a few seconds, a toy poodle was brought to them. Katherine entered the room with the dog and placed her on Mrs. Barclay's stomach. She immediately lit up with a huge smile that turned to laughter as Hester licked her face and wildly wagged her tail. Mrs. Barclay pulled the dog closer, kissing her neck and body, wrapping her arms around the tiny, exuberant bundle.

Jim Barclay watched, then turned to stare out the window.

Later, as Katherine left the room, the staff, who had overheard the loud confrontation through the closed door, gave her a silent cheer by mimicking clapping, displaying a thumb's up, or mouthing a thank you; gratified at being defended in their all too often thankless jobs.

"He'll be different now," said one.

Katherine wasn't so sure.

CHAPTER 16

Katherine took the stairs straight to Shirlee's office, conveniently located in the nursing home.

"I just lost it with a visitor." Katherine shut the door behind her and leaned against it. "Jesus!"

"Oh my! How so?" Shirlee stood up and came from behind her desk. "Come, let's talk." They hugged, then sat down in the comfy chairs across from Shirlee's desk.

"Jim Barclay! He's been shouting at the nurses for two years now. Same thing every time. Care is lousy, smell is bad; the patient, his mother, is in horrible shape. Nothing's right. As far as he's concerned, we're killing her. I finally let him have it by threatening him with a court order banning him from visiting."

"Sock it to him!"

"Oh, Shirlee, I lost my temper. I'll be lucky if he doesn't follow through with one of his lawyers and sue us."

"Were you right?"

"Yes, but the way I did it was wrong. I was also lucky I knew this patient. Because he's filed so many complaints, I'd already studied his mom's care plan and talked with the staff."

"So, my friend, how would you have handled it differently?"

"He's nothing new. The Jim Barclays of the world are part of our job. Before, I'd have nurtured him, let him become aware of his guilt, treated him with more finesse. Truth be known, I wanted to belt him, tell him to shut the fuck up. To make matters worse, his wife brings her talcum powder, a silk nightgown that needs to be dry cleaned, and perfume! They don't have a clue." Katherine rolled her eyes. Her voice was still a few decibels above normal.

"Wow! I guess he did make you mad."

Katherine looked around the room. Decorated in neutral shades to highlight the colorful African prints, Shirlee's office was an inviting place for people to sit and talk. "I'm tired of putting out these kinds of fires." Katherine voice lowered as she sighed deeply.

"Need a vacation?"

"Maybe more."

"Like what? A leave of absence?"

"Or retirement. I broached the subject with Peter recently."

"Katherine, if you retire, I retire! I've been mulling the idea over myself. My body and brain don't seem to move as fast. Let's face it. We're getting old." Shirlee laughed. Katherine tried but could barely manage a smile.

"We're not thirty anymore or even forty or fifty. I have, God willing, many years left, but the intensity and pace of this place has been, is, and always will be challenging. The work is never done. Shirlee, I wonder how many tens of thousands of hours we've put in?"

"Millions maybe. But I've loved most every minute of it. Look around, Katherine! This place is a national model. We've made our mark. I'm so glad we took this journey together."

"So, are we ready to ask for our gold watches and head off into the sunset?"

"How tired are you?"

"I'm not so tired that I can't wait another year or two. If I pull another stunt like today, maybe less. Besides, it'll take at least a year to get ready to pass the torch."

Shirlee peered over her glasses, looking maternally at Katherine. "Don't underestimate the people we've trained and mentored. I hate to break it to you, but if we died tomorrow, this place would go on just fine without us."

"Oh, God, you're right. This is Oak Place, not *our* place. We built it so it wouldn't live or die without us."

"We built it so we could eventually move in and enjoy the fruits of our labors. Did you know the waiting list for senior housing is close to three years? I've got to register my name."

"You could give up Harlem for Queens?"

"I've lived in Manhattan for forty-five years. That's enough. I'd miss my church, but I could visit regularly."

"Thanks for talking with me, old friend. I feel better." They smiled at each other, both grateful for their special bond.

"I have a feeling we'll be talking more about this. Might not be a bad idea to alert Jeff to our conversation."

"Oh, yes. He's still dealing with Mr. Riggins's suicide. And, he was called in the wee morning hours to tend to a resident who burnt her foot in that kitchen fire."

"I saw that from the morning report."

"Gotta go. Luncheon speech for volunteers. Thanks for listening. Love you." Katherine blew Shirlee a kiss as she walked out the door.

"Love you back."

❧ ❧ ❧

Katherine was the guest speaker for Senior Volunteer Recognition Day at the senior living complex. Some 200 hundred people were in attendance, the atmosphere festive. Students from a local culinary arts college had prepared a delicious luncheon of crab cakes, watercress salad, and assorted elegant-looking casseroles.

"Ladies and Gentlemen," began the president of the volunteer organization after lunch, "few people are as lucky as us to live in this marvelous place. And I mean *live!* Thanks to Dr. Katherine Eich and her wonderful staff, we can enjoy our golden years here. And when the time comes that our bodies or brains give out, we know we will be cared for with dignity."

Katherine went to the podium. Without notes, she began speaking.

"Do you all know that it takes a village to have a conversation? I mean, how many times have we finished each other's sentences because a word or a person's name eludes us? No, we don't have Alzheimer's disease, at least not yet." There was some laughter from the audience.

She paused, then went on. "Normal aging can be frustrating. At our age, our brains have accumulated a lifetime of knowledge. In our brains, there is a vast system of memory banks, like file cabinets. We don't always find what we're looking for right away, because it sometimes takes longer to navigate. In other words, we don't synapse as fast. Again, I repeat, this is normal aging. But, at least we have each other to fill in our temporary memory lapses."

Katherine made a few more points, then expounded on the value of volunteers, gave some statistics and began her closing statements.

"Without volunteers like you, Oak Place wouldn't be the stellar home it is. Our gardens are splendid because of you. Our flowers bring beauty to the soul, often to someone you may not even know. Our animals are loved and cared for because of you. And they are fed well because of the donations you bring in. Our music therapy program brings song where there was silence. Patients, now unrecognizable from their glory years past, sit up and sing. When reading to a blind patient, you bring light to darkness. When walking outside with a stroke patient, you enhance their world. You bring smiles and dignity to those who are suffering.

"Most of you have learned in your long lives that dignity isn't given to you on a silver platter. You cannot buy it. It takes work and effort, and people who care. Those of you whose health has been kind to you have helped others who are frail. I'm not saying you haven't had your share of suffering. Many of you volunteer despite your own disabilities or perhaps your own brushes with a serious disease. Some of you have lost the most significant people in your lives. We all attend way too many funerals. Yet, you still give of yourselves.

"I treasure you. Oak Place treasures you. I hope you realize the joy you bring. I hope you have found inner joy in your volunteer work, be it small or large in scope. Without a doubt, Oak Place would not have achieved national recognition without its volunteers. We have all worked together to make it happen, and now people from all over the world want to build their own versions of Oak Place. Yes, it takes a village to have a conversation, and it takes a village to make this place a model for aging.

"Thank you," said Katherine, placing her hand over her chest. "From the bottom of my heart, I thank you."

The audience stood up and cheered, congratulating Katherine and each other. Katherine hugged many of them before she left, each hug giving her a bit more strength to tackle the Jim Barclays of the world, face the deaths, the suicides, and even listen to a prostitute tell her story...

CHAPTER 17

S tella and Katherine were quietly enjoying a cup of tea on the patio outside the assisted living complex, watching the colorful clouds of the sunset above the Manhattan skyline when Stella began talking about Kevin. "As former owners and now big shareholders in the diamond mine monopoly, Kevin's family basically used cheap Black labor in the mines. And I mean very cheap, as in exploitative. He hated it and wanted no part in the business. He wanted human and civil rights for Black Africans.

"But I suppose that will all come out when I talk with the FBI, with you present, Katherine. Please don't abandon me now." Her eyes pleaded. Under her tough-as-nails façade, Stella was vulnerable. Katherine had witnessed this vulnerability in many older persons—too often, in fact.

"I won't," she assured Stella, reaching for her hand.

"Katherine, I *will* fully cooperate with the FBI, but I want something from them in return."

"And that would be…?"

"My son. Kevin and I had a son."

Katherine recalled an old cliché: *Oh, the twisted webs we weave…* She wondered how complicated this story was going to get.

"I got pregnant a few months after we met, but I didn't tell him. He was gone for many months, and we hadn't yet committed to a long-lasting relationship."

Stella took a deep breath. "I remembered holding that dear, sweet Jenny, a child of the streets, as she died from a back-alley abortion. I was scared, afraid to take that same risk. Imagine, Katherine, I was handing out condoms to hookers on the street, and one night it was I who didn't use one. It was so stupid on my part. We had one condom, but after downing a bottle of Dom Perignon, we made love twice that night. I wasn't going to burden him with my oversight. I took full responsibility. Or what I thought was full responsibility." She bowed her head and said quietly, "Oh, the mistakes we make."

"Back-alley abortions were scary. And dangerous. I don't blame you for rejecting that."

"Nine months later, I was in the hospital, having just delivered, holding this precious little boy for the first and last time. I had learned of a reputable adoption agency that I trusted would find him the home he needed. Back then, out of wedlock children were called bastards. I knew I couldn't give him the life he deserved."

"Oh, Stella, that must have been so painful. I remember from nursing school young girls birthing in hospitals, then giving up their babies. I often cried with them. Their grief was profound."

"My heart ached for an agonizingly long time. Still does, just not as intense. For years, I thought about him every day. Now, not a week goes by that I don't wonder what became of him. Did he have good parents? What's he doing? What does he look like?" Stella paused, then said, "You know, he would be almost fifty now. God, I hope he's still alive. I hope he's had a happy life."

"Have you ever tried to find him?"

"Not recently. Many years ago, I contacted that adoption agency, but they said they couldn't open the records unless both of us had contacted them. And he hadn't. I figured he wasn't interested, didn't care, or may have been angry that I'd abandoned him."

"How long ago would that have been?"

"The first time, it was forty-some years ago, and I've tried many times over the decades. My last attempt was about five years ago, but the agency was gone and there was no forwarding address. I finally decided it was not to be, and put that part of my life to rest as best I could. Besides, I didn't want him to know his mom was a prostitute, and was still having sex for money with a few clients well into my golden years, although most of my money came from being a respected Madam. Don't you love that word? Mad'em!"

Stella looked at Katherine. "You should see your face, Katherine. You don't think a woman can continue her *profession* into her seventies? Hell, Helen Mirren and Meryl Streep have nothing on me! Many men, especially in high positions, much prefer a mature woman who can carry on a conversation at cocktail and dinner parties. Some of the time, I was a just companion, nothing else."

"Stella, I don't doubt you for a minute. You're a beautiful woman, and I don't mean just physically. I can totally picture you intelligently dialoging with some king."

"Thanks for saying that. I knew there was a reason I liked you." She winked as she took a sip of her tea. "By the way, I serviced some kings; nothing special. Most flaunted over-the-top egotism. One was really nice but hated his life."

Katherine by now wasn't surprised by such statements from Stella. "I should have known." She also figured what was coming next. "Stella, I'm getting the impression you might want to use leverage with the FBI, maybe get something in return for sharing what you know. Am I correct?"

"How perceptive of you! And correct. I think I have the information they want, but I want to find my son. Do you think that might be possible?"

"Stella, that sounds like quid pro quo. They might not take a fancy to that," Katherine said while rethinking if Stella might need a lawyer.

"You mean I might really piss them off?'"

"That too."

Katherine thought for a moment. "Then again, maybe asking wouldn't hurt. The worst they could do is turn you down. But if anybody could find him, it's them. So, Stella, what is it that you know?"

"Let's save that for another talk. Right now, I'm late for my art class.

❦ ❦ ❦

The FBI had called again. Due to another pressing case, they weren't able to continue interviewing Stella for another week. But they weren't slacking off. They subpoenaed her bank statements from decades past, and Stella wondered if her phone had been tapped.

This made Katherine think about how to help Stella approach these guys without making it sound like blackmail, which they would almost certainly reject. Still, the chances of them using their time to track a child already gone for forty-nine-plus years was a stretch. It all came back to what they wanted and how badly they wanted it.

In the meantime, Stella had become introspective and saddened after her long-repressed thoughts about Kevin resurfaced. A period of her life she thought was over now re-claimed center stage, constantly occupying her thoughts. She tried to recall in detail the many conversations between Kevin and herself, including his feelings regarding his family, a family he despised.

"His parents treated servants without any respect or warmth," Stella told Katherine. "I remember Kevin telling me one of their gardeners had missed a couple of workdays because his sick child had to go to the hospital. They fired him. Plus, Kevin's two brothers were into accumulating wealth and buying expensive toys like fancy cars. Both parents and siblings mocked Kevin mercilessly as a 'kaffir lover,' a highly offensive term, the South African version of *N*-lover."

"Dear God, those words send shivers down my spine."

"Kevin thought of himself as different from his family because of two significant emotional events that shifted his priorities away from wealth and bigotry and into service. One was when a Black African man saved his life at great risk by helping him escape his car when it plunged into a canal.

"Kevin was young, having just gotten his driver's license. It was dark and rainy as he drove back from a social gathering at a friend's home. He had taken a curve too fast and lost control of the car. Though conscious, he was dazed and desperately trying to unlatch his seatbelt as the car sank. With water up to his neck, someone's strong arms reached into the car, unlatched the seatbelt and pulled him to safety. The next thing he remembered was lying on the ground by the canal and an older Black gentleman, dripping wet and wearing the clothes of a servant, hovering over him, urging him to take deep breaths. The man told him the police would be there soon, that he would be fine.

"Kevin remembered profusely thanking him and touching the kneeling man's shoulder. 'What is your name? Please don't leave me!' a shivering Kevin begged. But as the rescue sirens got louder, the stranger who had saved his life walked away, disappearing into the night."

"How frightening. Why do you suppose that kind soul left the scene?"

"Kevin figured he was probably out past his curfew," said Stella with disgust.

Katherine tried to visualize the scene Stella described. "I can only imagine all the personal stories of courage that took place during that vile system."

"That's why it's important for people to pass on their stories, like you've said in the *Writing Your Story* classes."

"Thanks for affirming that. You said there were two emotional events in Kevin's life?"

"The other significant event was meeting an Anglican church minister who was white but worked in the slums, trying to help curtail the tragic consequences of poverty. Kevin's family was churchless—no surprise there —but a friend had invited Kevin to attend church with his family. Katherine, while Kevin never quite grasped the meaning of God, he just loved that minister. They talked about justice and treating people with dignity."

"I always wondered how involved the white churches were in ending apartheid. Guess there weren't that many. Did Kevin ever say if this was a big church congregation?"

"It wasn't. Anyway, he began talking privately with this Englishman, Reverend Timothy Martin, who had volunteered for assignment to South Africa after having studied the teachings of Archbishop

Desmond Tutu. In a short time, he had set up two schools for Black children, both in need of decent educational supplies, but with a dedicated teaching staff. Children were learning to read despite the lack of books. Martin considered Tutu his mentor. Eventually, Kevin felt the same about Martin.

"Wow. Kevin knew Tutu?"

"He had met him, but it was Martin whom Kevin frequently interacted with. In fact, Kevin regularly sneaked off to help Martin, and he repeatedly stole small sums of money from the wallets of his parents and brothers to donate to the cause. He figured they would never miss the U.S. equivalent of a twenty-dollar bill among the bulging wads of cash they usually carried. Over the years, that sum became thousands of pounds in South African currency until 1961, when the pound was replaced by something called the rand. All along, Kevin told the grateful young minister that these donations were from his family, and thankfully he—or one particular family servant whom he trusted—was able to intercept all the thank you letters before his parents saw them."

"What courage for someone so young. His family never found out?"

"Well, they did eventually after Kevin decided pilfering what amounted to twenty dollars here and there just wasn't enough."

"When did that happen?"

"At nineteen, Kevin enrolled in a progressive university in Cape Town. The ideas he was exposed to there would fortify his transition from passive, status quo Afrikaner to anti-apartheid activist. He was honored when Martin first took him to hear Bishop Tutu speak, a man he admired greatly. He quickly became a student of South African history and heard the real reason, not his family's version, behind Nelson Mandela's imprisonment. Years later, Martin tapped his influential network to secure Kevin an envoy position on the Commission for Human Rights at the United Nations."

"So, it was Martin who got him to the U.S.?"

"He had to leave South Africa to survive emotionally. He also figured he could help end apartheid by working with other countries."

Both Katherine and Stella became quiet; Katherine reflecting on what Stella had shared, while Stella relived the emotion evoked by her words. With darkness upon them and a chill in the air, Katherine asked one last question. "How did he end up marrying a woman so different from himself?"

"Now, that's a story that could last well past midnight. But let's just say it was his family's money she was after. Some women, especially those without fairy godmothers, will do anything to fit into that glass slipper."

"Good one, Stella"

"It's always gratifying to ridicule that oppressive fairy tale."

CHAPTER 18

As Katherine passed the robustly growing oak tree planted in memory of Shirlee's husband, Darryl, who had passed away from muscular dystrophy some twenty-five years ago, she recalled a time when he was still alive.

A few months before his death, Katherine had run into Shirlee when she was on her way to visit Darryl.

"Hi, friend. Going to see Darryl?"

"Yes, it's our wedding anniversary and we're having dinner together, although Darryl is not eating much these days."

"Mind if I join you for a few minutes to say hello? Time's flown. I haven't seen him for a couple of weeks."

"You know how he loves to see you, but he's going downhill fast. This disease is really wreaking havoc on his body."

Darryl had been a stalwart in the New York Police Department. A striking six-foot-five inches, with the body of a football player, he could be intimidating when necessary. Underneath that exterior was a gentle and compassionate man. He had successfully climbed the ranks to officer status and had, before his illness, been assigned to the homicide department as a lieutenant.

In the spring of 1985, he had been accepted into law school, initially planning to attend part-time, with the eventual goal of working in the District Attorney's office. His symptoms were mild at first: some finger and toe tingling, a subtle weakness in his grip, fatigue. When they persisted, he became worried, as Shirlee, with her medical background, already was. His mother had died of muscular dystrophy, so a foremost concern was that he might be carrying the hereditary gene.

Rather than subside, the symptoms progressed, which neither of them could continue ignoring. The tests came back positive and

Darryl, still in his thirties, was forced to accept a future of disability and premature death.

Shirlee was angry. Darryl had been raised in the projects and on the streets of Harlem. Life had not been easy. With his parents deceased, he spent much of his time with his brother, making sure he didn't get into trouble. Later, as a street cop, he worked his way through the City University of New York. Then, with a well-earned opportunity at his doorstep, he found himself faced with this horrid diagnosis.

He refused to be angry at his circumstance, but Shirlee was angry enough for both. Katherine remembered long walks and talks with her as she processed their future, starting with him having to resign from the police department as his physical stamina deteriorated. "It's just not fair! He's worked so hard! Dammit!"

Even before his confirming diagnosis, Darryl and Shirlee were aware of the hereditary threat of this debilitating disease and had abandoned their wishes for children. Darryl and Shirlee knew they'd been cheated, but taking reproductive control assured that their generation of his family's mutant gene would also be the last.

Over the years, Darryl's symptoms progressively worsened. His muscles weakened, causing difficulty in walking. Eventually, atrophy confined him to a wheelchair. He needed help with most activities of daily living, including toileting. When he could no longer firmly grip a spoon, Shirlee helped feed him. A health aide was hired to care for him when Shirlee was at work. Finally, when Darryl's limp body no longer offered adequate assistance to people trying to lift him, Shirlee and Katherine transferred him to Oak Place's nursing home.

As she resigned herself to his fate and her anger diminished, Shirlee focused on his care. She visited him daily, often clearing her lunch schedule so she could be there to feed him. On some days, Katherine, who loved Darryl, joined them. He had been a kind and supportive friend for many years.

Watching him decline hurt everybody. Jeff, also his friend and now his physician, felt particularly helpless as Darryl's care became increasingly palliative. But Darryl wouldn't accept anyone's pity. Even though he had lost his physical ability to care for himself in the most intimate ways, he refused to let it destroy his self-respect. Most importantly, Darryl never permitted muscular dystrophy to extinguish his sense of humor. Always cracking a joke or appreciating the comedy in spontaneous events, he encouraged joy and laughter in the present, his bleak future be damned.

"I feel it won't be much longer," said Shirlee one day almost matter-of-factly. "Lately, his breathing has become more labored. He has trouble catching his breath."

"Like the beginning of the end?"

"Yeah, afraid so," Shirlee had said all those years ago. "He'll be forty-nine on his next birthday. It might be his last."

"Shirlee, he has really fought this battle. He's taught me what the concept of dying well means."

"How so?"

"He really knows what's important: his relationship with you, his brother and family, his friends. He knows what matters. He defines dignity even when it seems he has none left. Muscular dystrophy has robbed him of almost everything, but it has not taken his mind. In that way, he's still the Darryl I know and love."

"Thank you for saying that. You know, Jeff has been so helpful in preventing him from suffering. Bless that man."

Katherine and Shirlee walked arm-in-arm until they reached Darryl's room.

"Just what I needed," said Darryl. "Two beautiful women to grace my day. How's your morning been?"

Conversations flowed as they filled him in. Katherine noticed a change in just the short time since last seeing him. She sadly assumed he would die of respiratory problems, maybe pneumonia. His weakened diaphragm muscles wouldn't be able to help him.

"You know," said Darryl, "I was just telling a friend about the time you two squatted in that Hell's Kitchen dilapidated brownstone in order to open a homeless shelter."

"Oh God, Darryl. You didn't!" said Katherine.

"Not our finest moment," Shirlee added.

"No, it was a fine moment. What other two women would have done what you guys did?"

"You mean go to a swanky Fifth Avenue church where lots of women were wearing full length minks, and ask for money?" asked Katherine.

"That wasn't the big deal. It was what you did after they said no that was the big deal. I still can't believe you fed fifty homeless people baked beans, cabbage, and hot dogs for breakfast, then took their gaseous colons to that church for Sunday service."

"Darryl, we were young smartasses with major attitudes," said Katherine. "I've been trying to forget that for decades."

"Well, they gave you five hundred dollars, didn't they?"

"Darryl, may I remind you that they threw it at us and told us to get the hell out!" Shirlee said.

"You got your shelter, didn't you? Creative nonviolence at its finest."

"We got our shelter for one winter before the city evicted us," said Katherine. "But you're right, Darryl. We did house families, helped the parents get jobs, and got their kids in school."

"Hey, love, we were pretty obnoxious even though we were trying to do good," added Shirlee.

"Yeah, Darryl, we demonstrate in different ways now," said Katherine.

Darryl laughed. "Nothing you do will ever surpass that farting Sunday! By the way, whose idea was that?"

"Hers!" yelled Shirlee and Katherine simultaneously, each pointing at the other, rolling their eyes and laughing.

On that day, Katherine made a promise to see Darryl more often. Moreso, she pledged to spend more time with Shirlee, who had been his devoted caregiver for over a decade. He was dying well because she was by his side. Now, as if on fast-forward, she was facing his imminently fading life.

Over the following weeks, Darryl physical strength went downhill steadily until he was totally helpless. Finally, impaired brain function led to confusion and memory loss. In the winter of 1993, while recovering from another bout of pneumonia, he died peacefully of a heart attack in the middle of the night. Per his wishes, no extraordinary medical intervention was administered.

His funeral, standing room only, was in the Oak Place Theater. While most didn't know Darryl personally, they knew Shirlee and came to support her.

⁊⁊ ⁊⁊ ⁊⁊

In all the years since, Shirlee, still a beautiful woman, dated sporadically. But no other man ever took Darryl's place in her life. Instead, Oak Place became her life. On her days off, she did service work for her church in Harlem. She had never been religious previously, but she found solace in hymns and church suppers. The many church members who surrounded her became her extended family, and she became surrogate mother to more than a few of their children and grandchildren.

Katherine and Shirlee's friendship remained strong, and Katherine always included her in many of her own family functions. Besides, Jill loved her Aunt Shirlee and always wanted her present, especially during holidays. She often accompanied Katherine's family to their A-frame in Pennsylvania, where she had her own bed. Jill relished having Aunt Shirlee in her room; they would stay up late talking and telling stories. Shirlee also went on vacations with Katherine, Peter, and Jill; once to Europe and once to Japan.

They had come so far since their days in graduate school, where they had taken every class together. Each continued to remind the other about the passing years. "Where does the time go?"

Every time Katherine passed the memorial oak tree, she flashed on Darryl, if only for a second or two. It helped her stay focused instead of dwelling on trivia or depressing situations. By remembering his journey, she could reframe the negativity around her. And, she had to do that often.

On this day—standing in front of the oak tree—she held a letter from Jim Barclay's attorney. "Help me keep this in prospective, Darryl, and do what's right," Katherine said out loud. She had been reported to the Department of Health for unprofessional conduct. The complaint also accused the staff of negligent care and endangering a patient—Barclay's mother. Mediation had been offered, but Barclay refused. So, the medical records had been subpoenaed and a preliminary hearing had been scheduled.

CHAPTER 19

The gentle knocking on her open office door stirred Katherine from her thoughts. It was Jeff.

"Got a minute?"

Katherine smiled. "For you, Jeff, always. I've been thinking about you since Mr. Riggins's death." Jeff sat down. Leaning back in the cushioned moss green chair, he crossed his legs.

Katherine's office, with its living room atmosphere, invited people to relax. One side was sliding glass doors, curtains rarely drawn, opening to a welcoming fountained patio among many year-round green shrubs. A small, round mahogany conference table used for work sessions was tucked in a corner. One could usually smell fresh coffee. The earth tone walls were filled with paintings, most done by residents. Absent were framed diplomas, citations, and award plaques.

For most visitors or colleagues, she came from behind her desk to sit next to them in the comfy chairs and sofa surrounding a coffee table. Occasionally, and if necessary, she used her desk to affirm her authority, directing people to sit across from the desk in the more rigid chairs.

"Jeff, how are you doing?" Katherine asked as she sat down beside him. "Coffee?"

Jeff shook his head. "No thanks. Had two cups already. I'm okay. Sort of. I'll miss Riggins. He was a wonderful man and I admired him. Besides being a musical talent and role model for the choir, he was still so engaged in society."

"I agree. You know, he was the one who helped us plan the location for many of our raised garden beds. For each, he would calculate the amount of daily summer sun they would receive, helping us decide where to plant what."

"Not surprised. He was an environmental activist. As a retired scientist, he tackled climate change like his house was on fire and his grandkids were in the attic. He wanted to leave them a better world, and hated it when he was diagnosed with cancer. He felt cheated because there was so much yet to do."

"Damn, Jeff. There's never a good time to die. Always something to live for."

Jeff's eyes watered; a tear streamed down his cheek. He always cried easily and never held back. "I went through the what-ifs and if-onlys. Did everything but ask him if he was contemplating suicide, which, as I replay it in my head, didn't seem warranted. He accepted that he was facing a life limiting illness. He told me he was getting everything in order, which included former colleagues taking over an environmental project he was dedicated to, that is inspiring teens to get involved in the climate change movement. I told him we could manage the pain and that he'd have a peaceful death."

"I wonder why he opted out early?"

"He had suffered with late life depression over the last few years, but he told me the antidepressant was working and didn't want to increase the dose because it made him foggy. I don't know if he had stopped taking it, and neither does his wife."

"Well, cancer can certainly exacerbate depression."

Jeff nodded. "Plus, Mrs. Riggins told me he was having serious issues with the discomfort. He told her he felt like roaches were eating him from the inside. He hated roaches, and she said it was driving him nuts."

"I bet."

"He didn't share that with me. But it seems to be a holdover from his youth in central Mississippi, a youth spent in poverty. Apparently, roaches and spiders were common in his childhood home, even in his bed. He told his wife that some had looked as big as mice to his young boy's eyes, complete with pincers. He told her he had often been afraid to go to sleep."

"That would definitely freak me out."

"Hell, yeah!" Jeff rolled his eyes. "Anyway, the Resident Education Committee wants me to do a talk on late life depression and suicide in older persons. The timing is right."

"I agree. Another teachable moment after another tragedy."

"Katherine, on the home front, I also have some good news and not so good news to share. The good news is that my number one son, Eric, is finally getting married to Carrie."

"Wow, that's fantastic!" Katherine had always liked Jeff's future daughter-in-law. "Haven't they been living together for about ten years now?"

"Come on!" Jeff said with a laugh. "It's only been eight. She's not pregnant, so I'm not sure why. But Amy and I are happy. They're a solid couple and good for each other. And guess what? They want me to sing as Jeff at the wedding ceremony and as Jessica at the reception. So now I have to rent a tux *and* get a new dress!"

"Oh, such a hardship! When did you ever not like dress shopping?" They both laughed.

"The dress will be easy. Accessorizing will be a bitch. Plus, he wants me to start the reception as his father, then later change to Jessica. Can you imagine? As if I can just throw on my makeup!"

"Oh, you poor man!" Katherine said, still laughing. "But you're lucky. You've got Amy to help. She's got Jessica down pat."

"Oh, Amy. Amy…" Jeff looked down and his laughing ceased. "Amy has a cancerous lump in her breast."

"Shit! That sucks!"

"Big time. She's hoping to get off with a lumpectomy. The doctor isn't even sure she'll need chemotherapy, but I'll probably encourage her to do the rounds. It'll squelch any threatening cells."

"Oh, Jeff, I'm so sorry. How's she doing? How does she feel?"

"She's known too many women who've died of breast cancer. She likes her odds, as I do, but she also knows it can be a cruel disease. You know, Amy and I are in the last stages of our professional life and looking forward to some heavy duty grandparenting with Justin and Kailey. Proves again that you never know. Life can change in an instant."

Justin and Kailey were Jeff's preteen grandchildren from daughter Amelia. He and Amy had always spent a lot of time with them and were planning a two-week camping trip out West. Their grandchildren adored them, especially when they were treated to new adventures.

As health professionals, neither Jeff nor Katherine seemed too panicky about the early-stage diagnosis. To lighten the mood, they chatted more about wedding details. Then Katherine changed the subject.

"Jeff, how much longer do you think you'll work?"

"What? You want me to retire? Is that a hint?"

"Hell no, but *I'm* thinking about it. Shirlee too."

"We've sure been through a lot together. I don't know. Retire. Hmmm. Sooner rather than later, I suppose. We have some great docs working here. Oak Place is in good hands. God, am I really getting close to seventy? So, have you set a date?"

"No, I just started thinking about it. Been doing this a long time. Long days are not as easy as they used to be. Neither are irate, unreasonable people."

"Oh? What happened?"

"Not much." Katherine smiled sheepishly. "I only told a visiting bully to tone down or I'd kick him out. It wasn't my finest moment. Now, he's playing one-upmanship by ordering me to appear in court and face a professional firing squad."

"He pissed you off that much?"

"You've never seen such an adult temper tantrum. He was like a bulldozer rolling over all the staff."

"So, Miss Perfect has faltered? Give yourself a break, Katherine. Being professional with jerks isn't easy. Assholes exist. Even here."

"Yeah, but I used to be more patient with them."

Jeff chuckled. "I have a hunch you're talking about Jim Barclay."

"How did you know?" Katherine rolled her eyes.

"Dear God, Katherine, I hope you leveled him. What a repugnant monster! One time he told me I was probably working here because I couldn't handle a job in private practice. Called me a physician reject. That was after he demanded I prescribe antibiotics for his mother because she had sneezed twice. I refused!"

"God, I'm surprised he didn't want you to send her to the ICU!"

"You know, although I've seen my share of adult temper tantrums, they can still ruin an otherwise perfectly joyous day. And it's hard not to take it personally."

"Well, he does go right for the jugular."

"He's one toxic dude. Thank God he only shows up twice a year."

"You can say that again."

"Fight him, Katherine. If you need me to testify, I'm in."

Jeff got up after his cellphone signaled his presence was needed elsewhere. They hugged. Of course, in that moment, the affair that never was came sneaking back from the depths of her mind. Despite the passing years, it always did after these types of conversation. Katherine quickly pushed those thoughts away. She wasn't about to go there.

CHAPTER 20

"Coffee. I smell coffee." Katherine was still groggy when she heard the coffee cup with its accompanying aroma placed on the night table next to her prone body. She listened to the hard rain outside, happily knowing she didn't need to get up for work or anything else. Pressing the front of his body to the back of hers, Peter nestled next to her. She could hear the radiators cranking from the turned-up heat.

"Good morning. Want to sleep some more?"

"Hi, honey. No. I'm awake. Thanks for bringing me coffee."

"Looks like it's going to be a rainy day." Peter rubbed her hair and shoulders. After a while, Katherine sat up to sip some coffee, as did Peter.

"I love rainy days like this."

"Especially when we don't have to don raincoats and find the umbrellas."

Katherine touched his hand. "What a nice dinner at Jill's last night. Our daughter is quite the chef. That's one gene you passed on to her."

"I'll take credit even though it was my mother's gene."

Katherine turned toward him and laid close, her head on his shoulder, their legs intermingled, her hand stroking his gray-haired chest under his pajama top. For many minutes, they just touched and massaged each other under the covers as the room warmed up.

"You feel so good."

The blankets were pushed away and they undressed each other from the waist down. While they left their tops on to avoid getting chilly, Peter put his hands under her nightshirt and gently rubbed her breasts. Katherine massaged his arms and neck.

Their bodies were different than many, many years ago, but their lovemaking, while less athletic, was just as enthusiastic. They each knew what the other liked. While they didn't make love as often as in their younger years or before Jill's birth, they still made love a couple of times a week—slowly, with lots of touching, and a passion that remained after all these years. They were still drawn to each other in so many ways. While they no longer sweated their way to orgasm, it was satisfying and intense, a release from the pressures of the week, a chance to bond and reconnect mentally and physically. Making love was enjoyable.

Certainly, their sex life, as well as their marriage, had its ups and downs over the decades. Sometimes, sheer exhaustion, a result of parenting or their work schedules, curbed the pleasurable ritual of sexual gratification. At times, sex had become robotic, totally physical, more like screwing rather than lovemaking. There were phases when they weren't really connected even as their bodies were going through the motions. Quickies prevailed, sometimes conspicuously infrequent.

Like so many couples their age, they had been through it all: erectile dysfunction, atrophic vaginitis, body aches and pains that caused positioning adjustments, body image issues, hormonal changes, medication side effects, you name it.

But in the last few years, especially since Jill had left them empty nesters, they had reinvigorated their love life. Growing old together took on new meaning. Their trust in each other was stronger than ever.

Eventually, Peter reached over and retrieved the lubricant from his drawer. Katherine took some and placed it on his penis. He took some and gently rubbed her clitoris. After several minutes, her muscles tensed before she quietly climaxed. They started kissing again with increasing passion. Half an hour after the coffee was placed beside her, and Peter's ED drug had assured a firm, sustained erection, they finally progressed to intercourse, their bodies moving in sync, still touching and kissing, rain pelting the window. After Peter ejaculated, they laid together a while, relishing the moment.

"Ummm, so nice," said Katherine before getting up to wash herself.

"I agree," said Peter as he rinsed off in the sink. Both then went back to bed to finish their now cool coffee and read the newspaper. They talked, reciprocally voiced 'I love you,' sipped a second coffee, and read till ten before deciding to take a walk in the rain, which was now just a drizzle.

Katherine and Peter lived on a quiet street on the Upper West Side on the third floor of a lovely brownstone with a roof garden directly off their bedroom. It was rustic and far from posh, but it was comfortably furnished and inviting. Its spacious living room/dining area had a fireplace, with one section packed with books in floor to ceiling mahogany bookcases. Past the updated kitchen, there was a large bath and two bedrooms, one also serving as a study.

They had lived there for almost three decades, raising daughter Jill on a street where they knew most of their neighbors. They closed off the entire street once a year for a block party, complete with food and music reflecting various ethnicities. They had once seriously considered moving to Midtown, closer to Queens and Oak Place, but their love of the neighborhood won, practicality a distant second.

Instead, Katherine bought a car, but she only drove to work occasionally, choosing to take the eco-friendlier subway that stopped two short blocks from Oak Place. On most days, she could make it to work in half an hour.

The car also served as transportation on weekends to their A-frame cabin on a lake in northeast Pennsylvania. As a young child, Jill ran in the meadows and played in her treehouse with neighboring friends, many of whom were also weekenders from the city. Many afternoons, they lazily paddled their rowboat to favorite fishing or swimming spots. Before bedtime and while telling stories, they roasted marshmallows on an open fire. Although they loved New York, the cabin was a perfect respite from the pace and sounds of big city life. And Jill would always have fond memories of crickets singing her to sleep in her loft bed.

CHAPTER 21

While walking between buildings toward the therapeutic gardens, Katherine noticed Stella painting on an easel in the chilly but calm air. She was wearing a wide-brimmed hat and a mid-calf flowered skirt, looking elegantly bohemian. Upon approaching, Katherine saw the outline of the Oak Place complex, complete with the garden's blooming roses and hydrangeas.

"Looks good," Katherine said, admiring the rough-sketched landscape portrait.

"Haven't gotten very far yet, but I wanted to do the flowers first because I needed color today," Stella replied. "How are you doing?"

"So far, things are going smoothly. No big crises."

"I admire you and the tough job you have making this place so uplifting for old folks. Got a chance to sit and talk for a few minutes?"

"A few. I always enjoy talking with you." Katherine sat on the bench next to Stella.

"Today would have been my mom's birthday. It's conjured up memories for me, especially the last time I saw her. Painting flowers has made those memories easier."

"How so?"

"One day after years of no contact, I picked up the phone and called my mother. Oh, how many times I'd thought about calling, but never finished dialing the number because I was afraid my dad would answer. Finally, I did. And luckily, she answered."

"I imagine it would be scary if your father answered. When was that?"

"Oh, I don't remember. Maybe sixty years ago. I would have hung up if my father had answered. Anyway, I told Mom I was okay, living in New York City, and that I missed her. At first, my mom's voice was soft and loving. 'I am so sorry,' she said. Then, in the next millisecond, her voice turned to anger, jumping multiple decibels. 'But why haven't you called sooner so I didn't worry? This is no way to treat your mother! I thought you were dead!'

"I answered her honestly, telling her I couldn't let Dad touch me again, that his cruelty left me with many scars, physically and emotionally."

Katherine knew this story was not going to end well. She stared at the painted flowers before looking back at Stella.

"My mom was silent at first. Then she started scolding me. 'Oh Christ, Stella, it wasn't that bad! And he's changed now. He promised he would and he did!'

"Talk about denial, Katherine! It was like she had totally erased those horrid years. Still, I couldn't let her off the hook. I asked her if he still beat her.

"'Not really. Well, very rarely,' was her answer. Then, as if to justify his behavior, she gave a feeble excuse. 'Usually only after I have done something stupid, really stupid.' She told me my dad had diabetes and poor eyesight and walked around hunched over like an old man. I think she was trying to tell me that he could no longer hurt me, that I needn't be afraid of him anymore. She begged me to come home, crying and telling me how much she missed me, promising to bake my favorite apple pie."

"What a wounded woman," said Katherine.

"Yeah, totally beaten down."

"Anyway, Katherine, in a weak, almost nostalgic moment, I decided I ought to make that trip, even though it had *disaster* written all over it. Get this—I fantasized they'd ask for my forgiveness. How hopelessly naïve, not to mention extremely unrealistic—like the beast turning into a prince."

"Where was your home?" asked Katherine.

"Kentucky, the rural mountains, far from the fancy racehorse farms and big mansions that dotted the rolling hills. My part of Kentucky was dusty and dirty, very few paved roads, with junked-up, dingy trailer parks. Half my town never even went to high school.

"When I got there, the steps to my parent's trailer creaked and caved slightly when I put my weight on them because large sections of board were cracked and worn thin. The front door screen was ripped. Inside, everything was filthy, from the frayed curtains to the dirty carpets and the dingy furniture. A large TV was the centerpiece of the room, just like when I lived there. The remotes were parked conveniently next to a butt-filled ashtray on a wobbly metal tray table next to my father's recliner. Dishes were piled in the rust-stained sink. The cheap paneling had a few unframed pictures held in place with tape, edges torn and yellowed with age. There were fake flowers caked in dust. The whole place smelled of mold."

"So, you knew poverty firsthand." Katherine tried to imagine the scene.

"Oh yeah, I knew. But it seemed much worse than when I lived there, much shabbier. It was truly a dump. The dump of horror. When I had to go to the bathroom, I went outside behind my car. I sat on the vinyl kitchen chairs for fear of bugs in the slipcovered furniture."

"I've visited places like that more than a few times," said Katherine. "But I've never lived it like you did." It was quiet as they stared at Stella's painting.

"My once beautiful mom was hesitant, beaten down and slouched over, filled with self-loathing. She was still making excuses for my father, puffing on cigarettes, and saying the infamous empty words, 'I love him.' I had very mixed feelings for her. She was the textbook picture of an abused woman. But, she had failed to protect me and wouldn't accept that my father had raped me. It was hard to forgive her for that."

"I've listened firsthand as battered women blamed themselves while continuing to profess love for their abuser. They believe the abuser when he says it'll never happen again, while simultaneously begging for forgiveness and giving them flowers. The peace doesn't last long, though. It's a vicious cycle."

"Yeah, so true, and get this. I thought I could rescue my mom like

I rescued prostitutes. I blurted out, 'Mom, let me get you out of this hellhole!'"

"Let me guess. She said no."

Stella nodded sadly. "My mother's hands trembled as she lit another cigarette and said, 'I'm fine. I am fine, honey dear.' We talked for maybe fifteen minutes longer. Then there was the sound of a car door shutting. My father was home. My heart started beating rapidly. She lit yet another cigarette. We were silent as he entered. She got up nervously to meet him. As if to prepare him for reuniting with me, she said with a gallows laugh, 'Honeybun, surprise! Look who came to visit.'"

"Oh, Stella, I'm anxious just hearing this."

"He stared me up and down. I was purposely dressed simply so as not to divulge my financial status. He didn't smile, not a hint of pleasure on his face.

"'Yeah, well, so what took you so long?' he finally snapped as he walked past me. 'Too good for us?' Then he shouted from the living room, 'What happened to Honor Thy Father and Mother?'"

Katherine swallowed hard and slid forward to the edge of the bench as if anticipating the violence to come. "Oh, dear God."

"I thought to myself, that bastard is quoting scripture no less. A man who never set a foot inside a church getting Biblical, quoting the Ten Commandments. Katherine, I knew I had to keep my wits about me because I felt the urge to kill him!"

It was anger, not sadness, that Katherine saw on Stella's face. "But I gathered my thoughts and told him I figured he didn't want me. Then, get this, Katherine. I wasn't going to say it, but I did anyway. I looked him straight in the eyes and said, 'Besides, I couldn't stand the beatings!'"

"'You fucking little bitch!' he yelled. 'Come to criticize? Well, I never gave you a beating you didn't deserve! You were a badass child and a floozy, too! You ungrateful scum! You were never worth the food I put in your mouth.'"

Katherine put her hand over her mouth and said, "Dear God, I am so, so sorry, Stella."

"He frightened me all over again. I felt like I was one comment from getting whacked in the head, so I remained silent. Mom started crying. I started crying. I realized there was no point in staying any longer. Mom walked me out to my car. I tried talking to her for a while longer, but she was panicky and kept looking toward the trailer like he was watching, already armed with some instrument of torture. I figured he would demand that she reinforce him, and condemn me so as to justify the abuse he had inflicted on me. I handed her five hundred dollars and told her to take the money and leave. That was the last time I ever saw her."

Katherine was silent. She reached for Stella's hand and held it tight. Stella stared at her painting before violently throwing the paintbrush on the ground. "Even these flowers can't erase the trauma," she said.

Both were silent for a while.

"But you finally did find love and beauty in your life," said Katherine. "You worked hard, and you broke the cycle."

"I suppose I did. You know, Katherine, for a long time, I believed I didn't deserve a man like Kevin."

"You know you did."

"Yeah, I know now, after thousands of hours of therapy."

"What happened to your mom?"

"She stayed with my dad, and he died a year or so later. She told me about his death in a letter, the first one she had written since my visit. She wrote like a fourth grader. Of course, she asked for more money. Within three months, she hooked up with another man, so she said in her next letter, the same man who had given me a hundred dollars for a trick so many years ago. I guess she couldn't bear to be alone without a man in her life, even a wicked deadbeat. I heard they died in a car wreck."

"Did you send her the money?"

"Yeah, I did. Doubt she used it for self-growth."

Katherine got up, retrieved the paintbrush and removed the freshly cut blades of grass sticking to the hairs. "With all that dysfunction, was there anyone who had a positive influence when you were growing up?"

"I had an aunt, Aunt Sylvia, who was my mom's stepsister. She was a hard-working waitress, kind of reminded me of Flo, the character in the TV sitcom, *Alice*. She was rough around the edges, confident, and a good, loving person. She was married to a brawny lumberjack, my Uncle Floyd, who also grew beautiful roses. He loved his mom and respected women. A gentle man."

"Sounds like good people," said Katherine, smiling. "Were they close by?"

"They lived an hour away and I saw them infrequently, but she became my role model, as did Uncle Floyd. The last time I saw her, I was fifteen maybe. I was too scared to tell her my circumstances, although I suspect she knew, because she asked a lot of questions about my bruises. One week after I visited her, a social worker arrived at our house, inquiring about my welfare. Dad was livid and later threatened to kill whoever had reported him. I figured it was her, but never told anyone."

"Did the social worker take it further?"

"She asked me how I was doing—right in front of my dad! I lied and said I was fine, that my bruises came from falling out of a tree. I didn't say anything else because I was afraid of what he might do to Aunt Sylvia if he found out it was her who had reported him. And no, I never saw that social worker again."

"What happened to your Aunt Sylvia?"

"She died of breast cancer not too long after, right before I ran away from home."

"So, you lost the one person who cared enough to risk helping you."

"That about sums it up. But there was one piece of advice she gave me that I've never forgotten. One day, she held my face in her hands and said, 'You are a beautiful and intelligent woman. You can be whatever you want to be. Don't let anybody hold you back or take you down.' Then she hugged me tight.

"Those were simple words most kids probably hear all the time from normal, loving parents. As a child, I heard them just that once. But the impact was enormous. I repeated them over and over in my head until I believed them. It's so heartening that words said in casual conversation can turn one's life around. I doubt she had any idea how much she gave me that day. I regret never having told her."

Stella lowered her head. "The next time I heard similar encouragement was much later in my life, first from my therapist and then from Kevin."

CHAPTER 22

Katherine stared into space, shaking her head. Because her secretary understood the impact of the message, she had waited to tell Katherine personally rather than leaving a note on her desk. Theodore Oak had died, the man who started it all with a phone call over three decades ago. The man whose Uncle Samuel had died suffering, exploited, neglected to the point of torture, and robbed of his wealth and dignity by charlatans and gold diggers.

Katherine took some deep breaths, then picked up the phone. "Hi, Jeff. I was just notified that Theodore Oak has died." Jeff was silent. "Seems like he died in his sleep of a heart attack, but I haven't talked with the family yet. I wasn't available when they called."

More silence. Then Jeff said, voice cracking, "This is a sad day for us, for Oak Place. What a legacy he left us."

"Yes. Without him, we wouldn't be here."

"So very true. I've often thought how easily he could've lived luxuriously off his uncle's millions. By the way, did you ever see his home in Ohio?"

"Never did."

"He lived simply. It's been about ten years since Amy and I traveled there and stayed with him for a couple of days. Salt of the earth, both he and his wife. Such a welcoming home, conspicuously lacking any pretention, which he abhorred."

"I know. He showed us in so many ways. When I picked him up once at the airport, he was *carrying* the same frayed suitcase he had had for years, probably decades. For his next birthday, I surprised him with one with wheels."

Jeff laughed. "You know, he tried to teach me to play golf. What a hopeless endeavor that was! We laughed our way through five holes, quitting after I lost a whole bucket of balls."

"You klutz!"

"Yeah, I was robbed the genetics of athleticism."

"I'll call and get details on the funeral, but I do know it's on Saturday. We should probably fly out Friday afternoon. Will you bring Amy?"

"I doubt it. She's knee deep in wedding plans and still not her old self since the lumpectomy and chemo. Besides, she never knew him like you and I did."

"Yeah, Peter will probably feel the same way. You know, Jeff, Theodore changed the face of aging in this country, all the while being a humble high school teacher, then a guidance counselor. Oh, I'm going to miss him. He was like a second father to me."

"You got that right. And just because he lived a long life, it doesn't take away any of the sadness of his loss. He changed our lives, trusted us with an opportunity, believed in our mission..." Jeff's voice drifted off.

"And trusted us with a ton of cash and miniscule bureaucracy," Katherine added. "I remember being so nervous that I'd screw up, questioning myself. I was afraid I couldn't live up to his expectations, until he pointed out that they were really my expectations. His principle requirements were that we didn't lie or cheat. He once said, 'Oak Place will succeed because it deserves to, not because we manipulated the system. Our strength will be that we *were* right, secure with proof and evidence.'"

"And we were the proof," said Jeff. "A lot of people making a fortune in the nursing home business wanted us to fail."

"I remember once when I flunked miserably at convincing a foundation to grant us money, a lot of money. I asked for $1.5 million. They gave us $2500, telling us that our stats seemed too good to be true, that they wanted a few more years of research. What a punch in the face! I could hardly refrain from telling them to go to hell. Sensing my ego was deflated, Theo figuratively picked me up off the floor, dusted me off, and told me to get revenge by proving them wrong.

'Make them regret their decision. Sure, if you want, be depressed for a day or two. Then cheer up, get back in the saddle and get stronger. Old people are depending on you to keep fighting.'"

Katherine continued, "Jeff, as we speak, I'm dealing with a demented resident whose family ruthlessly robbed him of his savings, then vanished. The courts are requesting he become a ward of the state and we assume guardianship. Oak Place started for this very reason. It seems so surreal. Even after all these years, I've never gotten used to it despite having been around this block God knows how many times."

⁂

The afternoon skies were dark as the plane taxied for takeoff. Like so many times before, Jeff and Katherine buckled up and began working, this time writing their respective eulogies. Others would speak—family and friends—but his children had insisted both Jeff and Katherine share the story of Oak Place's founding, and how their grandfather and father had wanted Samuel Oak's tragedy to be the inspiration for justice, a shining model for America's elderly.

"Ladies and Gentlemen," said the pilot over the intercom a half hour into the flight, "Toledo is experiencing multiple severe thunderstorms and we have to divert to Pittsburg."

Once on the ground, they learned that all flights to Toledo had been cancelled. Stranded, Katherine and Jeff were left with the decision to wait it out and hope to make the funeral the next morning, or rent a car and drive through the night in severe weather. Once they were confirmed on a 6:00 a.m. flight to Toledo, they decided to wait it out.

The airport hotels were booked solid because of the weather delays, but they were able to book a single room with a king bed. Within an hour, they were both in the bed, laughing at the irony of it all.

"Well, here's our opportunity after all these years!" Jeff said, laughing.

"Dear God, we were supposed to do this when we were young, had firm bodies, and could handle the guilt!"

"Excuse me, but my body is still firm, and neither of us could have ever handled the guilt!"

"Did you bring a dress? Can you be Jessica for the night?"

"Yeah, where's a nice wig when you need one? Hey, let's order room service. I'm starving."

Katherine's cellphone rang. It was Peter, worried about the weather. "Yeah, we're in a hotel in Pittsburg," Katherine told him. "Booked on a 6:00 a.m. flight." While Katherine talked to Peter, Jeff called Amy.

Waiting for room service, they both went back to working on their speeches until there was a knock on the door.

"You get it!" Jeff demanded, grinning.

"Ha! Fuck you. You get it!"

Katherine laughed as Jeff threw a pillow at her.

"That does it!" Katherine yelled, returning the assault by throwing her pillow at Jeff.

Katherine reached for her purse, but another pillow hit her on the back of the head as she went to answer the door. "Really? We're going to have a pillow fight?" The laughter was just what they needed. Tired, grieving, nervous about their accommodations and worried about making the funeral, there was nothing to do except act like a couple of kids.

Both in the same bed for the first time, Jeff's back was toward Katherine while she finished her eulogy and nibbled on a sandwich. Katherine glanced over at Jeff while thinking to herself, *Who would have thought that on this night, circumstances beyond our control would put us here?* All kinds of thoughts raced through her mind, but none of them suggested she snuggle up next to Jeff. She didn't realize that Jeff was going through the same thing.

She had barely dozed off when the 3:30 a.m. alarm went off. She woke Jeff by semi-gently placing her pillow over his head before retreating to the shower. While showering, she heard a loud knock on the bathroom door before it opened. Without entering, Jeff yelled, "Katherine, I really have to go. Can't hold it. Please, I promise not to look."

"Sure, come in," replied Katherine, safely behind the opaque shower curtain.

Some minutes later, he was still standing at the toilet. "Sorry, my flow takes a while these days. Been putting off seeing the urologist."

"No problem, except I'm turning into a shriveled prune in this shower."

"Sorry. Come on, get out. I won't look."

"Will you please hand me a towel?"

With the towel tightly secured, she exited the shower. He was now sitting on the toilet with his head down so as not to see her.

"We have got to stop meeting this way," said a smiling Katherine as she turned on the faucet. "Learn from a nurse. Running water helps you pee," she said, leaving the bathroom and closing the door behind her.

"I'm already past that point," Jeff sighed, at that moment more worried about his enlarged prostrate than anything else.

Both Katherine and Jeff regained their composure as they checked out of the hotel. At the funeral, their eulogies brought the crowded congregation to tears, and the family members hugged them tightly for sharing untold stories about the origins of Oak Place, a tangible remembrance to one man's dedication.

CHAPTER 23

Katherine made her way to the taxi. Stella was already waiting in the back seat, smiling from ear to ear, in an expensive-looking black suit with a polka dot blouse, looking like she could model for the cover of a magazine. "I'm so glad you're letting a little old lady take you to lunch. I love my apartment, but sometimes I just have to get out."

"It's kind of you to ask. This is a nice respite from my day. By the way, where are we going?"

"A place Kevin and I often frequented. After all these years, it's still open. Third generation owners. Small and cozy. Do you like French cuisine?"

"Steak tartare?"

"Me too. Yum."

Their destination restaurant was an elegant brownstone on the west side of Midtown. After they settled in at a table, they ordered coffee and sparkling water.

"Katherine, does your work entail traveling?"

"Leaving tomorrow for a conference in Denver sponsored by the Council on Aging. I'm giving a speech."

"Oh? What about?"

"Actually, I'm not sure. I had one planned, but it seems so boring and theoretical like a hundred others I've done. Been thinking about changing it to make it more personal, more intimate. Lately, I've been doing a lot of soul-searching. Truth be told, right now I'm sick of statistical analyses, project hypotheses, graphs and charts, with people as numbers and data. For years, I've been making academic speeches about this. But something is changing in me."

"Why don't you practice your new speech on me?"

"Stella, you don't want to hear my lecture." Katherine chuckled as she spoke.

"Try me. Besides, you've done more than your share of listening to me. Now it's my turn to listen to you. What do you want to talk about?"

"I want to talk about aging and loss. Actually, my own aging and losses."

"Keep going…" Stella leaned forward, arms crossed comfortably on the table.

"Professionally, loss has always been there. Now, I'm also experiencing loss on a personal level. Lately, Stella, I feel like it's gripping me with tentacles, intensifying. The older I get, the more I see my contemporaries dying. My own departure is in the neighborhood. I'm in line. Someday, it'll be my turn."

"I do wonder how you do it, Katherine. Dealing with old people all day, every day. It must take a toll?"

"Stella, I'm asked that a lot. How can you go through day after day watching older people confront their mortality? Watching them die? You know what, Stella? It's an honor."

"An honor?" Stella frowned. "Didn't expect you to say that."

"Really. It is an honor to help patients and families through old age, helping them die with dignity. And living well before they die."

"It must get depressing."

"Oh, yes. It can be and has been depressing. A short while ago, I hugged a woman whose husband, with stage 4 cancer, had just committed suicide. In the thirty years I've been at Oak Place, I've hugged thousands of widows and widowers, sons and daughters, their friends, and, of course, the dying. And trust me, death doesn't get easier with practice. Hugging the bereaved doesn't get easier either unless you become dispassionately robotic. At times, I *have* been robotic when I've been overwhelmed with sorrow and have to almost sanitize my emotions or the sheer amount of pain cripples me. Sometimes, I even ask myself how many more of these wrenching grief hugs do I have left in me?"

"Oh my," said Stella as Katherine began to cry.

"I've comforted older persons whose grandchild just died in a car accident, or in Afghanistan, or in the mass murders of Newtown, Connecticut. Everybody says parents shouldn't have to bury their children. Well, grandparents shouldn't have to bury grandchildren either.

"Still," said Katherine, drying her tears with a napkin, "it's a privilege to work with older adults, a privilege beyond imagination. They come to you to share their lifetimes and last stories, when they're most vulnerable. Hopes and dreams, family and friends—all in front of you—inviting you in to walk their path for a while, until they inevitably go off alone. And so many of them, like you, Stella, are wise sages. What lives you've all lived."

Katherine and Stella sat silent as the steak tartare was delivered to their table, beautifully presented on a bed of greens. The fresh crusted bread was still warm.

"It's not easy being old," said Stella, "but that should not prevent us from enjoying such a feast. My hip is worthless, but my palate still works."

Katherine took a bite and chewed slowly, savoring the food before speaking. "I have always talked about it not being easy to be old, but now I'm living those difficulties. As I age, I will live them more, involuntarily, of course, because aging toward death is, after all, relentless and unyielding. And it's not just the final death, the one that puts us in a grave, but also the mini deaths along the way: loss of vigor, health, hair, teeth, careers, cars, freedoms we took for granted, watching former athletes in motorized scooters, or a Nobel Prize Laureate who can't remember his name any longer. And, oh, the chronic diseases that slowly clutch your body before that final stranglehold."

"You're describing me!" Stella said. "Thankfully, I still know my name. Oh, that unknown lurking before us. But that's the way it is. Death is inevitable. Funny, though, I'm not as scared as I thought I'd be."

"Glad to hear that," said Katherine as she buttered her bread. "I'm talking about retiring. Maybe that's why loss is so foremost in my mind. Leaving Oak Place will be a death for me, a huge loss, not to mention a major adjustment."

"Oh, no! That *is* depressing."

"Add to that, I have a friend that's been diagnosed with breast cancer. Another friend is dead of colon cancer. I'm burying friends in greater numbers in greater frequencies. We all know what academics call this: bereavement overload. I'd prefer to call it hell. This is my stage of life now. I've lived long enough for this to happen to me even as I've watched it happen to others for decades. Oh, yes, it can be depressing. And it is getting harder despite all my practice. I'm finding myself wanting to hold tighter to family and friends."

"My dear Katherine, retirement?" asked Stella, trying to digest this breaking news. "Oh, my! What will Oak Place do without you? You're not leaving soon, are you?"

"Nope. Can't leave until you finish your story," Katherine replied with a smile, before enjoying another bite of tartare.

Stella touched Katherine's hand. "I never realized how taxing your job is. Grief is all around you."

"I've seen grief in all its forms: frozen emotions, anger, denial, complicated mourning, people who want talk about it, people who never talk about it, people who want to blame someone and file lawsuits. And then there are the people who, crippled with grief, will curl up and die themselves or waste away, becoming apathetic and immobilized, who will never move on or never learn from a death. Listen to me! I'm talking a mile a minute, lecturing you."

"No, don't stop. This is fascinating."

"Others, especially families, can be really obnoxious, so much so that health care professionals want to run the other way when they see them coming. They yell and scream as if we should cure rather than render dignified palliative care. They're the ones I'm losing patience with."

"No surprise there. I bet you have more than your share of difficult people."

"Just last semester, I was teaching a university course when a student announced in a shrill, whiny voice, which Katherine mimicked, 'My grandmother has Alzheimer's and is in a nursing home, but I just can't go see her. I can't stand to see her like that.'"

"If there's one thing I can't stand, it's a whiny woman," said Stella.

"Let me tell you, Stella, I know I should have maternalistically said, 'Let's talk about those feelings, my dear, sweet child. It must be so difficult for you. It'll be okay.' Instead, I looked her in the eye and firmly said, 'Why don't you grow up?' Like you, I hate whining. As I recall, I was having a rather post-menopausal day." Stella burst out laughing.

"Then I asked her, 'What does your grandmother mean to you?' The student talked lovingly about experiences from cookie making to road trips for soft custard on hot summer days. There was clearly a mutual love between her and her grandmother. I asked her not to abandon her grandmother, and take the risk of losing it emotionally, which was really her biggest fear. And for God's sake, touch her; show the dear woman some affection.

"She did go, and the visit was not easy. She continued to visit, talking to a grandmother who didn't understand her, but reacted to her soft, increasingly tender voice. She hugged her, reminisced, thanked her, and told her she loved her. At the funeral, she smiled through her grief, knowing she had said what she needed to say, thankful she hadn't stayed away and surrendered to her fear of old age and death. It was a learning experience for her...and me too."

Reaching for a second slice of bread, Stella said, "Tell me something, Katherine. Do you think being religious helps the dying?"

"For some people, religion provides great comfort. It makes death less frightening when they feel they have a place to go. Some return to religion after a lifetime of ignoring it. I've watched old people join certain churches because 'they give good funerals.'"

"You're kidding! And what about the non-religious?"

"I've watched non-believers also. To contradict an old cliché, I've seen more than a few atheists in the foxhole."

"Wow, you *have* seen it all. And I thought I had life experience."

"You know, Stella, we really live in an age-phobic society."

"You'll get no argument from me. After all, I wasn't in the most age friendly profession, if you know what I mean." Both smiled. "Once, I thought about starting a 'mature-only' escort service, one that helped old men with alternative positioning, ED, that sort of thing. But instead of 'prostitutes for seniors,' I'd have called it 'senior sexual surrogates for seniors, the 4-S Club!'"

Katherine laughed. "I have no doubt you could have made that a success. Truly, there is a need." She paused. "You know, Stella, you're like no other."

"Enough about me. I find it fascinating listening to you."

"I've stayed in this field because there's something to be learned from death and there's a lot to be learned from our elders. But now, more than ever, I'm having trouble separating my professional life from my own aging and thoughts of death."

"Are you afraid of death?"

"Death is the easy part. It's the dying that sucks. And trust me, there's never a good time to die. It's highly inconvenient. Always the next graduation, wedding, some celebration…"

"Like me not wanting to die till I find my son. Then, of course, I'd like to have the time to get to know him. Why did it never occur to me that you've had to deal with so much sadness?"

"A few weeks back, I went to the funeral of a resident. Only three people were there, including me. She came to us already having advanced Alzheimer's, so none of us knew her. Now that's sad."

"I bet it's also hard on your staff."

"When we admit a person to the nursing home, they know, I know, and their families know that the bed we put them in will most likely be the bed where they die. The staff likewise knows their ultimate reward for providing superior care and establishing a relationship with patients and their families will be an invitation to the funeral. We don't often witness our patients getting better. What we do witness is the downward trajectory toward the end of life. We are also vulnerable to compassion fatigue."

"Personally, I want to go out suddenly. Big heart attack, plane crash, anything but slow."

"Well, Stella, I hate to tell you, but ninety percent of older adults will go out slow with Alzheimer's, heart failure, or something like cancer."

"You mean I only have a one in ten chance of dying quickly?"

"That's about it."

"Damn, now that is depressing. Personally, I vote for calmly falling asleep and never waking up."

"Stella, things have changed for me."

"What's that?"

"I'm becoming the age of the people I've been caring for all these years. Don't get me wrong. There have been some great role models for me…"

"But you think you might become a burden soon?"

"Yeah, sort of."

"I'm learning about burden. I dread it. I want to die before I have to get my butt wiped. Katherine, I'm closer to the end than you, even though I can reframe aging to a degree. By that I mean this: I'm an old woman who looks great, but I'm falling apart physically. A walker is now part of my wardrobe."

"I wish I had known you years ago."

"No, you don't," Stella said reaching for Katherine's hand again. "Trust me. I'm at my best now. Aging does have its perks."

Katherine helped Stella up. As they walked out, Stella said, "By the way, do trash the graphic charts and academic verbiage."

"Thanks to you, I just did."

CHAPTER 24

"How did you meet Kevin Finchley?" asked Agent Gultowski. He and Agent Wilson had settled down in Stella's comfortable chairs and were sipping coffee, which they readily accepted this time.

"At a cocktail party. I'd come with another man who had gotten quite drunk and was becoming more obnoxious by the minute. When he wandered off in search of more bourbon, Kevin approached and asked if I needed any help. He knew the guy and, well, confirmed he was a pig.

"We were able to talk for a while. It was stimulating conversation. I knew instantly he was a special person. 'Pig' reappeared and proceeded to feel me up and paste wet, liquor-scented kisses on my cheek, all the while speaking in sexually explicit language. I finally told him to get lost. Later in the evening, Kevin offered take me home."

Katherine, sitting next to Stella on the loveseat, could see in her face that she was anxious, perhaps speculating which direction this conversation might go. She wondered if the FBI knew Stella had been a prostitute.

"When was that?"

"Let's see. I'd just been to Vermont to see the brilliant-colored leaves, so fall, late 1960s."

"Were you paid for your services that night?"

"No," Stella replied with an immediate change in tone. "Not by either man."

Katherine tensed, realizing if either Wilson or Gultowski became judgmental, Stella would not respond well.

"Gentlemen, now it's time for *my* questions. Why are you here and why do you want to talk with me? I can't help you much if I don't know your motives. What can you tell me about Kevin's death?"

Katherine watched the two agents look at each other, noticing their unwillingness to become interviewees instead of interrogators. Katherine could see that they didn't know when to get pushy and when to back off. It was obvious they preferred a more formal approach, but Stella could easily get them to tone that down, especially after she had baked them coffee cake that she served on fine china with petite linen napkins. They wanted to be in control, but Stella's resistance to being treated aggressively was an obstacle. At the moment, she held the ultimate trump card and could end the conversation. Katherine wondered if Stella knew there'd be limits to that.

Initially, Katherine assumed this investigation was not a top priority for the FBI, considering the age of the case and because they had sent these young agents who were clearly just starting their careers. Perhaps they were assigned to obtain preliminary information before more seasoned agents were brought in. Still, she listened to every word so as not to let her guard down. She knew better than to underestimate the power of the FBI, especially since she didn't even know whether Stella had committed criminal acts.

Jeb, perhaps the more senior of the two, relented. "A great deal of money was taken from the Finchley family's diamond operation. Millions. The prime suspect was the son, Kevin Finchley, who denied it. And he certainly didn't live a lifestyle that pointed to his guilt. In fact, he sold his rather luxurious home that had been given to him by his family for something much simpler. We learned that his wife was livid."

"Glad you've been doing your homework," Stella said. "She was in it for the money, nothing more."

After taking a sip of coffee, Gultowski took over. "So many diamonds were missing that the apartheid government, to whom the family was very loyal, got involved. They claimed the diamonds had been taken out of the country illegally, even implying they were blood diamonds. They accused Finchley of sending money to various guerilla movements in Africa whose motives were to kill whites and topple governments. It was common knowledge that blood diamonds, or conflict diamonds, were entering South Africa from countries such as Sierra Leone and the Congo. Yet Finchley's family insisted Kevin was aiding rebel factions with his own source of diamonds unearthed from his own country."

"That's utter bullshit!" Stella exclaimed harshly before pressing her lips tightly together.

Walker continued. "Finchley was open and vocal about his negative feelings for apartheid, and the government intimated that he was a huge thorn in their side. In the meantime, Finchley was increasingly more active with anti-apartheid groups and foundations. He supported nonprofits whose purpose was to help Black Africans achieve education and start small businesses. We also uncovered information that he had worked tirelessly for the release of Nelson Mandela."

With this last statement, Katherine noticed that it seemed they were endorsing Finchley. *Perhaps,* she thought, *they had done more extensive homework.* Their tone was more sympathetic, as if they were talking with Stella not to her. Katherine was also beginning to understand why Stella had loved Kevin.

Gultowski took over again. "The apartheid government, acting on the blood diamond accusations from the family, pressed charges. He was indicted for theft and treason. Without any specifics, the prosecution said there was plenty of evidence. He was jailed for a while but was released on bail and, of course, his passport revoked. A pretrial hearing drew national attention, especially when Finchley was uncooperative and used it as a forum for his political views...."

Stella interrupted, "Surprise, surprise. He already knew he was doomed."

"Several weeks later," said Gultowski, "he disappeared and was eventually found brutally bludgeoned to death, literally tortured: fingernails removed, teeth drilled, eyes gouged. By the way, the circumstances surrounding his death seemed to have been suppressed in the media. Later, a Black miner was accused of aiding him, but died in a car crash before charges were filed."

"Oh, that dear, brave man." Stella paused, imagining the pain he must have endured, but not wanting to lose control. It was obvious she wanted his story to be told and was holding her emotions at bay. "When did that happen?"

"September 1, 1990."

"I was never sure of the exact date. Alistair Winthrop, a longtime friend of Martin's and a surrogate father to Kevin, knocked at my apartment late one night to give me the news in person. He had been in South Africa at the time of Kevin's death. But because he suspected his phone was tapped, he waited a few weeks until his next trip to New York. Apparently, in a coverup, the news reported that his death was ruled accidental. But Winthrop knew the truth."

After a brief silence, Stella went on. "I was devastated, but not surprised. Kevin was a man embarrassed by his family, as well as his country. He so wanted to change the way it was. Kevin was ahead of his time. It was analogous to being the son of a slave owner in 1860s America. One who was appalled by slavery and wanted to fix it."

"Okay, Stella, we need to know the history of your relationship with Finchley," said Gultowski, his tone now more empathetic as he called her by her first name for the first time.

"As I told you, we were together over twenty years, till 1990. I didn't see him continuously. Sometimes, he'd be gone for months. But when we were together, it was marvelous and stimulating. After a time, he bought me an apartment near the United Nations. He even put it in my name. In fact, I just moved from that apartment to live here at Oak Place.

"We had a wonderful time together. He was a good man, a moral and ethical man. I'll tell you right now there were no conflict or blood diamonds. He'd have never used them to supply guns to any group or any country. He was a pacifist, believing change should come about only through nonviolence. In the sixties, he studied the creative nonviolence of Martin Luther King, Jr., listened to his speeches, watched his marches, and saw the reactions to those marches."

Katherine was riveted by Stella's description of Finchley. She stared at the African sculptures around the room as Stella talked.

"With insufficient public support against apartheid in his own country, I remember him quoting King: 'In the end, what will hurt the most is not the words of our enemies but the silence of our friends.' We talked endlessly about how he wanted to use King's strategies in South Africa." Stella paused again, resuming with the one question weighing heavily on her mind. "Why, after all this time, are you here now? He's been gone three decades."

"His brother never really let the case drop and became more and more active once his parents were either dead or incompetent," said Gultowski. "He made no bones about his hate for Kevin and how he'd destroyed the family name. For years, it seemed the family mines were producing significantly fewer diamonds, and they suspected theft. When they finally sold their shares to a much larger government-run corporation, they received considerably less than hoped for. Now, his brother has Alzheimer's, and it seems his nephews and a niece are not satisfied, continuing to accuse Finchley of stealing diamonds worth millions and using them to supply rebels with weapons. In other words, they suspect a stockpile of diamonds still exists. Just recently, they produced documentation to that effect."

"Fucking bullshit! Forged, I'm sure," said Stella. "Lies, lies!"

"Consequently," said Walker, "governments are involved once again. With accusations that blood diamonds entered this country, the CIA, who had been involved initially, referred the case to the FBI. We're charged with finding out if they still exist—and if they do, who has them."

"His living relatives probably depleted their trust funds," Stella retorted.

"Regardless, the FBI is investigating because of the charge of theft of international money allegedly used illegally for weapons. We have to follow up."

"And you think I might know the answers? Tell me this. How did you get my name?"

"The family gave it to us. Apparently, they learned there was some type of relationship."

Katherine had been silent throughout this exchange, but her mind was reeling. Did Stella know something about the money's whereabouts? She wondered when Stella could or would ask for the big favor: finding her son.

"Can you help us?" asked Brian.

"Either of you guys want more coffee?" Stella asked as if she needed time to gather her thoughts and decide what to do next.

"Sure," said Walker to the surprise of everyone. Stella, using her walker, went to the kitchen.

When she hadn't returned after a few minutes, Katherine went to check on her and found Stella hunched over the sink, eyes wet again.

"I'm sorry. I know this is hard for you," said Katherine placing her hand on Stella's shoulder.

"Fingernails removed! Teeth drilled! Jesus! Fuck! All for mother-fucking money! He was murdered for believing in justice. I wish I had tried harder to see him again. I could've supported him when he needed me the most. Oh, Katherine I'm so consumed with regret!"

Walker was at the kitchen door listening. Stella turned to him. "I wonder how many more were killed to perpetuate a brutal, oppressive system. What he did was tantamount to publicly condemning Hitler. And he paid dearly. His own family was fueled by greed. He married his wife, that bitch, only because she lied to him during their court-ship about wanting social justice, all the while craving a piece of his family's fortune." Stella started crying. "Goddamn her! And damn me for abandoning him! How can I ever make it right?"

Stella turned to Katherine and reached for her as she started to fall against the kitchen counter. Katherine helped her regain her balance.

"I'm feeling lightheaded and need to lie down for a few minutes. Please tell them for me what I want from them."

Katherine helped Stella to her bedroom before coming back to the kitchen. Walker looked at Katherine. "What does she want from us?"

"She wants to find the child she and Kevin Finchley had."

Walker sighed. "Jesus! If she knows about the money, she could be in big trouble." He was obviously connecting the dots between getting information from Stella and finding her child.

"I haven't a clue what, if anything, she knows about the money. But I do know she's distraught right now."

"Seems obvious she's talking to you when we're not around." Walker's frustration was growing.

"And?" Katherine was irritated. "Look, Jeb, of course we talk, but we are *not* conniving or lying."

"So, she was a prostitute?" Walker asked as if to verify what he already knew.

"Yes, but she and Kevin fell in love." Katherine was caught off guard but knew better than to lie to an FBI agent, even a young up-start who was about the same age as her own child. "And," she added firmly, "prostitute is not a word you should use again to describe her. In fact, she spent a good deal of her life helping young girls and wom-en get off the streets. She counseled them, guiding many back home to worried parents, as well as helping them complete their educations. She took great risks to free them from pimps. She may have been a prostitute on her first date with Kevin. However, their relationship grew into much more." Now she was staring, face firm, straight at Walker.

"I'm sorry. I think I'm beginning to understand."

All their phones had been going off for the last few minutes. Finally, each answered calls that instructed them to be somewhere else.

On the elevator, Gultowski turned to Katherine. "Look, seriously, we're talking many millions of dollars in diamonds here."

"For God's sake, Brian, have you done the math? We're talking about something that happened thirty years ago! They still expect to find the money?"

"Yes. It's a seemingly old case, but evidence indicates stolen dia-monds are still hidden somewhere."

Gultowski's concern became clear as he continued. "Look, we've got to get some answers soon or Stella Cordrey will be charged as an accessory to international smuggling. And Dr. Eich, if you're suppressing any relevant information, we'll charge you with withholding evidence. Please understand. This is serious."

With that, they marched out to their sedan. Katherine watched as they drove off, reflecting on Stella's repeated descriptions of Kevin's altruism. She was finally certain of one thing—Stella knew where those diamonds were.

CHAPTER 25

Katherine was still focused on Gultowski's menacing words as she made her way to the memorial service. She presumed both he and Walker were being pressured for answers.

The volunteer organist, a resident in senior housing, was playing a slow, solemn version of "What a Friend We Have in Jesus" as Katherine walked quietly into the chapel and took a front seat next to Jeff, Shirlee, and two other nurses from the nursing home. The retired minister, also a resident, sat up front in a simple black robe with a somewhat frayed yellow and blue scarf draping down, most likely the same one he had donned for decades in his large Presbyterian church. Next to him were the ashes of Rita Jenkins.

Katherine had been to funerals like this before. An empty chapel, no one there save a few Oak Place employees, all of whom were thinking the same thing: Who was the deceased? Today, it was Rita Jenkins. Except for her short, six-month residency in the dementia unit, they knew nothing else about her. This mute woman was unable to fill in the blanks. One day, she stopped eating and drinking, and death quietly came calling.

Before coming to Oak Place, she'd been discovered living alone in a rundown tenement, incapable of caring for herself and—according to the other tenants—abandoned by her family.

As a ward of the state, Katherine became her legal guardian, and Rita Jenkins was lovingly cared for by the staff. Except for her name, nobody knew anything about her life. A teacher? A mother? Somebody's dear friend? Nobody knew. Using her social security number, Oak Place learned she was born in 1931 in Minnesota. Katherine wondered, *How was it that a person came to the end of their life surrounded only by strangers; her life summarized with a generic eulogy?*

For many months after her admission to Oak Place, social workers had tried unsuccessfully to find family and friends. Her landlady thought her often staggering, drunk daughter had moved to New Jersey or Pennsylvania, but left no forwarding address. Nobody else ever came to visit that the landlady knew of. And, as the dementia took its toll, Rita Jenkins was incapable of telling her story, or paying the rent.

The police were finally called when the odor coming from the dark apartment, electricity turned off, became overwhelming. Her decomposing cat had apparently succumbed to starvation, and Rita was emaciated and caked in feces. There was no food in the apartment, and she didn't even know her name. An ambulance was called. The hospital re-nourished her body, but they couldn't awaken her brain enough to learn anything about her. A judge ruled her incompetent and she was admitted to Oak Place. She constantly held tightly to a single possession from the apartment; a previously filthy but finally bleach-washed raggedy teddy bear, perhaps representing a child, that was cremated with Rita and now rested with her in the cardboard box.

Katherine fantasized about what Rita might have been like in her youth—maybe dancing in a field of daisies or playing with her dog. Or perhaps helping sell war bonds during World War II. Could she have welcomed home returning soldiers? Maybe she cooked a decadent apple pie. Maybe she had sewn her own clothes, as well as those of her family. Where was her child? And were there other children?

Katherine, Jeff, Shirlee, and the nurses were in their own deep thoughts about the life lived and now departed. But all anyone could do was think what might have been. All knew that drugs were too often the sad reason children abused and then abandoned their parents.

The minister stepped to the podium and said out loud what everyone was thinking. "How did it come to be that no one can tell us about this life, what made her worthy of being remembered. Somewhere in the depths of this is a legacy, but we know not what it is. However, no one is without worth in God's kingdom. Perhaps there is someone whose life was changed because of her." The minister bowed his head as if the impact of his words profoundly affected him and he was trying to comprehend that he—for the first time—was at a funeral where nobody knew the deceased.

When he raised his head, his sadness was apparent. He looked out at the congregation of five. "The inscription on the Tomb of the Unknown Soldier says, 'Known but to God.' Here and now, we know a name, and nothing else. Still, we honor her for whatever gifts she had, and gave. We ask God to take her into His arms and bring her peace."

Dying in obscurity, she would go to a pauper's grave that no one would visit. At Oak Place, there were currently thirty guardianship residents, all demented, and hundreds more who had departed over the years. Like Rita Jenkins, they were known but to God. Katherine, Shirlee, Jeff, or some of the staff always prepared a funeral in the Oak Place Chapel. "Nobody deserves to have no one attend their funeral," Shirlee had once said. Today, she said, "I hope she experienced at least some love and happiness in her life. I would like to think she shared some kindness, that someone thanked her, and someone remembers her."

❧ ❧ ❧

After the funeral, Jeff, Katherine, and Shirlee decided to have a working lunch together. They settled in a booth at a crowded neighborhood deli, with waitresses scurrying about carrying six-inch high pastrami sandwiches and cooks ringing bells as orders were ready. Katherine found it difficult to engage. Instead, her thoughts were occupied with the FBI interrogation of Stella and yet another funeral of yet another abandoned elder.

"Katherine," said Jeff, snapping his fingers, "you seem like you're in left field."

"Sorry. This FBI thing has got me rattled. I've become close to a woman who just may have smuggled millions of dollars of diamonds out of South Africa."

"Do you think she did?" Shirlee asked.

"I hope not. Maybe. I don't know."

"Not to change the subject," said Jeff, "but would it help you to reengage if we talked about sex?"

That caught Katherine's attention. "What?!"

"I'd like to discuss the reemergence of STDs, again, for the umpteenth time."

Given the advanced age of many residents, turnover was understandably high as people transferred to different care levels or died. That meant sex education programs had to be made available regularly. Over the years, they had noticed that when a bunch of older people, especially singles, live in close proximity, many rediscover their sexuality and sex drives, some with gusto, as well as multiple partners.

Back in the 1990s, Jeff, Shirlee, and Katherine had thought they had seen it all. Yet they were surprised when an almost epidemic proportion of sexually transmitted diseases presented in the Oak Place Medical Clinic.

"Mrs. Clayborn, you have venereal warts," Jeff had said (circa 1993) to a seventy-two-year-old widow after she complained of painful white spots on her labia.

"How did I get that?" she had asked timidly, as if not wanting to know the answer.

"Unprotected sex," Jeff had replied matter-of-factly.

"Oh my," she had said, bowing her head. "I guess I've been a bad girl."

"Not at all. Lots of older people are sexually active. It's healthy and fun. Besides, I'm not here to judge you."

In that same month, Jeff saw five more cases of venereal warts, three cases of herpes and one case of gonorrhea.

"Methinks we need to do some educating," he had said after telling Shirlee and Katherine about the problem.

"Egad!" Shirlee had said, shaking her head.

"Egad is right. And this is over and above all the cases of female cystitis I've seen due to Viagra-induced penises creating excessive friction from intercourse without a lubricant."

"Ouch!" Katherine had said. "That's got to hurt."

"Plus, might make you reassess society's expectations of age-related celibacy," Shirlee had added. "I mean, people don't want to think their cute little old grandma or grandpop are doing it!"

Shirlee had then gotten on her soapbox. "Look, these old people grew up in an era where sex wasn't talked about. Most have been ignorant of some sexual issues all their lives. They hardly taught their kids about sex. But now, as they collect Medicare and pensions, some are re-experiencing a yearning for sexual intimacy, or discovering that orgasms still feel good."

Katherine's rant had followed. "You know, our senior housing is sometimes like a college dormitory. People in and out of apartments doing a whole lot of experimenting. Some might feel liberated for the first time in their lives. And more and more are not feeling any desire to remarry, thus avoiding any turmoil regarding their children's inheritance. They just want intimacy."

Jeff said, "We've got a lot of sexually active seniors who think their condom days are over. I mean, they know pregnancy is not a concern but never thought about STDs."

"Maybe we should make both condoms and lubricants available," Shirlee had suggested.

"Is that possible? What would it cost?" Jeff had asked.

"Why don't we call the lubricant jelly salespeople?" By now, their smiles had turned to giggling.

"Okay," Katherine had said. "Sex education for seniors? Do we need to get cucumbers and teach them how to put on condoms?

Jeff was holding his belly, laughing. "You guys!"

"Wait a minute!" Shirlee had said. "Maybe we could pass out lubricated condoms?"

"Not kidding, Jeff," Katherine had said. "Some of these very wise sages haven't a clue how to use a condom."

"Maybe we should do a class on sex toys like vibrators and dildos," Shirlee had said. "Sex isn't just for couples, you know. Some of these people still view masturbation as *sin*." Shirlee emphasized the word 'sin' and raised her hands like an evangelist at a Bible rally.

"Preach on, Shirlee!" Katherine had said. "Should we get samples of sex toys?"

"Of course!" Shirlee had agreed. "If they've never had a sex toy, as I suspect many haven't, they need to know what's available. I'm sure they won't ask their grandchildren."

"Yes, let's call it the Oak Place Sex-a-rama!" Jeff had said, causing all three to go into full-on laugh mode.

"Maybe some good erotic films, using only older persons, of course," said Katherine as Jeff and Shirlee leaned in over the table, still laughing.

"Why not?" Shirlee had said. "This isn't the dark ages, and erotica is not porn."

"You mean films complete with wrinkled dicks and flopping breasts?"

"Maybe we could get Bob Hope to narrate an introduction," Katherine had said back in the 1990s. "He's an older person now."

"Bob Hope?" Jeff had said. "He must be almost a hundred by now!"

"How about bringing in Dr. Ruth as a guest speaker?" Shirlee had suggested.

"Now you're talking!"

Thus, the Oak Place Sex Education Program was created. Attendance soared and the incidence of STDs dropped almost immediately. Shirlee even went to all the neighborhood pharmacies and convinced them to carry self-lubricated condoms. And yes, Jeff passed them out freely.

One pharmacy went so far as to publicly display lubricants with a sign that said, "LUBRICATE!" Sales went up dramatically.

Shirlee's stash of vibrators and dildos was always a hit. The masturbation class, Enjoying Solo Sex, was the most popular, particularly for women not partnered.

Katherine taught a class on sexual positioning in one's later years, especially relevant for arthritics. "Let's talk about the spoon position," she would start. Katherine loved teaching and even with all her administrative duties and research projects, she always found time to regularly do a class or two.

Jeff talked about drugs that affect erectile dysfunction, as well as sex after menopause. His classes were standing room only.

Jeff, Katherine, and Shirlee were straightforward and serious during their talks. Furthermore, residents trusted them when they proved to not be the moral police. Still, since many residents were hesitant to raise their hands and ask questions, hundreds of index cards were distributed so questioners could remain anonymous. When word of the Oak Place sex classes got out, older persons from across the city came.

"Is it me, or are half the people in this class coming from outside Oak Place?" Katherine commented after one class. "I hardly recognized anyone."

Jeff, Katherine, and Shirlee were unfettered when it came to curriculum. Shirlee summed it up. "Thank God we don't have to worry about what the parents would say."

※ ※ ※

And so today, after a particularly sad funeral, the threesome sat in a restaurant and decided that updated sex education classes—initiated years ago—would resume.

Katherine thought back to her lunch with Stella and how she joked about starting a 'mature escort service.' She would be a great teacher. *Bet Stella could even teach me a few things*, she thought.

CHAPTER 26

Two days later, Stella again met with Gultowski and Walker in her apartment. "In the late 1980s sometime, I don't remember the exact dates, Kevin twice smuggled diamonds out of South Africa, diamonds he assured me were mined from South Africa, not some other African country. He brought them to our home and said he was going to use them for human rights, although I don't recall him mentioning specific organizations." She paused for a moment, then continued. "Oh, how mesmerized I was by that valuable contraband totaling maybe one hundred precious diamonds. I'm talking about big diamonds, already cut, like the kind Elizabeth Taylor would've worn."

Katherine's assumption was verified. Stella had known about the diamonds. She looked at Gultowski's and Wilson's stoic faces, then at Stella, wondering if the truth would set her free, or land her in jail.

"Did he say if they were certified?" asked Walker.

"He did and they were, although the certificates were forged. Kevin knew a lot of people in low places. Smuggling was rampant back then, well, until a strict, formal, government-mandated certification process was initiated."

"You mean the Kimberley Process Certification?" asked Walker.

"Yes, that's what it was, I think. It was a long time ago. And Kevin did his smuggling way before that. He was dead before Kimberley laws. And when I visited him in South Africa, he gave me more diamonds to bring back to the U.S."

"You took that kind of risk?"

"I loved him, *and* the cause. He told me they were going to be used for the nonviolent anti-apartheid movement, as well as education and medical care. I didn't think for a minute I was doing anything wrong or immoral. Besides, I'm from the streets. It kind of got my juices flowing. By then, I wholeheartedly believed the money should fund schools rather than Bentleys."

Go girl, thought Katherine.

"To get them through security, I hand-painted some of them with various colors of lacquer so they looked like sparkling glass rubies or sapphires. Then, I glued them into cheaply molded foundations so they formed large brooches. By the time I was done, the costume jewelry pins, while striking, appeared to have come from a second-rate tourist shop. I covered the other diamonds with clay, baked them till hardened, hand painted each one and strung them into a necklace. They were beautiful. On my person and in my luggage were several million dollars' worth of diamonds, all concealed in an assortment of pins and necklaces. I declared them as worth $465, complete with phony receipts."

"And you got them through customs?" Gultowski asked as Wilson and Katherine just stared at Stella. "Jesus!" Everyone except Stella was sitting on the edge of their seats.

"I was scared to death. My palms were sweaty and my heart raced as I waited in line for customs officials to search my suitcase. Some classic 'ugly American' tourist wearing her Ramar-of-the-Jungle hat and toting some six suitcases was yakking endlessly about her private safari. Then, in the front of the line, guards forced a man and his suitcase to the side. I couldn't hear why, but they were rough with him, shouting, and finally drawing their guns. My intense paranoia made me think he was smuggling something and got caught. I was worried I'd be next."

Katherine was in awe. The guts, the courage it must have taken.

"By the time it was my turn, I had managed to compose myself. I knew if I didn't, it was over. The guard looked through my suitcase, then at me. He grabbed the pins. 'Where are these pins from?' he sternly asked.

"A gift shop downtown, I told him. Aren't they lovely? I couldn't resist buying them for myself and my family. He held the pins in the air towards the lights, angling them in different directions. Then he scratched one with his fingernail. That really petrified me. I had used two coats of supposedly scratch-proof lacquer, but would it pass the test?

"'Show me the receipts!' he snapped gruffly, again staring straight into my face. Yes sir, I said. But he only glanced at them. It was the gems that got his full attention.

"He kept studying them carefully, first closely, then with his hand outstretched once more towards light, he twisted and turned them for what seemed like a lifetime, before saying, 'My mother would love one of these.'"

Katherine took a deep breath and grinned. *Wow,* she thought.

"I smiled, knowing if he tried to find the store, he'd realize I was lying. I told him they were made by a team of African women, emphasizing—really emphasizing—that they were the last ten in the store. I told him the saleslady said more were being made but that it would take about two weeks before they received a new shipment.

"To add to my nervous tension, he called a colleague over. 'Look at these brooches! Never seen anything like these.' His colleague began the same ritual of examination, minus the scratching. 'Where is that store again?'"

"I was vague, acting like a tourist. I told him the store, small like a kiosk, was downtown near a farmer's market. He wasn't as interested in the necklaces, perhaps because they looked like other tourist baubles. After a grueling several minutes, he let me pass." Stella sighed with relief, perhaps as she'd done on that day decades ago.

"Go on," said Wilson.

"I was nervous the entire plane ride home. My mind was plagued with 'what-ifs.' Did he hear me when I said more pins *wouldn't* be available for two weeks? I fretted that he might go there after work and discover I'd given him a phony address. He could alert authorities in New York and have me detained on arrival. Thankfully, that didn't happen."

Katherine realized she was anxious just listening to the story despite knowing Stella had made it safely.

"In the end, it wasn't the perfect crime, but I got away with it. I did, though, age several years in those hours."

"So, what did you do with them?"

"Took me two full days to restore them to their original sparkle. I had to burn the lacquer off; that was laborious. The necklaces I broke with a hammer. They all went into a safe deposit box on Fifth Avenue, along with the other diamonds Kevin had smuggled and the forged certificates, which he sent separately by private carrier. Kevin insisted I have a key so I could access them in case something happened to him."

"And....?" asked Walker.

"And...are you going to help me find my son?" There was an immediate, abrupt shift in Stella's tone.

"Let's not change the subject," Walker said, apparently unwilling to negotiate. They wanted the rest of the story.

"Actually, let's do," insisted Stella.

"Ms. Cordrey, please!"

"Stella! *I would like you to call me Stella!* Listen, there were no blood diamonds! Never! None! And I am going to prove it to you so you can close this case once and for all."

"If there're no blood diamonds, how do we know the money wasn't spent on lavish luxuries? That's still theft."

"Lavish luxuries? Kevin died for what he believed in! And it wasn't fucking gold toilets! This compassionate man deserves something for his ultimate sacrifice. His son should know who he was. So, will you help me?"

Walker and Stella stared at each other, as if daring the other to blink first.

"You know where the diamonds are, don't you?"

"I do. And I have every intention of telling you. But I need your help," Stella said to the agents in desperation. "I repeat! This man had a son who should know who his father was. Please, I beg you!"

"Your son was born a long time ago," Walker said, pursing his lips and rubbing his chin.

"You're the FBI!"

"I suppose we can make some inquiries."

"I want more than 'I suppose!'"

Katherine thought she should say something. She felt pulled into Stella's story—and her life. "Look, I think this is, ah, a reasonable request," she said out loud before thinking, *Jesus, can't I express myself a bit better. I'm being a shitty advocate.*

"Would you be willing to come down to our offices and talk with our supervisor? Only he can make that decision," Walker said.

"You name the time and place and I'll be there. And Katherine comes too. I say nothing more without her being present."

Katherine, tense about how things were unfolding and the sheer magnitude of what had happened years ago, chimed in, "You sure, ah, you don't want a lawyer?"

Stella began visibly sweating. She cradled her head in her hands, her elbows resting on her chair's armrest. She raised her head and said in a clear voice, "I don't need one. It will soon become apparent to *all* of you that I have not committed an egregious crime or threatened any country's national security. "Now, if you will excuse me." Stella got up, walked to her bedroom and closed the door firmly behind her.

Gultowski and Walker knew better than to follow her. Katherine's mouth was half open.

CHAPTER 27

Katherine and Shirlee settled into a corner booth at a nearby coffee shop, mugs of steaming lattes in front of them. "I'm so glad you were available," Shirlee said, squirming nervously.

"You're not going to give me the news that you're retiring, are you?" Katherine raised her eyebrows as she peered over her glasses.

"Not yet. I'll reserve that for a dinner date at the Ritz, with you paying."

Then Shirlee gleefully blurted, "David Livingston asked me out!"

Katherine smiled widely. "And you said?"

"I said yes! We've known each other for years, but I never wanted to mix my professional and personal life. I don't know if I did the right thing, but I guess I'll find out." Katherine was still smiling at her dear friend. Hand over her mouth, Shirlee started giggling, and Katherine couldn't help but join in.

David Livingston was one of the principal architects of Oak Place, having designed the original buildings. Now, when something was to be constructed or redesigned, they contacted him. David was a senior partner at a major firm in Manhattan, but gave his time generously to Oak Place. Over the years, he'd spent many hours in Katherine's office. In fact, he worked closely with many of the staff to get their feedback on new construction ideas. He charged very reasonable rates for half his time. The rest of the time, he worked pro bono.

He had worked closely with Shirlee in designing state-of-the-art educational and activity classrooms for the residents. They had a wonderful relationship, full of respect, but not without laughter and joking with each other. She had consoled him when his wife of thirty-five years died. She knew what it was like to bury a partner.

"This takes our relationship to a whole new level. What if it's a bust?"

"Shirlee, he's not asking you to marry him!" Both women laughed like schoolgirls.

"I don't know. This is a whole new thing for me."

"What? Dating? It has been a while for you, hasn't it?"

"Yes, and well, you know…"

"Know what?" Katherine said. "Wait a minute. *Because he's white?*"

"You don't have to say it with such emphasis."

"Is that it?" Katherine and Shirlee stared at each other, both suddenly serious.

"This is new territory for me, Katherine. In the sixties, I wouldn't have considered it. Dating a white man was not what militant Black women did. They were against everything we valued. Society and—in particular—white men, were the oppressors of Black people. I swore I'd never date one. Katherine, these old tapes keep playing in my head. They're stupid, I know. But now that this opportunity is presenting itself, I'm conflicted. I've even surprised myself by my reaction. I feel like a phony, preaching for integration yet segregating in my personal love life."

"Methinks you are letting the past get in the way of a potentially nice friendship."

"Katherine, we already *have* a nice friendship. Maybe that's how it should remain. God, I feel like I've become, at least in this part of my life, a rigid old fart."

"Maybe you have," said Katherine calmly.

"Gee, thanks."

"It's not too late to change, you know. Do you like him?"

"Yes. Very much."

"Are you attracted to him?"

"I knew it! I knew you'd go there. Hey, I've seen a million white dicks in my nursing career, but this is personal, intimate, different. Come on, Katherine!

"Like you, I've evolved. We're older now. Who cares? We don't do things these days just to conform. Besides, this is New York City, not Smallville, Mississippi. It took David guts to want to take this to another level. Maybe he's already thought about it long and hard. And I might also add, there are interracial couples all over the place. We're not living in a *Guess Who's Coming to Dinner* society any longer."

"Yeah, yeah. I know."

"Shirlee, ever since I've known you, you've always embraced diversity. This is something you can handle. So, where does he want to take you on this date?"

"He has tickets to an opening night play. We're going to dinner before the play."

"That's special. Sounds like a nice date, no strings attached. I'm sure he's not going to insist on getting you in the sack."

"But if there are more dates, then what? What if this relationship tanks and we still have to work together professionally?"

"Cross that bridge when you get to it."

"Easier said than done. Plus, I haven't had intercourse in, I don't know, a long, long time."

"Shirlee, you can do this. You're an assertive woman." A thought dawned on Katherine. "Wait a minute! You really like him, don't you?"

"Shut up!" Shirlee sighed, covering her face with her hands.

"Hell no, girlfriend. I can tell you're attracted to him. So, what do you like about him other than being such a kind person and a great architect?"

"He's a good man, really compassionate, plus he's fit and healthy. This would be easier if he wasn't a WASP."

"But a wonderful WASP! Don't let that stop you. So, do we need to go dress shopping?"

"I feel like I'm in college again." Shirlee said, nodding her head.

"So, he makes you feel young?"

"Yes, but both of us are old. What if he gets sick? I certainly don't want to have to take care of him. Been there, done that."

"Oh, now we're going from a first date straight to caregiving? Shirlee, think! Aren't you jumping the gun a tad too quickly?"

"I know, I know. Guess so. How about that black dress I wore to the residents' opening play?"

"Too matronly."

"Get a grip, girl. I'm not a sex object."

"Getting testy, aren't we? I'm not talking about a strapless see-through."

"I haven't had a date in so long. Dear God, with a white man, no less."

"The world will not go to hell if you date a man outside your race. And just maybe you'll be an inspiration to others. By that I mean judging someone by the content of their character, not the color of their skin."

Shirlee quickly raised an eyebrow. "Quoting Martin Luther King, are we? Okay, you've made your point."

"I mean it. It's time we listened to ourselves about all this racial equality we've been advocating for all these decades. Besides, you've already said yes to David. Maybe you've already moved past all that."

"When can we go shopping? God, I'm so fat."

"Stop with the self-deprecating! You look as amazing as ever. How about tomorrow night?"

"Sounds good," said Shirlee before saying, "What if he can't get it up?"

Katherine almost choked on her latte. "For goodness sake, put some Viagra in your purse along with lubricant."

"I can't do that! Maybe he has a heart condition. And you know I can't prescribe drugs."

"Shirlee, you're making me crazy!"

CHAPTER 28

Stella looked stunning, almost regal, for the ride to the FBI offices in Manhattan. Her silver hair was tucked loosely in a French twist, with a few long, curly locks hanging down around her face. She wore a navy blue suit with a culotte skirt and comfy, flat, slate gray boots. A sapphire pin at her shoulder held her bold, color coordinated scarf in place. Instead of her walker, she had substituted a sturdy, custom carved African mahogany cane because she wanted no part of the adjustable metal canes that clicked annoyingly with every step.

Katherine was filled with nervous anticipation. She had stayed up late talking with Peter, who'd taken an interest in Stella's story. "I can't believe I'll find out what a rebel who loved a prostitute did with all of them diamonds."

Peter told her he wished he was still working for *The New York Times*. "I think this would be a compelling story. Dear God, I hope the son is found."

Gultowski and Wilson met them in a waiting room and escorted them to the office of Special Agent Mark Beder, a balding man who looked to be over sixty. He rose from his chair when they entered, extending his hand first to Stella and then Katherine. "Ladies, thank you for coming. Please, let's sit at the conference table."

The stately office was dark wood throughout, with a bookcase loaded with memorabilia directly behind the desk, where a framed triangularly-folded American flag rested. Black and white photos covered the walls, including Beder with two U.S. presidents. Katherine, uneasily realizing he must be at the top of the command chain, sat down next to Stella on one side of the rectangle table, while Beder sat on the other side, Gultowski and Wilson at opposite ends. Bottles of water were offered.

"So, in return for information, you want us to find a long-lost child?" asked Beder, opening a folder, on top of which was an 8 by 10 photo of Kevin Finchley in front of the United Nations. Stella stared at the photo, as did Katherine.

"Thank you for not beating around the bush," Stella said. "This is not quid pro quo. I consider it cooperation. Besides, the story I'm about to tell you is as old as Methuselah. I can't imagine it being a pressing risk on today's national security."

"It is quid pro quo," said Beder. "Prove to me the diamonds weren't used for weapons. If they were, I don't care how old the story is. And don't think I won't throw a little old lady in jail if she lies to me."

Katherine squirmed in her seat. This guy knew how to play hard-ball. Even Stella came to attention. The room was eerily silent.

"Look, Agent Beder," said Stella, "you and I both know I'm going to tell this story regardless. In fact, Kevin's reputation and legacy are more important to me than finding my son. For God's sake, he died for this!" Stella was getting emotional, and Katherine ached for her.

"Please understand, though," Stella said, "I'm begging for your help. All the other doors are closed."

Beder acknowledged with a nod. He showed no emotion. "Start talking."

Knowing Gultowski and Walker had brought Beder up to date, Stella started her story where she had left off. "By the time Kevin and I smuggled all the diamonds we could get, Kevin was able to get them appraised: $155,998,000 and change." Katherine gasped, eyes open wide as Stella continued. "The diamonds had been split up into five or six piles and several appraisers were hired, one for each pile, so as not to call attention to them."

"Oh my God," whispered Walker before clearing his throat following a stern look from Beder.

"When was this?" asked Beder.

"It was the late 1980s. I remember because Ronald Reagan was still president and he had refused to condemn apartheid. Can you believe? Our own president vetoed the Anti-Apartheid Act! *That* was infuriating!" Katherine's heart sank. One of the photos on the wall was of a younger Beder and Reagan.

"Why did he smuggle the diamonds out?" asked Beder. "Couldn't he have just converted them in South Africa and used the money as planned? And what, exactly, was his plan?

"All the banks, politicians, and police were friends of his family or they had strong business connections. Kevin figured, correctly, I think, that any scheme to convert diamonds to money, locally or nationally, would quickly raise red flags. No, the diamonds needed to be transported out of South Africa first, and then reallocated without his name attached."

Beder peered over his half glasses and waited for Stella to continue.

"By this time, Kevin was constantly looking over his shoulder. He was disheveled and gaunt, but he was still very vocal about his distaste for Reagan's position. He knew the South African government was pressuring the U.S. to revoke his visa in an effort to ban future entrance into the States once he left. He feared deportation could come at any minute. Mind you, I don't think they knew yet the extent of his diamond smuggling activities. At least, no accusations had been rendered. I urged him to defect. He knew if he returned to South Africa, his safety would be in jeopardy, but he wanted to continue his fight not only here, but in his homeland. He rejected my pleas outright."

The room was silent as Stella paused and took a deep breath. Her hands were trembling.

"What a sad time," she said, shaking her head, her voice cracking. "He kept telling me it was too dangerous to stay together. I realized my wonderful relationship with the only man I ever loved was about to be taken from me, forever. Our last night together in New York felt like a funeral, the death of what we had compounded by an uncertain future. He told me we wouldn't be able to communicate because he already feared for my safety."

"Did you ever see him again after that?" asked Beder.

"Yes," Stella said quietly, looking down. "I just couldn't *not* stay in touch. I went to South Africa against his wishes and concerns for my safety. We were only able to spend two nights together, even though I was there almost two weeks. That's how paranoid he was about me being implicated. It was like he was dying of cancer and we were saying our final goodbyes. That last night was nothing but tears. We ordered room service and truly hoped there could be a future for us. In hindsight, it was wishful thinking. He promised me he'd make it back to the States, but it was not to be."

Stella started crying and Katherine reached for her hand. "I'll be okay," Stella said. She blew her nose and looked at Beder. Despite the tears, there was renewed strength in her voice. She wanted her story told.

He gave her a moment to compose herself, pushing a bottle of water towards her, which she accepted. She fumbled with the top and Beder intervened, opening it for her.

"How did Finchley get the diamonds in the first place?" he asked.

"One worker in his family's mines, a guy named Milton, knew of Kevin's work against apartheid. They had apparently met in the underground anti-apartheid movement through Timothy Martin. Did your agents tell you about Martin?

"Yes, the minister." Both agents nodded.

"Mind you, all the mine workers were Black, and the supervisors who managed the mines were all well-paid, apartheid-believing whites who treated the Black workers terribly. In fact, some were indentured because of bogus debts Kevin's family said they owed. Some were promised a percentage of profits after years of service, but Kevin said that never happened. All were paid miniscule salaries and were regularly subject to humiliating searches after their shifts to make sure they hadn't stolen anything."

Stella took another sip of water. "Kevin had approached his mine worker friend, Milton, who was also a lay minister in a Black church. He promised that if he could smuggle out some diamonds, he would make sure the proceeds went to help Black communities. I guess Milton agreed to help because he, and for that matter all the workers, hated Kevin's family for how they were treated. Milton saw Kevin as a spy, a friendly white spy. Knowing the dangers involved, he was tight-lipped and didn't divulge Kevin's identity to the other Black workers."

"What trust he must have had in him," said Katherine. She wondered if Beder was disturbed by her speaking up. He didn't say anything; his attention was only on Stella.

"Kevin trusted Milton with his life. Anyway, Milton was aware he could be searched daily, therefore the only way to smuggle out the diamonds was to swallow them whole, which he did, using laxatives to ensure they came out the other end before going back to work the next day. Kevin ate the diamonds too. He liked to tell me they tasted better with mustard and relish."

"So, Kevin and Milton swallowed the diamonds together?" asked Beder.

"Yes. Milton had secret hiding places in the mines where he stockpiled up to half of what he mined. And that mine produced lots of diamonds." Stella took a sip of water, still trembling. "Kevin knew that diamonds can be detected because they fluoresce under X-rays, which, of course, his family used randomly on the workers. They didn't care that frequent X-rays had physical consequences. So, on days the diamonds were swallowed, Kevin was present in the mines and basically escorted his friend safely past the X-ray machines by pretending to be talking about recruiting hard working Africans to the mines or some such attention-diverting conversation. Since he was a member of the Finchley family, the despicable mine overseers let him pass. 'Hello sir,' they would say as Kevin and the minister strolled by security checkpoints. By the way, Kevin counted every ingested diamond. While he trusted Milton, he felt compelled to discourage any temptation."

"That must have been enormous temptation for a poor man," Katherine said.

"Kevin generously compensated him for the risk he took. In

retrospect, it was quite dangerous for both men for reasons over and above getting caught. There was always the fear that the larger diamonds would become lodged somewhere in the intestinal tract, leading to obstructions. So, Kevin and his accomplice took care to eat only diamonds with smooth edges and of a certain size. But some were still pretty big."

"When did the smuggling stop?" asked Walker.

"It stopped abruptly. The family discovered the scheme after Milton foolishly ate a diamond when Kevin wasn't there, and it was discovered on an X-ray. Milton had just been X-rayed the day before, so he mistakenly assumed they wouldn't do it two days in a row. That was monumentally stupid. I'm sure when they questioned him about his relationship with Kevin, they tortured him. I don't know if he caved, but shortly thereafter, he and one of his sons were killed in a head-on collision with a truck, a Finchley mine truck, of course, after which the police started accusing Kevin of embezzlement."

"Do you think the family had Milton killed?" said Wilson.

"Kevin had no doubt," said Stella.

"Was it the family that reported Kevin to the police?"

"Yes, of course."

"You know, Stella," said Beder, "Kevin was embezzling. He did commit a crime."

Stella shot back, "The real crimes were injustice, apartheid, the silencing of Nelson Mandela and the stealing of tribal lands, especially those that coughed up precious gems! He was South Africa's Robin Hood."

Everybody in the room took a deep breath, even Beder.

"I know you said it stopped abruptly, but how long did this go on?" Beder asked.

Stella frowned. "I don't know. However long it takes to steal hundreds of diamonds without getting caught. Probably a few months, maybe a year."

"Please clear up something else. You said Kevin hated his family and the family business. Why, then, would he work there?"

"The money. He wanted the money for his causes. So, he started lying to his family about the extent of his disgust. He actually acted happy. He kept his feelings and underground activities private, so they foolishly thought it was just a stage he'd gone through. He even lied about his job at the United Nations. Oh, and one more thing. They needed Kevin."

"How so?"

"The family knew Kevin had the respect of the Black workers in the mines. Once, when the workers threatened a strike, the Finchleys were desperate to dispel tensions. Kevin was able to settle things. After that he realized the timing was perfect for hatching his smuggling scheme."

"Did anybody question you about your role in all of this?"

"Funny you should ask. Much later, after I learned of Kevin's death, this South Afrikaner calls me, telling me that Kevin told him to look me up when he came to New York. His words were all sexy-like. He was up front about knowing I was a 'reputable, full-service companion.' He claimed to want those services, even asking my fee. But I knew Kevin would never do that to me. In fact, Kevin and I had talked about ways his family would try to get to me if they found out about us."

"What happened?"

"I saw him, of course. I wanted to get as much information as I could from him. It took about three nights and me charging him three thousand dollars for a couple of hours a night to learn that he was, in fact, a private investigator, probably hired by the family.

"I was a very pricey lady. God, he was so bad in bed! But he thought he was a Don Juan. A real fellatio nut; pun intended. I was grossed out. Oh, excuse me. Is that too much information?"

Beder was smiling, clearly not shocked. "How did you figure out he was a PI?"

"The questions, all the questions. He wanted to know every-thing about Kevin. Not subtle at all. I kept asking, 'Kevin who?' and pretending I'd forgotten his last name. I admitted to having some *flings* with 'this Kevin somebody,' but I told him I wasn't one to pry into my clients' personal lives.

"One night while he was snoring, I searched his wallet. Right there were his PI business cards. How stupid can you be? Anyway, after those three nights, Don Juan must have figured I was useless to him. I'm sure I succeeded in convincing him I knew nothing. I was rather proud of myself, not to mention nine thousand dollars richer."

"How did you know you succeeded?" asked Gultowski, speaking for the first time.

"I acted like a damn floozy, a dimwit, played stupid to the hilt. Even dressed like a prostitute, just like the old days. Anything to convince him that Kevin would have never given the diamonds to me. It must have worked. Oh, and I had another thing working in my favor. Kevin and I had kept our affair very private. Only one close friend of Kevin's knew about us, and we trusted him not to talk. That was Alistair Winthrop, dead now of cancer. In fact, if we went out publicly, I wore a wig and introduced myself as Heddie Blakely. We were incredibly careful. You know, I wonder if that PI ever tried to look up Heddie."

"What happened to the PI? He never contacted you again?" asked Beder.

"I guess he left. Never heard from him again. My last words to him were, 'Say hello to your Kevin friend. Tell him to look me up when he gets back to town.' It broke my heart to say that because I knew Kevin was dead."

"Anything after that?"

"No, nothing. Apartheid was ending, but dreams of a reunion with Kevin ended with his murder. I watched the events unfold in South Africa, saw Nelson Mandela become a free man in 1990 and get elected president in 1994. You know, after his release from prison, Kevin got to meet Mandela. It was sometime in mid-1990. He was so honored, and it obviously reinvigorated him. He talked endlessly about Mandela during those special last times we communicated."

"So, what happened to the money?" Beder asked.

"I can't wait to tell you, but first I need to find a ladies' room. I've been here almost two hours."

"Do you need me to go with you?" asked Katherine.

"I think I can negotiate the handicapped bathroom stall by myself. Give me a few minutes." Gultowski jumped up to assist and Stella put her hand around his arm. "Thank you, Brian. Which direction are we going?" He escorted her out the door.

Katherine's cellphone went off while Stella was in the bathroom. There had been another kitchen fire at the senior housing, with extensive smoke damage. Two people had been taken to the hospital. Upon Stella's return, Katherine announced, "I have to go. A fire at Oak Place has been controlled, but there are damages and injuries."

"I won't go on without Katherine being present," Stella reminded Beder. "Put me in jail if you have to."

"Tell me this before you leave," said Beder. "Are there any diamonds left?"

"No. Not a one."

❧ ❧ ❧

"Stella, I feel I'm not doing that much to help you," Katherine said in the cab on their way back to Oak Place.

"More than you will ever know. This is the first time I've ever told this story. Thank you for taking the time to listen to an old whore." She patted Katherine on the knee in a matronly way, giving her a sly wink.

Reaching for Stella's hand, Katherine said, "You know, I've never considered you an old whore. Old maybe, but never a whore." Their laughter seemed to echo in the car as Katherine's phone went off again. More ambulances had been dispatched to Oak Place.

CHAPTER 29

"Let's go to the lake this weekend," said Peter. "I want a break after days of grading papers. I need to unwind a bit. I've been burning the candle at both ends." Peter loved their rustic, cozy lakefront A-frame. Large windows let in light during the day and displayed the stars at night, making it feel like they were outdoors. Except for some open space in front of the house, mature trees (maples, oaks, and beech) were everywhere.

"Sounds like a great idea," Katherine responded enthusiastically. "Shall we invite anyone else?"

"Truth be known, I'd like a weekend just with you."

"Oh, I forgot. We've been invited to Jill's for dinner on Friday night. She has a new recipe she wants to try on us."

"Can we postpone?"

"Maybe. Or we can go to the lake afterward. We could keep each other awake while driving."

"Okay, that works. I'll call her to share our plans and see if she can have dinner earlier."

The rest of the week passed uneventfully. All residents transferred to the hospital for smoke inhalation were discharged. Although the fire was contained to one apartment, the smoke had spread to two other apartments and the hallway. Cleaning companies had already made massive progress in reducing the smell of smoke. With the fire emergency behind her, Katherine was able to complete her most pressing issues by Friday. Peter finished grading his students' papers. It was a good time to get away.

❧ ❧ ❧

"Dinner was outstanding. You've really got my mom's cooking genes," Peter said to Jill after a delicious eggplant parmesan. As they leaned back in their chairs to digest a bit, Katherine and Peter heard the pop of a champagne bottle being opened in the kitchen, along with the clinking of crystal.

"I'd like to make a toast," said a joyous Jill on reentering the dining area while holding hands with Sean. "Mom! Dad! We're going to have a baby! You're going to be grandparents!"

Katherine and Peter could hardly contain their excitement. Joy was on everyone's faces as they hugged and kissed. When Peter proposed a toast, Jill just wet her lips. "No drinking for me," she proudly announced.

"How far along?" said Katherine, barely able to contain her jubilation.

"Almost four months, and we don't want to know the sex. So bring on the green and yellow."

Jill and Sean had been married for two years. Jill was an English teacher at a New York City public high school and already had her Master's. Sean was a third-year resident in internal medicine at Harlem Hospital, studying public health. Both wanted to live and work in New York.

"Sean, have you told your mother yet?" asked Katherine.

"No. Tomorrow we will take the train to New Jersey and surprise her. It'll also be two years since my dad died, and I was planning to spend the day with her anyway." Sean's dad had died in a horrific car accident during a snowstorm as he rounded a curve on a country road. A truck on the opposite side of the curve slid into his lane and hit his car head-on, killing him instantly.

"How is your mother?" asked Peter.

"She still struggles, but she's slowly moving on. She stays busy volunteering since she retired from teaching and loves taking care of her grandchildren. My brother told me she had a date last week. My Aunt Edi, Mom's sister, divulged that news because Mom was hesitant to tell us for fear we might not approve. We'll have to straighten her out on that. He's an old family friend whose wife died of cancer. Really nice guy."

Katherine said, "Your mother is such a wonderful person. She'll be so excited for you."

Both Katherine and Peter were wide awake on the drive to the lake. The excitement triggered lots of conversation. Katherine talked about making a list of items they needed to buy in preparation for baby visits. "Let's see. We'll need a crib. I can probably get a used one at Goodwill."

"And don't forget a highchair and stroller."

"Oh Peter, that baby will visit in his or her own stroller. But we will need a highchair."

In bed, with her head on Peter's shoulder, they watched a 1938 movie, *The Adventures of Robin Hood*, with Errol Flynn and Olivia de Havilland, although Peter was snoring before King Richard was found in Sherwood Forest.

The next morning, Peter was up early and had taken a walk around the lake before bringing coffee to a groggy Katherine. "Hi, Grandma."

"That sounds so strange."

"You don't look like a grandma."

"How sweet of you. Just think. They can bring their child here for weekends just like we did."

"And so can we when they need a break. I can't believe this place will have another pattering of small feet. Do you think we'll need a crib and highchair for here too?"

"Dear God, you're really planning ahead!"

"It's my grandchild! And it will also need a swing set. Why did I let you sell our old one?"

"It?"

"Well, until we know if it's a boy or a girl..."

Peter jumped back into bed, putting his cold hands under Katherine's butt. "Oh, your hands are freezing!"

"Thanks for warming them up."

They cuddled and talked. After his hands warmed up, Peter rubbed Katherine's breasts. More foreplay soon led to intercourse in a rocking chair near the bed. With Katherine sitting and Peter on his knees, they laughed and kissed. They lubricated, then he penetrated, Katherine wrapping her legs around his back as he thrust, both enjoying the moment.

"I love making love with you," said Peter. "Who says us old people can't do it right? It's never gotten boring with us."

"We do conjugate well together, don't we?" Katherine responded with a big smile. "By the way, you missed the big Robin Hood sword fight last night."

"Resting up to fondle you this morning. Want me to warm your coffee?"

The weekend revitalized them. They walked hand in hand in the forest, planned next spring's garden, and assessed the leak in the rowboat—not for the first time. "I think we can patch it," Peter said.

"Jill's not going to let you put her baby in a thirty-year-old boat with more patched holes than a colander. What we need is a new boat."

"It floats just fine. Besides, I'll get a baby life jacket."

Eating dinner in front of the blazing fireplace, Katherine brought up retirement again. "Sometimes I wish I had a job that was under forty hours a week with no on-call responsibilities."

"Grandma's getting tired, is she?"

"Oh, I don't know. Last week was an intense week. Lots done and still mostly gratifying." There's a big part of me that doesn't want to give that up. I love working with older people. I love Oak Place. That's not the problem. And I'm at the height of my career. Guess you could say my wisdom is at its pinnacle. But…"

"I knew there was a *but* coming."

"I want to refocus on research and education. I'm tired of day-to-day administrating. Too many hours. I don't want to stop working. But I want more flexible time."

"Have you thought about passing some of your responsibilities to one of your VPs?"

"As a matter of fact, yes. Sonia Miller, to be exact. She's just completed her doctorate, is showing great promise and has told me she could see herself remaining at Oak Place. That, of course, could change. Some other organization might steal her away with an offer she can't refuse."

"It sounds like you've got the future figured out. So, you pursue figurehead status? Is that it?"

"Possibly. I'd never leave Oak Place without a long-range plan of succession. There's too much at stake."

"So, what do you want to accomplish before you leave?"

"Good question. I'd like to write another book and maybe do more teaching or consulting. But I don't want to travel as much professionally. Airports and hotels with plastic plants in the lobby are growing old. I don't care how much money they pay me. It's exhausting. Last week, Shirlee asked me where I'd given my last speech and I had to look it up on my calendar."

"And where was it?"

"Kansas City."

"I can't keep track of your whirlwind travel schedule. How about teaching a course at a university? Most would hire an expert of your caliber in a heartbeat. Then we could grade papers together in the wee hours."

"I've thought about it. It might be a good way to cement my legacy. Maybe I could even do some weeklong seminars about Oak Place at Oak Place."

"I think you might be onto something."

"Yeah, it might work. In fact, last week I had this lady call me from Tupelo, Mississippi, a salt-of-the-earth type person. She kept apologizing for never having gone to college. I told her that didn't matter as much as her attitude. And, oh, was her heart in the right place! I also had a call from the president of a corporation that owns eight nursing homes in Minnesota. I could teach them right here about the Oak Place mission. It would be so much more than just giving tours."

"Care for a moonlight stroll?"

"I'd rather get under the comforter and have you massage my, um, shoulders."

"Should I take my enhancer?"

Sustained alone time with each other, while infrequent and maybe only for a weekend here and there, always strengthened their bond. Gone was the frantic pace, the falling into bed too tired. Instead, their conversations were longer, relaxed, more reflective, even funny. Once again, they promised to do it more often.

CHAPTER 30

"I know how challenging retiring will be for you," Peter said the next morning as they were sipping their coffee. They looked out the large dining area window with its view of the lake. Some autumn leaves were falling as trees swayed gently with the breeze. Others, still brilliantly colored, clung to branches, refusing to be displaced.

"What do you mean?"

"Lots of transition. You've been focused on Oak Place for so many years. One day soon, it'll be different. You'll walk away and your life will change."

Katherine mulled his words. "You're so right. Preparing for that is paramount. But I think I'm ready. Besides, I'm not retiring to a rocking chair. I'm still planning on working. Might not always be smooth for me and maybe I *will* regress. But I think I'll make it, especially with your support."

"And what about giving up your daily interactions with Shirlee and Jeff? Won't you miss that as well?"

"I will. We're a team. We built Oak Place together."

"Katherine, was it ever more than being a team with Jeff?" Peter looked out the window, avoiding eye contact.

Katherine's heart skipped a beat and her whole body tensed. "What do you mean?"

"Katherine, once upon a time, I think you and Jeff had strong feelings for one another."

"Peter, I *never* had an affair with him!" She was completely unnerved. *Oh my God,* she thought.

"I didn't imply that, although I appreciate that truth. I said *strong feelings.*"

There was a long silence.

Peter reached for Katherine's hand. "I'm talking about long ago. I almost brought it up a few times over the years. But each time, I was afraid of the answer. And worried it could have led to our separation. It hit me again just recently when you and Jeff were stuck in the same hotel room before Theodore Oak's funeral."

Katherine thought about lying or denying it. Maybe he would believe her.

"I love you," Peter said. "I also know you. Little nuances of your behavior were telling. I knew you were struggling, not recently, but perhaps at a time when our marriage was not so strong. Besides, I saw you look at each other once at an Oak Place function. It was that kind of look. Nothing definitive, nothing tangible, just subtle, and revealing enough for me to wonder."

Katherine was silent, stomach churning, pulse rapid. "I don't know what to say."

"Am I right?"

Katherine turned to Peter and held his hand tightly. "I loved you more. Much more. Nothing ever happened. I wouldn't have been able to live with myself if it had. I went to therapy. I realized I wanted to work on this relationship. I realized back then that Oak Place was all-consuming, that its success somehow defined my success. That, of course, was bogus. But I neglected our marriage because of my career."

"I believe you, and I know that's what you did. I even remember some conversations we had about how we could be closer. I thought Jeff might be having the same conversations with Amy."

"Peter, that was years ago. Those impulsive feelings subsided long ago. Nothing ever happened, not even in that hotel room. Today, Jeff and I have a wonderfully supportive, and very platonic relationship."

"Again, I believe you. I'm glad you and Jeff worked it out and I'm *really* glad you wanted to stay in this marriage."

Both sat quietly. Katherine, still astonished that Peter was aware of her struggle, felt cheap and dishonest. Peter knew. He knew! She suddenly realized the pain she'd caused, how he must have struggled as she did, worrying if or when the elephant in the room would be exposed.

Of course he knew, she thought. *How could he not? For God's sake, I went to therapy.*

Peter even asked at the time, "Why have you decided to see a therapist?" Did she really think he was so unaware? Then there was the period of no collaborative writing between her and Jeff. He had noticed that, too. What a red flag! She'd been so caught up in her own conflict that she hadn't even realized she was causing him pain.

He believed her when she told him there was never a physical affair, and that both she and Jeff had mutually agreed to work harder on their marriages. For his belief in her, Katherine was thankful.

She knew there would be more conversations. At the time, he had been doing the lion's share of childrearing while she and Jeff worked into the night on Oak Place projects. How much had she eroded his trust? How resentful was he? He had known just by the way she and Jeff had looked at each other. Had he laid in bed at night worrying about their marriage? She would ask him these questions. Just not now.

The affair that never was. Never consummated but emotionally stressful, probably teetering closer to disaster than she had imagined.

I wonder if Amy had suspected also, thought Katherine.

CHAPTER 31

Katherine arrived early to work. She was sipping coffee and going over her day's schedule when Jeff came in quietly, shutting the door behind him.

"Katherine, I'm going to take a leave of absence for a while," he said, holding back tears. "They found metastatic masses in Amy's lungs, liver, and brain. We're facing the ride of our lives. It's back to chemo and you know the drill. There's little hope she will survive this."

"Goddamn! Fuck!" Katherine exclaimed, eyes already welling.

"I want to be with her and care for her. The kids are really upset. Eric wants to know if he should delay his wedding. Nobody's thinking clearly right now."

"Jeff, I'm so sorry. It's just not fair."

"Cancer never is, but we are…" Jeff's voice cracked. Katherine jumped up and hugged him tight as they cried silently together.

After a few minutes, Katherine said, "Take as long as you want. What can I do to help? I'll call Amy later. Maybe we can go to lunch." Over the years, Katherine and Amy had formed their own friendship.

"I know she wants to talk with you, and she wants you and Shirlee in the loop. She's going to resign from work this week. She was planning such a beautiful set for this new stage production."

"Does she know when she'll start chemo?"

"Soon. Probably in the next week or two."

"She was so sick the last go-around. She can't be looking forward to this."

"Not in the least. And I'm afraid we're only buying time. It's looking quite grim. She's already talking about hospice and forgoing treatments with awful side effects. She wants to spend time with the kids and grandkids. I'm numb, scared, and so angry when I think about losing her. Can we take a walk?"

Arm in arm, they went outside. The chilly air was refreshing, but Katherine was hot like in her menopause days. "Hi, Dr. Jeff!" yelled a resident. "Heard we're getting our first snow soon." Jeff waved but didn't say anything. They walked quietly for a while.

"I'm not resigning. When this is over..." his words drifting as he tried to hold back tears, "I'm going to need to work. I don't know how life will be without her. She's been my rock." He began to sob.

CHAPTER 32

One date led to another and then another. Now seeing each other two or three times a week, David and Shirlee were fast becoming an item. He invited her to a company party, enthusiastically introducing her to his partners. Katherine and Shirlee seemed to be shopping more and more, both enjoying time together away from work.

"He's a classy guy with a full social life," said Shirlee. "For God's sake, he plays golf! My wardrobe is black-on-black flannel with comfy old-lady shoes for work. I need to bring it up a couple of notches. On Friday, we're going to dinner at a partner's house in Connecticut. "Methinks I'll be a minority, the token Black, except for maybe the staff."

"Stop, Shirlee. You don't know that. It's the 21st century!"

"I know, I know."

"Well, get off it!" Katherine said as she searched a rack in the store. "Do you like this blue dress? I think it has your name on it."

"I feel so funny shopping and thinking about the future while Jeff and Amy are facing such sadness and perhaps the end of their lives together."

"Yeah, Amy and I talked and she's really angry. She wants so much to see her grandchildren grow up. You know, she'll be sixty-two next month. How fucked up is that? Would you like to go to lunch with us next week, maybe Wednesday?"

"Absolutely. You know, that blue dress is too cutesy. It's not a cocktail party. I need some clingy satin slacks and a nice blouse, maybe with a belt and dressy vest. Jewelry might help. Can I borrow your jade stone belt and necklace?"

"I'll bring them tomorrow, but let's get the clothes first."

"Under the circumstances, it seems strange shopping for clothes. Trivial, really."

Katherine's phone rang. It was Kara, an Oak Place resident and one of Katherine's evening administrative assistants.

"Katherine, six or seven Oak Place seniors have been arrested."

"What?! Dear God, for what?" Katherine put the phone on speaker so Shirlee could hear. They huddled behind a dress rack, the volume turned down.

"Disorderly conduct," Kara replied. "It seems they were protesting climate change at the United Nations and laid down in the street directly in front of several horses ridden by the NYPD mounted police. The press has already called us."

"Where are they now?"

"Jail, I think. The press said they have footage of them handcuffed and being carried into a police van. None of them went voluntarily."

"They laid down in front of horses?" whispered a stunned Shirlee. "Oh, God!"

"That's not all. One of those arrested, a Mrs. Riggins, called our office and it seems none of them were planning this. They got caught up in the demonstration, impulsively deciding that gray hairs being arrested would send a strong message about climate change."

"Mrs. Riggins? The one whose husband committed suicide?"

"Yes. She said she did it to honor her late husband because he was so dedicated to environmental issues. And that's not all. Since they didn't plan this, they didn't bring their medications, including one man on nitroglycerine for chest pains. He thought he had one dose but apparently left it on his kitchen counter. He and the others are asking if we could go to their apartments and retrieve their medications. It seems they've decided not to pay their bail and will be spending the night in jail."

"Lord have mercy," said Shirlee.

"Wow! Who'd have thought?" said Katherine.

Katherine directed her assistant to get keys and retrieve the medications. "Please take a security guard with you. Also, alert PR. Our official statement is that they are autonomous adults. Do not give out any personal information, including any names."

"Katherine," said Shirlee, "seven seniors? They're probably on enough medication to fill a shopping bag, half of it in pill containers that won't be labeled. Good luck getting that through jail security."

"Okay, Kara, don't get all the pills. Too complicated. But do get that bottle of nitro over there. That's an emergency drug. Being in jail, he just might need it."

"Oh no," sighed Kara over the phone.

"Oh no what?"

"The media is here. They're taking video of the senior living complex. There's a reporter in front of the cameras."

Katherine searched her phone for the live broadcast.

"This is Meghan Rydell of WKYN News in front of the senior living complex at Oak Place, a nationally renowned residence for the elderly, and the home of seven senior citizens who defied police this afternoon at a demonstration protesting the United Nation's lack of environmental action on climate change. Mounted police apparently told these gray-haired seniors to move out of the area, but they laid down instead, one narrowly escaping being trampled."

The newscast was enhanced by footage of the residents—four women and three men—already being called The Oak Place Seven, holding hands, slowly helping each other get to their knees, grimacing, then managing to lie down on their backs in the street, horses' hooves only feet away. A sign saying, *Save the Planet for our Grandkids,* was attached to a walker. Another raised a sign over her prone torso: *You are Never Too Old to Fight!* The police reined back their horses, not wanting them to step on the frail elders, especially in front of cameras.

Apparently, several other Oak Place residents who had decided not to get arrested stood close by shouting, "It's never too late to act! You're never too old to start! Gray Power, Gray Power, yeah, yeah, yeah!" Among this group was Stella, firmly attached to her muscular, part-time assistant/chauffeur, her version of *Driving Miss Daisy.* For his services and road trips using his twenty-year-old Honda, she paid for this future physical therapist's tuition at Queen's College. He carried her sign, *Justice for our Earth.*

When the broadcast was over, Katherine and Shirlee were silent for a while before Shirley asked, "It's 6:30. Do we need to go back to the office?"

"They're adults. Old people not watching the news but being the news. What guts." Katherine smiled, proud of what she'd witnessed. "But, how is it that you go to a demonstration that's sure to be stressful and forget your nitro? And Stella was there. My God! In her pink sweats, no less. Thankfully, she decided not to get arrested. She's supposed to meet with the FBI again the day after tomorrow."

"That was Stella? I've yet to meet her. You know, Katherine, this is going to be a long night for those who went to jail."

"I know. Courageous old souls determined to make a difference. I hope they do."

CHAPTER 33

It was week's end before Beder made it to Stella's apartment. Having recognized her frailty, he had extended the courtesy of traveling to her home. She presented herself in another stylish suit as if decked out for a fancy lunch. Gultowski and Walker had been assigned to another case, so Beder was alone. Naturally, Stella had made coffee cake, which Beder, his ample belly already hanging over his belt, gladly accepted.

"I'm not leaving here until I know what happened to the diamonds." he said. "Then, if I am satisfied with the truthfulness of your answers, we will make some inquiries about your son. But no, and I mean no, searching for him until I get the truth that can be proven beyond a doubt."

Stella got up to fetch a black, three-ring binder she had set out in preparation for Beder's visit. "I think you will find everything in order here. But before I hand this to you, let me explain something."

Sitting with the binder in her lap, hands protectively resting on it, Stella said, "When I learned of Kevin's death, I was devastated and didn't even think about the diamonds for months. What jarred me into checking on them was a bill from the bank for rental of the safe deposit box. I promptly complied and then decided I'd better see if the diamonds were still there. Later that week, there they were, secure in that box, carefully rolled in a pocketed soft blue cloth. I counted all the diamonds myself.

"How many were there?" asked Beder.

"I don't remember exactly, but almost two hundred.

"In the meantime, Alistair Winthrop, Kevin's friend and a powerful man in the U.S. Embassy in South Africa, introduced me to Adelaide Mhala of Cape Town. She came to the U.S. as a nanny for some rich Afrikaner family. Ironically, she had worked with Kevin several years before at anti-apartheid events in Cape Town. When that family returned home, she defected and immediately applied to a nursing school in the city. Because of her perspective on apartheid and her connection to Kevin and other Afrikaners against apartheid, we became fast friends. Winthrop verified her need for asylum and helped obtain a coveted green card. I found her a comfortable, modest apartment."

"So, she knew about the diamonds?"

"Every detail. I hired her as my secretary. Are you ready for this? She helped me sell the diamonds and get the money back to South Africa. You see, I had finally gotten in touch with Reverend Timothy Martin. I told him I'd known Kevin Finchley, but didn't share details of our intimate relationship. I wanted to donate to Martin's continued work in his memory, as well as other efforts he felt were worthy to assist in South Africa's transition to full democracy. Martin and I corresponded and spoke a couple of times over the phone. All his letters to me are in this binder, as well as notes of our phone conversations.

"I finally experienced firsthand why Kevin admired Martin so much. Without ever having met him, I would have trusted him with my life.

"The first donation Adelaide and I made was for one million dollars to one of Martin's startup schools in the slums. I sold several diamonds on 41st street, wrote a check to Martin's cause and gave the remaining few thousand to Adelaide so she could pay her tuition for nursing school."

"You know Martin's dead now," said Beder, a hint of sympathy in his voice.

"Glad you've been doing your homework. So is Adelaide. She died of ovarian cancer two years ago, but not before she got her nursing degree and spent years caring for her patients, as well as her very fine husband and two kids, who by the way, call me Grandmama. She was a dear, dear friend and my link to Kevin's life, as was Alistair Winthrop, who died in 1995."

Stella took a deep breath. "When Martin suggested an organization that needed support, Adelaide did the homework. She knew most of the worthy programs in South Africa. If she didn't, she could verify their credibility through her numerous contacts. Within five years, some $150 million made it back to the homeland to start medical clinics, schools, and help progressive people running for office, which included the African National Congress that elected Mandela in 1994. Martin also recommended I donate to the Urban Foundation, whose mission, while fuzzy at times, was to raise the socioeconomic circumstances of the Black populace. I honored that request with several donations. Sometimes, I made the donations. Other times, Adelaide did. We didn't want to raise any red flags."

"And Martin didn't know who you *really* were or where the money was coming from? I find that hard to believe."

"He thought I was some very rich benefactor that Kevin had convinced to help the cause. I never let him believe otherwise because, well, I really was a very rich benefactor. All the money I gave was in Kevin's honor. Martin even wanted to name a school in Cape Town after him. But I firmly told him no, stressing that Kevin would not have wanted that. I was afraid that any naming would blow the lid off everything. I also demanded I remain anonymous. Truth be told, I believe Martin knew the money was not exactly kosher, if you know what I mean. Let's face it. He obviously had known of the accusations against Kevin, the pending trial, the murder. Anyway, he didn't press the issue."

Stella handed Beder the binder. "Here are our notes, receipts, thank you letters, everything, all with official seals from the Anglican Church. Adelaide kept meticulous records, ironic for me, because I had operated a cash only business with no records. Oh, sorry. I changed the subject.

"Anyway, you'll see that it accounts for almost all of it minus the couple million I kept for myself, something Kevin insisted I have from the get-go. 'My retirement,' he'd said. There is even a handwritten letter, notarized, plus his will to that effect in the binder. He wanted me to have a comfortable, simple life without ever having to prostitute myself again. I honored that—well, the simple life part," she added with a smirk. "After all, an extravagant lifestyle would have shamed him."

Beder was silent after Stella stopped talking. He turned the binder's pages back and forth as if checking numbers. Stella sipped a glass of ice water while studying Beder's reaction. Katherine tried to digest the magnitude of what Stella had done. Diamonds had been smuggled out only to be smuggled back in as much needed cash. The ultimate redistribution of wealth. Dirty money made clean. Monuments to materialism denied, instead being donated for schools and medical clinics.

"This shows your last donation was in 1999."

Stella nodded. "That's when the money ran out."

"Everything looks in order," Beder said after thumbing through the pages for a few more minutes while Katherine and Stella remained silent. "Of course, we will have to check this out."

"Be my guest. I've nothing to hide. It's too bad Martin and Adelaide aren't around to verify my story. But I suppose some minister at Martin's old church can vouch for it. Martin might have used some funds for things I don't know about, but I'm absolutely certain he did not spend it recklessly or selfishly."

"Did you pay taxes on this?" Beder's right eyebrow was raised.

"Well, certainly not on the money that went back to South Africa. After all, it was theirs, not the U.S. government's. As to the rest, well, not exactly, because I was afraid the IRS would want to know where the money came from. But, sir, I did calculate what the tax would have been and donated that amount to charity, an organization that helps prostitutes get off the streets. There are receipts for that also. And just so you don't think I'm a complete tax dodger, Kevin insisted I have a legitimate business, Cordrey Consulting. I paid taxes regularly."

"What did you consult about?" asked Beder, more curious than actually needing an answer.

Stella smiled before saying, "Everything! I was full service."

Katherine said, "I wish Gultowski and Walker were here so they could hear the rest of this fascinating story."

"I'll be sure to fill them in," said Beder. "You, Stella, have apparently made quite an impact on them, a positive one, I might add. It was a worthwhile experience for them. Did you know this was their first assignment?"

"Yes!" both Katherine and Stella said simultaneously. They all laughed.

"I've never told this story to anyone else," said Stella. "A huge burden has been lifted. In telling you, I'm honoring Kevin. He'd been planning all along to sell the diamonds and return the money for worthy endeavors. I merely followed through on his wishes as I had promised to do. I won't be in any trouble, will I? Do I have to go on trial in South Africa?"

"I can't imagine. These receipts prove they weren't blood diamonds. Upon verification, the FBI will close this case and notify the CIA. Plus, the money is gone, spent. With Kevin and Martin dead, I doubt the FBI will be interested in you now. And one more thing. You did all this twenty plus years ago. I'm sure a South African statute of limitations applies here."

Beder stood up and held her hand in his. "Miss Stella Cordrey, it has been a pleasure to get to know you. Kevin chose a very special lady to be in his life. I'm sorry he died so violently, but I must say I admire what he did."

"Thank you so much for your words. Would you like to see a photo of him?"

"By all means."

Stella retrieved two from her bedroom. One was a touching photo of them, arms swung around each other's necks, smiles gleaming, in front of the marquee for Shakespeare's *King Lear*. The other was a black and white of Kevin in front of the United Nations with the inscription, *'I will love you always, my dear Stella. So thankful you came into my life.'*

After Beder left, Katherine left too, but the thoughts of Stella, and what she had done, lingered. She found herself distracted while interviewing a person for a public relations position. *Smuggled out only to be smuggled back in;* these words kept going through her mind. *Dirty money made clean.*

⁂ ⁂ ⁂

"I've nothing more to hide," said Stella, sipping coffee with Katherine a couple of days later. "I'm old now, just trying to have some semblance of normalcy after this damn hip replacement and my heart problems."

"You've done good," said Katherine. "I doubt they'll throw you in jail now. Besides, the money's been gone for years."

"I do hope that they tell the family. In fact, here's what I would say to his family: I'm glad Kevin screwed you and got away with it!" Stella said the last bit loudly, startling Katherine.

"As you can see, Katherine, I've not one iota of guilt. All that money went to help apartheid victims and their ancestors. It also helped get Mandela elected."

Do you think his brother was the one who killed him?"

"He had to have been there because he was looking for information. He knew the questions to ask. Who knows if he personally did the torturing? But the lust for money and power causes people to do unconscionable things."

"Killed by his own brother. I can't imagine."

"It happens. After all, I was raped and tortured by my own father. Who knows what would have happened if I had stayed in Kentucky?" Stella paused, then smiled, "You can't imagine the relief at telling this story. I thought I would take these secrets to my grave."

"I feel honored to have been a part of this."

"By the way, Agent Gultowski called me yesterday."

"Oh yeah? Why?"

"To inform me that the FBI had notified the appropriate authorities in South Africa that they had closed this case. Everything checked out, and while he couldn't promise me they wouldn't bring a lawsuit, he knew they had used Black workers essentially as slaves to mine their diamonds. A lawsuit would not look good in the press, especially if the circumstances surrounding Kevin's murder might be investigated. Besides, South Africa, with its now democratic government, is probably not willing to pursue compensation for white people whose wealth came from the exploitation of Blacks, especially if that money was redirected to *help* Blacks.

"Gultowski also told me that he and Walker had made initial inquiries into my son's, I mean, *our* son's, whereabouts. Now that's a good job for those young FBI whippersnappers!"

"Oh, Stella, I do hope they find him."

"Oh, so do I. But if they can't, then I'll lay it to rest, hope he's had a good life, and the humanitarian genes of his father live on in him."

"Don't forget your wonderful gene pool. I hope he's feisty and compassionate like you."

"Thank you, Katherine. Oh my, I'm going to be late for my art class. Painting has been so relaxing for me—and I'm damn good too! Just imagine if I'd had the opportunity to become an artist before my hands started quivering. Ha!"

Katherine was walking away when Stella said in a barely audible voice, "What if they find our son and he's not interested in meeting me?"

CHAPTER 34

In a pathetic sight, with Hal leading him, Jake limped around the pasture, his head hanging low to the ground. Katherine knew it was cruel to let Jake suffer, but her concern for Hal interfered with her feelings of humane euthanasia for the horse. Hal caught Katherine staring and said, "Doesn't Jake look better today? I think he's going to have a full recovery."

Dr. Morrison, the vet who always cared for Jake and was as attached to him as anybody, came up behind Katherine, shaking his head. "What do you want to do?"

"I don't know. Hal's mental health is at great risk."

"I can give Jake more steroids to help perk him up, but it will only delay the inevitable."

"I know. Go ahead. Let's keep Jake alive until we can prepare Hal further for that dreadful day."

All day, Jake and Hal weighed heavily on her mind. She wasn't alone in her concern. Jeff spent a great deal of time with Hal, as did Shirlee. Slowly, Hal was coming to the realization that he couldn't save Jake. All the money and medicine in the world couldn't stop Jake's failing body from shutting down. It seemed even Jake was trying to tell Hal it would be alright, that he was old, didn't fear death like most humans did, and it was his time.

Sure enough, with more steroids, Jake lifted his head higher by early afternoon. Hal smiled at first. But when Shirlee asked him how long he was going to do this, he stared at the ground, knowing he could no longer deny Jake's suffering. Then, without saying the words out loud, he mouthed to Shirlee, "Okay. It's time." Katherine went home that night with a heavy heart. With Hal's permission, she had summoned the vet to euthanize Jake the next day.

In the early morning, Katherine, Shirlee, and Jeff arrived together to go straight to the stalls. From a distance, through the early morning mist, they could see Hal carrying Jake and sobbing uncontrollably. Jake's head hung lifeless. His tongue, now released from muscles no longer working, touched the ground as Hal walked. Hal gripped his body tightly, all four legs in the confines of a massive hug, while his head was buried in Jake's back.

"Oh, dear God," murmured Shirlee, already crying. Katherine, hands over her mouth, began sobbing, as did Jeff. Some residents were gathered, not a dry eye among them.

Jeff was first to approach Hal. "Don't touch me," he shouted. "You can't have him!"

"Hal, I'm not going to take Jake from you," Jeff said softly, tears streaming down his face. "But let's go to the bench and sit down." It was cold, but Hal was sweating from the weight of the horse.

Short of breath, Hal sat down. Jeff and Katherine helped place Jake's body on the bench, with his head on Hal's lap. Hal put his arms around Jake and pulled his head to his chest, his face now in the horse's mane. For a long time, there were no words, just crying. Some residents brought chairs to Jeff, Shirlee, and Katherine as if knowing it might be a while before Hal would let go of Jake. They all sat close to Hal, stroking Jake silently.

Thankfully, everyone stayed back, even two security guards someone had summoned. Suddenly, a whole class of children came by. "What's wrong with Jake?" asked one child just as the teacher realized the scene they had come upon. She quickly tried to turn them around to return to their classroom when some started screaming. "Noooo!" "Is Jake dead?" "No!" "He can't be!" Their piercing cries and high-pitched screams echoed throughout the complex, triggering more crying from the grief-stricken children.

Katherine jumped up to help console them, as did many residents. It seemed each person held a crying child suffering deeply from the loss. Finally, they were led away, surrogate grandparents holding them tightly.

Katherine returned to her chair. "Hal, Jake lived well because you took care of him. I've never seen such a bond between an animal and a human."

"Hal," Shirlee said, "bless the day you came into Jake's life and he into yours. We wish this end would have never come."

Hal said, "I just can't believe it. I never accepted that Jake could die. I don't think I've ever loved anything so much. I haven't had this feeling of overwhelming grief since Vietnam, when I held a dear buddy who was killed."

For the first time, he started talking about Vietnam. A horse was the catalyst to his repressed memories, a horse who had given him unconditional love despite his eccentricities. A horse, now dead, had helped Hal to live again.

"Can we bury him here under the oak tree?" Hal asked Katherine, barely able to speak.

"I'll arrange it." However, that was easier said than done. A trench digging machine would have to be brought in. Zoning would surely reject burying a horse, even a small one, on the grounds. A resident piped up and suggested Jake be cremated at a pet crematorium in Queens.

Hal agreed and got up to carry Jake to an Oak Place SUV that was summoned for the trip. Jeff offered to help carry Jake, and Hal accepted. Shirlee would go with him. He needed her now more than ever.

"Cut off some of his mane to give to Hal later," Katherine said to Shirlee.

By afternoon, Jake's stable was adorned with flowers in his memory. Apples and carrots were placed on the fence posts. His bright pink blanket hung on the fence, along with a framed photo. One bouquet came with a card thanking Hal for the loving care he had given Jake. Back in her office, Katherine, already ranking this day among the saddest in her life, was approached by some residents. "We'd like to do a funeral for Jake."

"Sure," Katherine said. "A small memorial service would be very appropriate."

"No. Small would be underestimating Jake's huge impact."

Katherine looked at the residents. "How big are you talking?"

CHAPTER 35

The residents wanted a formal funeral for Jake, which included inviting people from the surrounding community. The idea gained momentum, and more residents got involved. Even with threatening winter temperatures, the memorial was to be held outside by Jake's pasture. The area, now a shrine, was overflowing with flowers and memorabilia honoring the seven years Jake resided at Oak Place. A multidenominational altar would be brought from the chapel.

A retired Episcopal priest who resided in the senior living complex, and whose grandchildren spent many hours with Jake, volunteered to officiate. The choir wanted to sing about the love of animals and would include an original song by a resident, "All God's Creatures Great and Small." To accompany the choir, a cellist would be joined by a pianist on a portable keyboard. A retired bagpiper who had played for numerous police and firemen funerals over the years was also invited to perform.

Letters went home to the primary schoolchildren's parents, inviting them all to attend. More than three-quarters of the parents responded affirmatively. Children whose parents couldn't come were given permission to be paired with residents they knew who would accompany them to the service and post-funeral gathering.

The day was picture perfect: cool, temperatures in the upper forties, a windless blue sky.

When Katherine, Jeff, and Shirlee arrived at the service, they were overwhelmed by the sight. More than a thousand people were gathered: residents, people from the neighborhood, shop-owners, police and firemen—all those that Jake had visited when he made his rounds. Even former primary school students, now almost teenagers, were there. More chairs had to be fetched. The young gave up their seats for the elderly. Kids sat on the grass and sidewalks. Music played as people gathered. They brought down coats and blankets, scarves and hats. No one was going to let the cold keep them away.

Before the service began, people approached Hal with condolences, as if he were the surviving spouse. "I'm so sorry for your loss." Kids silently gathered around Hal, who was wearing a donated suit, and hugged him. One four-year-old boy would not let go of his leg, the father having to pry him away. Hal was too choked up to talk.

After the choir sang, Father Manning began. "We are gathered here today to honor a small creature who was a great friend to us all." Sniffling could be heard throughout the crowd.

"You know, I was in Manhattan the other day," he continued, "talking with someone who didn't know Jake or even any of the wonderful people at Oak Place. I told him about the profound grief being felt by all since Jake's death, and he said, 'But it was only a horse.'

"Only a horse? This blessed creature visited our school and made even the shyest child laugh. Jake made all people, young and old, want to reach out, to touch him. Only a horse? This four-legged friend brought families together on many an afternoon. When we visited Jake, we visited also with each other. We shared our stories and hugged our children and grandchildren. Only a horse? Jake could somehow reach into the depths of a demented mind, bring forth a smile, and move even a catatonic hand. His love was unconditional. And, because we loved him, he loved us. Oh, did he love us! He gave many of us something to live for. Yes, he was old, not unlike so many of you here today."

That brought laughter from the crowd.

"But he didn't let arthritis stop him. His work was being a therapy horse, and for most of his life here at Oak Place, save for the last few weeks, he was a workaholic.

"Thousands of hands touched him. Thousands of lips kissed him. Thousands of hearts rediscovered love. He generated millions of smiles and a good bit of laughter. In short, Jake brought happiness to us all.

Only a horse?" The good reverend waved his hand over the crowd as if acknowledging their collective grief. "Yes, a tiny little horse did all of this."

The audience was captivated. They all had their Jake stories, and Father Manning reiterated how important these stories were. At one point, he even had the kids raising their hands after asking if they had brushed him, combed his tail, or given him a carrot. The kids enthusiastically raised their hands in the air, collectively shouting, "Me! Me! I did that!"

"And how many of you had to help clean up when Jake chose to poop in your classroom?" The kids laughed and raised their hands higher. Some stood up to make sure their raised arms were seen.

Father Manning didn't let anybody forget the other animals at Oak Place, a hodgepodge of cats, dogs, fish, and a hamster named Sully. "While many of these animals are not as well known to everybody as Jake was, they are still valued for their service," Manning said. "Only cats? Only dogs? No way! Just like Jake was not only a horse! Animals give so much to us and we in turn give our hearts to them. When they leave us, we hurt."

Singing and music continued following Manning's remarks. Then Hal stepped up to the podium after Manning gave him an encouraging look. Hal had helped plan the funeral and been asked by Manning to speak. He didn't know if he could and told him he'd decide at the service. At first, he even declined to help with the planning, but later asked that photos of Jake be placed on tables near the service. There was an especially moving one of Jake and Hal taken some years ago by a retired *National Geographic* photographer that captured their delight in each other; Jake licking the laughing face of a kneeling, straw-covered Hal. The children's school had plenty of other photos to display.

"Thank you, Reverend Manning," Hal began, his voice shaky, "for your wonderful words. Just like the fine reverend said, for me personally, Jake was so much more than just a horse. When I could hardly relate to people, Jake stepped up to the plate. I received much more than his body heat on cool nights as we laid together. While I might have been the one with the lead rope, it was Jake leading me back to society and people. Everywhere we went, people stopped to pet him and speak to me. Slowly, my trust came back, my confidence reemerged, and my self-worth was born again.

"I thought therapy animals were for others. It never crossed my mind that Jake was also my own personal therapy animal. While he brought smiles to so many, he slowly, without me noticing, brought me back from the abyss, from the trauma of Vietnam. I never wanted that horse to die, thinking that if Jake died, well, so would I. When he became weak and frail and death lurked, I was so scared. How would I live without Jake? But now I know that I am going to live. In fact, more than just live. I'm going to make Jake proud, because I am becoming whole again. He loved me unconditionally. And he asked for so little in return."

Hal began to cry and children spontaneously rushed to the podium, surrounding him. One three-year-old girl ran up to Hal and grabbed his leg as her arm reached up to give Hal a tissue. Many in the audience caught the touching moment with their cellphones.

Tears streaming down his face, Hal blurted out, "Thanks Jake. God bless your soul." He took some deep breaths. Then, voice quivering, he looked at Shirlee. "And thank you, Shirlee, for believing in me."

The audience was silent as they watched the tender sight of children and the Vietnam vet embracing. Shirlee was in tears as Katherine held her hand and Jeff wrapped his arm around her shoulders. Between Jake's influence and Shirlee's tough love, Hal had been transformed. He knew Shirlee loved him as much as Jake had.

Hal took Jake's ashes, and with children still clinging to him, he put the urn in the freshly dug grave next to the stable. The children placed carnations over the urn. Hal threw in the first handful of dirt before he walked away, children trailing behind. Reverend Manning followed suit and invited people forward, who also took handfuls of dirt to place over Jake while privately saying their goodbyes. As they filled the grave, the bag piper played "Amazing Grace" as many sang along.

After the service, the outside tables were brimming with sandwiches and hot cider. People lingered well into the afternoon. Over the years, hundreds of funerals and life celebrations had been held at Oak Place, but none were as touching as this one for a tiny, beloved horse.

Hal was named chairman of the committee to select another pony. The first meeting would be held when he was ready. Later that month, he went to the primary school to talk about his loss. He was introduced as Jake's best friend and read a book by Fred Rogers on the loss of a pet. On another day, with Hal present, the children named one of the therapeutic raised beds, Jake's Garden, complete with a class-made ceramic tile. In this garden as the new spring began, they planted carrots, Jake's favorite treat. Hal showed off his new urn pendant necklace—given to him by Shirlee, Katherine, and Jeff—which held some of Jake's ashes and a strand of Jake's mane. When Shirlee clasped it around his neck, he declared he'd never take it off.

Hal started therapy again at the VA and began the long process of getting off the streets. Shirlee no longer had to pressure him to take a shower. Katherine gave him more work at the complex and a studio in a basement section of senior housing, where two on-call salaried maintenance crew resided. He helped pay rent with the disability benefits he started collecting. The furniture and contents were donated by residents, including the families of those recently deceased. Every day, Hal stopped by the pasture and quietly stood with his arms resting on the fence, envisioning the times when Jake was there and often putting a single flower on the grave, which now had a small, simple tombstone embedded in the ground with engraved words the children had chosen and Hal approved: Jake—Wonder Horse.

Some three months after Jake's death, when a child innocently asked Hal if Jake had a friend who would like to live at Oak Place, he made a beeline to Katherine's office to announce he was ready to begin the search for another miniature pony.

CHAPTER 36

Peter came back to the table where Katherine, Shirlee, David, and Amy were sitting and announced, "Jeff is still standing at the urinal. Nothing happening. Let's drink to enlarged prostates!"

Everyone laughed. Amy lifted her glass of wine. "Here's to a doctor putting off getting his personal plumbing opened up with that roto rooter operation."

"Ouch!" said Peter. "Nothing a dignified older man should have to face."

"Can we not talk medical for once?" asked Shirlee. "Especially not at a wedding."

"Yeah, why is it that you put a bunch of old farts together and they start talking about aches, pains, and elimination?" said Peter. "Someone called them organ recitals."

"Please, let's not get into bowel movements," said Katherine. "I hear that every day at work."

The atmosphere was joyous as about a hundred people witnessed the formal marriage of Jeff and Amy's son, Eric, to his long-time girlfriend, Carrie. Katherine, who had long ago become a justice of the peace for just such occasions at Oak Place, performed the ceremony. Eric held a special place in her heart, calling her Aunt Katherine since he started talking.

Katherine had very little to say because Eric and Carrie had written their own wedding vows. The simple ceremony was held in an elegant but cozy Victorian hotel's wood-paneled, wainscoted banquet room surrounded by flowers and the people they loved. An eighty-year-old Oak Place resident, formerly a NYPD officer and member of the city's solemn bagpipe band who had also played at Jake's funeral, led Carrie and Eric into the room with a beautiful bagpipe ballad. In fact, when the Oak Place residents had found out that Dr. Jeff's son was getting married, they all wanted to participate, including the Elvis impersonator, who wanted to sing Presley's song about out-of-control fools helplessly falling in love. Jeff had thanked him, but Elvis was before their time and they preferred the singing of someone like John Legend. He did, however, have the Oak Place dance band play for the older folk when the disc jockey took a break. The money he paid them would go toward new instruments and tuition for their annual trek to band camp.

At the end of the beautiful ceremony, people gathered at the tables—with large, flowered centerpieces—for wine, food, and song. Jeff, back from the bathroom, danced with his grandchildren, then with Shirlee, who, despite her arthritis, could still choreograph eye-catching rhythmic moves. They both worked up a sweat as they were urged on by the guests. Katherine, Jeff, and Shirlee were enjoying the festive atmosphere and being able to socialize away from Oak Place.

At ten, the lights dimmed on the dance floor and a spotlight focused on a gorgeous Jessica dressed in a sleek black dress studded with rhinestones, complimented with sapphire jewelry. Somehow, Jeff, with the help of Amy, was able to transform to Jessica in just under a half hour, complete with stick-on, long polished nails.

People went nuts. She was the most gorgeous woman in the room. While Eric and Carrie danced, he serenaded them singing, "I see leaves of gold, red roses too. And I think to myself, what a wonderful world." Then, Jessica quickly went into a rendition of Kool & the Gang's "Celebration." While singing, Jessica danced with the happy couple. Eric loved it, laughing and applauding his sexy father. Amy joined them, as did their daughter, Amelia. Later, when Jessica had performed a few more songs, she and Amy embraced tightly for a slow dance. They were beautiful together and looked lovingly at each other. Despite facing a life-limiting disease, Amy was feeling better after completing the last round of chemotherapy. She was wearing a gorgeous wig, no doubt from her extensive collection of theater costumes.

The reception lasted until midnight, when the couple took their leave for some sleep in an upstairs hotel room before their early morning flight to the British Virgin Islands.

"I know you're so proud of Eric," Katherine told Jeff. "He's a wonderful man."

"I'm very proud. As neither of us will forget, things were a little touch and go during his teen years. But he came out of it. And he's become such a great high school teacher. He knows how to excite kids about learning."

"And he's partnered with such a wonderful woman. Do you think they'll have kids?"

"I think not. At least that's what they said the last time we discussed it. Surprisingly, I'm okay with that. Don't feel compelled to spread my genes further. I've got two wonderful grandchildren and that's a blessing enough. Besides, Carrie's not interested in being a mom. All day, she mothers her third graders and prefers coming home to peace. I just found out that she stays after school most days mentoring at-risk kids. Spent a couple hundred dollars of her last paycheck to buy some of them shoes and clothes."

Katherine was so happy for Jeff as he beamed with pride. Life with Eric had not always been so joyful. He drank heavily during his teen years, getting in trouble with the law on a couple of occasions. Jeff and Amy were kind and patient parents, but this child had tested their steadiness, and their souls. Effective parenting won out, as did growing up past the hormonal chaos. Somewhere around twenty-one, in an epic turnaround, Eric apologized and asked for forgiveness. He rematriculated in college and worked full-time to make up for the scholarships he had squandered. Now, whenever he encountered difficult kids in the classroom, he remembered himself. He openly shared his past mistakes with students, something they came to respect him for.

"You seem lost in your thoughts," Peter said quietly to Katherine. "Ready to go home?"

"Just thinking about Eric and how long we've known him. It's wonderful to see him so happy. And yes, it's way past my bedtime. And look at the band. All of them are over seventy. The clarinet player is eighty-six. Half of them are falling asleep. Thank God Jeff hired a bus to transport them."

Shirlee approached. "My feet hurt and look how swollen they are. Just how am I going to make church tomorrow?"

"Dear woman," said Katherine, "with those heels you're wearing, no wonder. I'm just glad you didn't fall on your ass."

"I might be old, but I can still sport a pair of stylish pumps. Besides, I didn't see you shaking *your* hips so much. You're almost as stiff as David, who exposed his WASP genetics on the dance floor tonight. God, he really needs a good Black woman. He's pathetically dance-challenged!"

"That's why I love you, Shirlee. You never mince words. You headed home soon?"

"Yes, it's time. Let me go hug Jeff, ah, Jessica first."

Later in bed and still wound up from the evening, Peter and Katherine embraced, talking for an hour before falling asleep. Jeff and Amy did the same thing. Shirlee took a bath and elevated her feet. David, having gone home after dropping Shirlee off, took a strong muscle relaxer.

CHAPTER 37

"Hello, this is Katherine Eich."

"My name is Seth Noland," said a shaky voice. "I don't know where to start..." His voice trailed off. Katherine could hear his deep breathing through the phone.

"Hello, Seth. This doesn't sound like an easy phone call for you. Please, how can I help?" Katherine hoped her calming voice would help alleviate his anxiety.

"An FBI agent by the name of Jeb Walker contacted me regarding my biological mother, a woman named Stella Cordrey. Do you know of her?"

Startled, Katherine quickly responded. "I do! Oh, wow! She's been hoping to meet you for decades. Thank you for calling. I'm betting this is hard for you."

"I, I, ah, I'm scared to death." His voice quivered, and he took another deep breath. "The FBI gave me her number and yours. I was too terrified to call her."

"Where are you calling from?"

"Washington, D.C. How can I be sure she's my biological mother? I mean, this Walker agent told me the adoption records matched, but..."

"Your calling tells me you're interested in pursuing this."

"Uh, uh, yeah. I think so."

"We could do DNA testing to be certain." Katherine knew this was moot. The adoption records matched, so DNA confirmation would be no surprise.

"What's she like?"

"I've found her to be fascinating," said Katherine. "It's been my pleasure to get to know her. She's eighty-four and lives here at Oak Place in assisted living."

"And my biological father? Has she said anything about him?"

"There's so much to tell you, but I think you should hear it from her, not me. I will tell you this. She's never forgotten you and has never given up trying to find you."

There was silence on the other end. "Seth?"

"Yes, I'm still here."

"Are you willing to meet Stella? It would mean so much to her." Katherine didn't want to run the risk of scaring him off but was unsure how to proceed.

"I, ah, guess so."

"Tell me about yourself," Katherine said, wanting to get a sense of who he was.

"I live in D.C. with my wife and two daughters. One daughter is in college in upstate New York. My parents, already older when they adopted me, are deceased. But they were wonderful. I'm a history professor. How is it that the FBI calls me?"

"They needed some information from Stella, and she asked if, in return, they could help her find you. She'd exhausted all other avenues. Seth, she really wants to meet you."

"Do you know why she gave me up?"

"Seth, you need to hear that from her." Katherine voice was gentle, but she firmly believed that Stella's story should come from Stella.

"Was she married?"

"It is a beautiful love story. Your father was from South Africa and worked hard to end apartheid starting from its inception back in the 1950s. He was a United Nations Special Envoy for Human Rights. Stella helped him." Katherine was telling him more than she wanted.

"Tell me more…"

"I know Stella would want to tell you the story," Katherine repeated. "But I can tell you that it has been my honor to know her. She's a courageous woman who generously helped Black South Africans achieve a better life through education, decent medical care, and equal rights."

"She did? Really? Okay, you've convinced me. How can I possibly pass up this opportunity? Still, I want to be sure she's my birth mother." Katherine could tell from his voice that his anxiety had lessened.

"Let's start by you giving me your date of birth and the name of the adoption agency. I can get our attorney to help us confirm the match."

Seth shared what he knew. He apparently had the adoption papers in front of him and confirmed he was born in New York City. Both the adoption agency and his birthdate matched what Stella had told Katherine. While Stella's name had been omitted from the birth certificate, a decades-old letter from the defunct agency confirmed she was the birth mother and Kevin was the biological father.

"Seth, can I tell Stella you've called?"

Silence.

"Oh, wow, I, ah, guess so. I guess I need to go for this. No, let's wait. I need to digest this some. I want to talk more with my wife and children. Please don't tell her I called just yet."

"Why don't you call me back in a week?" Katherine suggested, not wanting to leave things open-ended. "Can you give me your phone number and email address?" Seth complied and promised to call within the week.

"Oh my God," Katherine said to herself after she hung up, a huge smile on her face. She could hardly contain herself. Walker and Gultowski had found Stella's son. But she had promised Seth she wouldn't tell Stella. Somehow, she'd have to avoid Stella at all costs for fear of divulging what she had just learned.

CHAPTER 38

Peter had breakfast waiting as Katherine hurriedly walked to their kitchen, fidgeting with the papers she was stuffing inside her briefcase. It had been months since Jim Barclay had yelled and screamed over the alleged negligent care of his demented mother, after which Katherine had confronted him and threatened to suspend his visits.

Peter hugged Katherine. "You'll be fine, honey."

"Oh, Peter, thanks for the vote of confidence. I think I'll be fine, but Jim Barclay might be full of surprises. Plus, he's attempting to destroy my professional reputation. Jesus, he has the soul of a dishrag."

"Remember how many times you've told me not to take it personally? It's time you listened to yourself."

"Oh, I know, I know. I could do that for *myself*, but when he falsely accuses my staff of negligent behavior, I see red. The son of a bitch. And his poor mother. How did such a sweet woman birth such a monster?"

"Katherine, you know better than to say that."

"Oh, you're so right. I'm totally unnerved. Forgive me if I don't eat. My stomach is already churning. I need to get to the office and talk with our lawyer."

Fixated on the court appearance in one hour, Katherine entered the elevator to an enthusiastic, "Hi, Katherine! Isn't it a great day to be alive?" As always, Maria had a wide, captivating smile that, when on full mode display, deepened the existing wrinkles on her face and exposed the dormant ones. Maria was the epitome of aging positively. She was also a member of the infamous Oak Place Seven, who had protested the world's lack of involvement in climate change and laid down to block horse police at the United Nations, resulting in being arrested and jailed.

Not sure if she could handle Maria's just-be-happy attitude, she attempted a smile. "Hi, Maria."

Then something happened to Katherine. She stopped obsessing over Barclay and focused her attention on the extraordinarily radiant woman in front of her, a gift at the precise moment she needed one.

Maria was like a magnet for many, including Katherine. She defied all the stereotypes: old equals ugly, old equals inert, old equals waiting around to die. At eighty-five, Maria refused to let old dominate her life. "God knows," she would say, "I don't want to be thirty, forty, or even fifty again. I've already been those ages. Not interested in repeating them."

One year, she went to Africa by herself. "Most of my friends want to stay close to home, or more appropriately, chained to their cardiologists. To hell with my cardiologist! I wanted to see a giraffe in the wild. I figured the Serengeti would be a good place to die if it's my time."

Last year, she tethered herself to a muscular twenty-two-year-old and jumped out of an airplane. "I never fully experienced the world from 10,000 feet," she had said. Her completed bucket list also included riding a motorcycle with her grandson. And not just a thirty-minute jaunt to say she had done it. No, she spent almost a week riding with him through the mountains of Colorado. "It was exhilarating!" she had proclaimed upon her return. "He's a good driver and such a brave person to take his grandma, who, thank God, was wearing Depends when we went off-road on bumpy trails. I did spend one night under the stars in a sleeping bag, but having to use the bathroom twice during the night posed logistical problems. I can't squat like I used to, so I opted for motels."

She earned her Ph.D. at the age of seventy-nine. Her dissertation was on women in the former Yugoslavia. "My mother was Croatian and I wanted to understand her life and what she had been through under Tito and communism."

One time, an elderly man remarked, "You're lucky to be so healthy!"

She shot right back. "I have hypertension, degenerative arthritis, atrial fibrillation, and probably some things I don't even know about. So what! Should I just whine and shrivel up?"

Some people avoided Maria as if her positive attitude meant eccentric or crazy rather than just wanting to live every moment. Others were drawn to her contagious positivity. When one woman went snorkeling in the Bahamas, she came back and proudly announced it to Maria, almost as if to one-up her. "Oh, you wonderful soul," said Maria. "Got any photos?" She did, of course.

Maria inspired other residents. She encouraged them to take risks. "If you don't try, you'll never know," Maria had said. Couch potatoes avoided Maria, which was just as well. She wasn't interested in reruns of *Family Feud*.

Like the lives of so many other seniors, Maria had experienced her share of suffering. She had been married twice, her first husband dying at forty-three of a massive heart attack, leaving her with two young teenagers to raise. Her second husband, who she thought was loving and kind, turned out to be a brutal abuser, and she ditched him after he beat her in a drunken rage. She was open and out front about her experience, which had landed her and her children in a shelter for abused women.

"I totally misjudged him," she had written to her family in her unpublished autobiography. "His supposed kindness came with so many stipulations. Dinner ready when and how he wanted it. Be there at his beck and call. He also isolated me from my family and friends, and treated my kids like dirt, all of this after I married him. I should have noticed the signs, but in my loneliness and desire for companionship, I was blind."

After that, Maria never married again, although she had one long-term relationship that ended with his death from cancer. Instead, she had concentrated on being a good mom and always being there for her children, both of whom went to college and now had families of their own.

Now that Maria was in the senior living complex, they visited her often. "So Mom, what adventure are you planning this time?" they would often ask. Her son, Rob, had long ago stopped trying to talk her out of things. "She'll do what she wants when she wants."

He did worry about her, which is why she usually told him *after* she had done whatever. "Guess what I did yesterday?" was how the conversation would start.

"Maria," Katherine said as she exited the elevator, her mood much improved. "You're such a role model for the residents. And me too, for that matter."

"I've got a lot of living to do. And not much time to do it. Tie me down in my coffin, not a moment sooner! Guess what I'm doing today? Going to the zoo with my granddaughter and her preschooler, my great granddaughter."

Seeing Maria gave Katherine the energy to fight. She was right to have confronted Jim Barclay on the day he yelled and screamed, and she knew it. She had set boundaries and quelled his unruly behavior. Most importantly, there had been no patient neglect.

It was a short hearing, with the case dismissed. Oak Place's lawyer was prepared with documentation of Barclay's biannual rants, and the medical records showed no physical or emotional abuse. In fact, a physical examination by a third-party doctor confirmed that Mrs. Barclay was well cared for.

Barclay was livid when the judge confronted him for his disorderly behavior and produced a court order forbidding Barclay from visiting Oak Place. Katherine then proposed to the judge that Barclay be allowed supervised visits with his mother if either a social worker or security guard was present.

"That's bullshit!" he yelled, his angry retort confirming what the judge already suspected.

"Pipe down, Mr. Barclay," the judge said, "before I throw in a contempt charge."

"I am transferring my mother to another facility!" As Barclay ranted, Katherine felt completely vindicated. Barclay really was a dysfunctional human being.

Later, Katherine asked the staff to alert her when that transfer request came.

It never did. And Barclay never came back.

CHAPTER 39

"The cancer is in my brain. I'm not going to lick this," said a teary Amy to Katherine and Shirlee several months after the wedding.

"Don't give up, Amy," said Shirlee. "You've got to fight. You still have quality time left."

"I'm starting to get bad headaches. I don't want to be a burden."

"They can control your pain," said Katherine, although she wasn't sure her pain could be completely controlled. "Talk to the doctor about getting the right medications. And, you could never be a burden to anyone. You've spent your life caring for others. It's your turn to let people care for you."

"Last night I had diarrhea in bed. Jeff helped me wipe my butt and change. That was pretty humiliating."

"He's a doctor, although nurses do that so much better," Shirlee said, forcing a smile. Amy rolled her eyes and smiled back.

"Please stay close to Jeff. I worry about him."

"We've got that covered," said Katherine. "And we'll stay close to you too."

"As recommended, I'm going to try radiation on my brain tumor to see if they can shrink it. I'll do that for a while, but I'll not do chemo again." Amy began crying and her tears glistened as she said loudly, "I'm not going to be endlessly sick just to live longer, or maybe I should say suffer longer! It's not worth it to me. It's just not!"

"The doctors can stop the suffering. Pain can be controlled," Shirlee said, halfheartedly repeating what Katherine had already said. She knew the end was near.

"Oh, Amy, I'm so sorry this has happened to you." Katherine began crying as did Shirlee. They each reached their hands across the table. For a while, they stayed that way, holding hands tightly, silently.

Amy looked at both Katherine and Shirlee "I'm talking a lot to

Jeff and the children. I'm trying to fill them in on pieces of my history. They all know my death is near, lurking and waiting, sooner rather than later. Recently, I've had this strong urge to leave a more detailed legacy, silly as it sounds. The other day I was wondering if I'd taught Eric to add oregano to our favorite lasagna dish, a recipe that was handed down from my mother. Suddenly, at that moment, I was consumed with adding fucking oregano!"

"That is important to remember," said Katherine, smiling.

"In a way, it's like when you go on vacation and one hundred miles from home, you wonder if you left the coffee pot on," said Amy. "Well, right now, I feel like dying is similar, only on a much greater scale. I'm consumed with what I forgot to tell people."

Amy wiped her tears. "You know, when I was seventeen, I was elected vice president of my senior class. A boy named Gerald, whose cystic fibrosis had stunted and distorted his growth, came in second. The next day, as I disembarked from the school bus, Gerald was there waiting and approached me, arm out, to shake my hand and congratulate me. I was so touched and even felt guilty about winning. Sure, I might have been the cheerleader and perky *Miss Popular.* But in that moment, I knew I was no better than him."

"Must have been significant for you to remember all these years later," said Katherine.

"Shortly after graduation, he succumbed to the disease. And you know what? Neither my kids nor Jeff knew about this short snippet of my life. Yesterday, I felt compelled to tell them. I feel driven to fill in the blanks to somehow, I guess, prove my life was a series of meaningful memories. My stellar resume of accomplishments seems miniscule next to some of these other consequential encounters in my life."

"They're not going to forget you," said Shirlee in a soft voice while shaking her head, "even if they do forget the oregano and don't know all of the stories."

"Amy," said Katherine, "they might cherish memories of you that even you may not remember or think were significant."

"Yeah, I suppose. Look guys, let's try and have a nice lunch and not dwell on this. I've done that too much already. Please, I want to be distracted for a while. I want to stop the maudlin talk that only increases my depression. And for God's sake, I don't want pity."

"Okay," said Katherine. "I'm having the clam chowder. But I want to say one more thing. We'll be there for you every step of the way. You have quality living left. Besides, I want to hear some more of your stories."

"You're wonderful friends. I love you both." The death and dying conversation thus ended abruptly, replaced with more stories and laughter. "Did I ever tell you about…"

After sending Amy back to her apartment in a cab, Shirlee and Katherine decided to walk before taking the subway back to Oak Place. Arm in arm, they started making plans to help Amy and her family through the last months—perhaps weeks—of her life: making food for family and visitors, being there to help, and supporting whoever needed it, including each other.

Shirlee changed the subject. "This is probably not a good time given our lunch with Amy, but David and I had an amazing evening last night."

Katherine's head rocketed from sadly staring at the sidewalk to Shirlee's face. After a few seconds, she said, "You made love?"

"Girl, did I say that?"

"It's all over your face."

"It was very nice. He's gentle and slow. I felt very comfortable. It's been a while for me. Him too. We had to work out some kinks."

"Oh, Shirlee, how nice. You're glowing."

"He told me he loved me. Actually, he said he's loved me for a long time."

"Holy cow, Shirlee! And you said…?"

"Yeah, I love him. And I told him."

"Jesus! What a milestone!" Katherine paused for three seconds. "What do you mean by kinks?"

"He's past seventy. It took a while for him to get an erection, and

I needed enough lubrication to fill a bucket. My arthritis made one position…well, let's say uncomfortable. He got a cramp. We're going to have to work on our sexually aging selves, with all its complexities."

"Did he say he loved your beautiful body?"

"He did, even if it *is* full figured. And you know, for a white man, his body wasn't bad either."

"No comment!" Katherine laughed out loud.

"You know, this isn't going to be without glitches. He's got kids. He told me that our racial differences wouldn't be a problem, but I think we may have to cross that bridge."

"You're a beautiful woman inside and out. You've made their father happy. They're going to love you."

"We'll see. They might be worried I could take their happy father to the altar, thus amending his extensive estate. Of course, I don't give a hoot about his money. I've got my own, thank you. But I'm not going to worry about that now. In fact, I've invited the whole kit and caboodle to my home on Sunday. I'm making some soul food. Might as well initiate them properly."

"All his kids are coming?"

"Yep, all two of them."

"Grandchildren?"

"No. His three grandchildren are all grown up, and the youngest is in college. He started his family early. All have their own lives. So, it's just his two children, one with a spouse. The other is divorced but bringing his girlfriend.

"Katherine, he wants to retire and travel. Wants me to come with him." Shirlee tempered her excitement as she gauged Katherine's reaction.

"Oh my." Shirlee's last words hit hard. Katherine knew Oak Place losing Shirlee would be huge.

"Yeah, I know. Haven't said yes yet, but we're not getting any younger. And both of us are still healthy. He wants to see Yellowstone and I want to see the Grand Canyon."

"They have great mule rides down the canyon."

"I'm not getting on no damn mule!"

Both women laughed as if attempting to reduce the impact of what Shirlee was saying, which, for Katherine, had quickly gone from elation to "Oh my God." But talk of imminent retirement would have to wait. Katherine didn't have the energy to pursue the subject just then.

"Scared of a mule? Come on, brave one," said Katherine. "Peter, Jill, and I did it one winter break. It was fun."

"Liar! I remember you saying you were peeing in your pants as your mule negotiated the switchbacks."

"Well, I do recall saying once was enough."

"More like, 'I can't believe I lived to talk about it!'"

After more chitchat, Katherine turned serious again. "I saw Stella this morning near the gardens and avoided her. There's big news about her long-lost son. In fact, he called me."

"Oh? Did you find out this morning?"

"I've known for a week, but I promised her son I wouldn't tell her. I did tell him some things about who Stella was."

"What? Who gave you permission to share her life, then keep that secret? You're running the risk of Stella getting really pissed off at you."

"I know…"

CHAPTER 40

"What a beautiful dress," Katherine said to Stella, who was wearing a long, informal paisley lounging dress with a beaded belt.

"Thank you, my friend. To what do I owe this special visit, even though I'm glad you're here. Seems it's been weeks since I last saw you. How about a cup of tea?"

"Sounds nice. Let me help."

"Oh, sit down. Let a little old lady wait on you."

Katherine nervously sat down, fidgeting with her cell while Stella went to the kitchen. Seth had called back that morning and given her permission to tell Stella the FBI had found him.

"In fact," he had said, "if I get the nerve, I might even call her myself."

He planned on coming to New York within the week if Stella's schedule permitted. His college student daughter, Melissa, would be meeting him. Apparently, she had been instrumental in convincing Seth to meet his birth mother.

"Dad! You've got to do this! It'll give you a full history of your heritage. Don't you want to fill in the blanks? And mine, too? Your birth father was a special envoy to the United Nations. Don't you want to learn more about that?"

"Truth be told," Seth had said, "I needed my daughter to push me. She's so curious. I'm just plain scared. My wife and other daughter wanted to come also, but we felt it might be too much, all four of us descending on this woman. Hopefully, there will be plenty of time for everyone to get to know each other."

"Tea's ready," called Stella from the kitchen. "Do you want sugar?"

Katherine couldn't keep still, so she got up and went to the kitchen to help, then carried both cups back while Stella made her way to her chair and sat down. "Something tells me this isn't a social visit. You seem tense. Is the FBI looking for me again?" She winked and smiled at Katherine.

"No," Katherine said. Then, unable to keep it in any longer, she said, "But your son is!"

Stella's eyes widened and she put her hand over her mouth. "Oh my God." The shock was evident on her face. Her lips were quivering, she was breathing rapidly, and tears were filling her eyes and beginning to stream down her face. "Oh my God," she repeated.

"He called me last week but asked me not to tell you. He wanted some time to digest this incredible new information and talk to his family before contacting you. This morning he called again. He would like to visit you this Friday with his twenty-year-old daughter, who's in college in upstate New York. He was hoping that would be convenient for you. Stella, I'm sorry for not telling you sooner, but I was afraid he'd panic and..."

"Oh my God, Katherine, forgive yourself," Stella said, reaching for Katherine's hand. She tried to take a sip of her tea, but her hands were trembling. "I've been waiting for this day for so many years. I just can't believe it. You talked with him twice? What's he like? What did you tell him about me?"

"He seems really nice. A history professor at a university in Washington, D.C. He has a wife and two kids."

"A history professor. Wow. I always hoped Kevin and I would create an intelligent child."

"I didn't give him many details. I wanted you to do that. Also, he doesn't know that Kevin is dead."

"Thank you, my friend. Oh, wow! This Friday? Oh, so much to do. I'll have to go food shopping. Will they be here for lunch? Dinner? Where do I start? Katherine, can you be here?"

"Sure. Wouldn't want to miss this! They're meeting me at my office at 10:00 a.m. Apparently, they're both taking trains to get here the night before."

"I have a granddaughter!"

"Two actually, one in college, one a junior in high school."

"Where do I begin…"

"Stella, there's no hurry. You'll have plenty of time—in fact, the rest of your lives."

"For me, that might not be that much time. What if he doesn't like me?"

"I can't imagine that. What's not to like?"

"But I abandoned him."

"You gave him a loving home. He said his adoptive parents were great. *Abandon* is not a word you need to use."

"My confidence level is about minus ten right now."

"You're the strong, brave woman who smuggled millions of dollars in diamonds out of South Africa. That courage is still inside you."

"Dear God, What's his name? I forgot to ask you, what's his name?"

"Seth. Seth Noland."

After talking for an hour, Katherine left, even though she wasn't entirely sure Stella was okay. Stella remained in her chair; her mind flooded with memories of Kevin while playing out various scenarios of her impending conversation with a son she had only known as a newborn baby. Where would she start? Would he allow her to hug him? Who would he look like? How could she explain things? How would he react to being half South African? What kind of history did he teach? American? World History? Ancient?

One question took center stage in her mind. Should she tell him she was a prostitute? Yes, of course she would, but how much detail should she reveal? She didn't want to scare him away. There was always the chance he would find her morally repulsive. And she had the granddaughter to contend with, too. What parts of her life should she take to her grave?

"I am who I am," she said to herself. "The good, the bad, the ugly." Her confidence rose as she thought about her life. He'd have to take her as she was. She hoped he'd stick around for the whole story—her autobiography told again—the second time in one year, and only the second time in her entire life.

Her phone rang. "Hello?"

"Hello, is this Stella Cordrey?"

"If you are selling something or doing a survey, this is not a good time."

"How about if I want to talk to my biological mother?"

"Oh, dear God! It's you." Stella began crying, so much so that she couldn't talk…or catch her breath. Seth began crying too, so nothing was said for a couple of minutes.

When she could speak, Stella asked, "Were you raised by a nice, loving family?" First things first.

"Yes, I was. My parents are deceased now, but they gave me a great home. Plenty of love to go around. After me, they also adopted my sister."

"All these years, I worried about that the most; whether you had a good home. I'd have never forgiven myself if it were any other way."

"You can stop worrying about that. I'm well-adjusted. No major dysfunction or mental quirks. I also have a great family myself."

Stella laughed. "Thank God! A normal man with a normal childhood."

"Very normal. Sometimes boring."

"I'm so sorry I gave you up. But I knew I couldn't give you a normal life or normal anything."

Silence again.

"I understand. Really. I do. Please, if you need to forgive yourself, do it. *I forgive you.*" Stella hung tight to those words. I forgive you. She was overwhelmed and relieved. She began to calm down. For the first time, she thought she might, just maybe, fully forgive herself.

"Thank you, Seth, for saying that. My friend, Katherine, tells me you're coming here on Friday with your daughter. You can't imagine how happy that makes me! I've been looking for you for a long time. Decades! I wish I could've met your parents and thanked them personally. What were they like?"

"My mom stayed home to take care of us kids. She volunteered with various organizations, especially the local thrift store. My dad worked in a steel mill. His leg was injured in the military, but he worked the assembly line with the best of them. They both worked hard to give us kids an education and a better life. Salt of the earth people. My sister is also a teacher."

"Oh, how wonderful." Tears of happiness streamed down Stella's face.

"Your turn. Tell me something about you—and my father."

Stella told him just about everything. Except for holding off on the prostitute part, there was no hesitation, no guilt or remorse as the floodgates opened. "I didn't have such a loving childhood. In fact, I was abused in every way. I ran away at sixteen to escape. The scars have never quite left me, but I managed to pick myself up and work my way through college. Your father was from South Africa, also from an abusive family, mostly emotional abuse. He was very much against apartheid and spent his life trying to end it. That's what brought him to the United Nations, where our paths crossed."

"Where is he now?"

"He died in South Africa in 1990. He was assassinated. He was a wonderful man who fought his whole life for justice and paid the ultimate price." She paused. "I still miss him so much, Seth. He's the only man I ever loved." Stella could hardly get the words out before sobbing.

The phone call lasted over an hour, neither wanting to hang up. So many questions.

"I really want to meet you and get to know you, Stella. Your history is my history."

"What's your last name?"

"Noland."

"Seth Noland. I like the sound of that. Tell me, is it Doctor Seth Noland?"

"It is."

"What type of history do you teach?"

Seth paused and took a deep breath. Then, barely able to speak, he quietly said, "World history with a concentration on social injustices in societies, including apartheid."

The silence that followed spoke volumes.

CHAPTER 41

The progression of Amy's metastatic brain tumor was swift and painful. Life prolonging treatments were discontinued. Her headaches became unbearable, necessitating mega doses of narcotics to quell the throbbing, medications that rendered her semiconscious and sometimes disoriented.

Jeff scheduled caregivers round the clock. Family and friends maintained vigils at her bedside in two-hour shifts during the day and evening hours. Katherine and Shirlee took their turns, and their nursing skills often brought Amy some relief. Shirlee found that a cold compress on a certain area of her head helped. They also darkened the room so light wouldn't trigger the auras that frequently preceded severe migraines. Hospice was called, bringing palliative care professionals with specialized skills.

When Amy was awake and fighting to be aware, she groaned in pain. Her final mission became expressing her love to those she held close. Her semi-demented, ninety-three-year-old mother made this difficult as she looked skyward, loudly repeating over and over again, "God, why don't you take me instead? Why my beautiful little girl?" Her multiple outbursts made one day particularly challenging, prompting Katherine to gently take her arm and lead her outside for a walk, giving Jeff and Amy some peace from her mom's understandable, but constant, torment.

The refrigerator was jam packed with food from friends and neighbors. The grandchildren gave everyone some relief. Jeff took breaks to read them stories, barely concentrating, and repeatedly interrupted by Amy's moaning. They peppered him with their questions. "Why is Grandma so sick? Why can't you make her better? Is she going to die soon?"

"Yes, soon she will stop breathing," answered Jeff honestly. "Come. Let's rub her head." He wanted the grandkids to take part in caregiving, even if only with small gestures.

A few hours later, Jeff said in frustration to the hospice doctor who had just walked in the door, "Enough! She wants to be awake and pain-free, but she can't have both. We're beyond that. Let's stop the suffering!" The doctor agreed and administered a combination of medications that almost immediately stopped the pain, and put Amy in a deep sleep. She would never fully wake up.

For two more days, her loved ones touched her gently, including her grandchildren. They talked to her as if she were awake. They gathered around the bed and told stories to Amy and each other. Everyone said their goodbyes. They took comfort knowing Amy wasn't in pain.

Late one night, Jeff was alone with Amy, lying by her side. Her breathing had become sporadic. He rubbed her hair and face and shoulders, and thanked her over and over again—reminiscing about their life together. Finally, the next breath didn't come.

He placed her head on his chest, closed her eyes and hugged her. Then he paced the room, talking to her the whole time. He sat in a chair for almost an hour staring at her lifeless body. Then he cuddled beside her again, still talking, while he positioned her arms over her chest before rigor mortis set in. He sobbed out loud at times; other times he cried quietly to himself.

A few hours later, still in the early morning darkness, he began awakening people, some who were in the apartment and others who had gone home.

"Hi, Katherine," Jeff said into the phone. "She's gone."

Katherine laid in bed, so many things running through her mind. She was relieved the early morning phone call hadn't awakened Peter. She thought about death, and what it would be like if she lost Peter. She could only imagine, and it was frightening. She remembered a colleague once telling her that a death not learned from is a wasted death. For many minutes she pondered what she would learn from

Amy's dying and from her death; her thoughts interrupted by Peter's hand on her shoulder.

❧ ❧ ❧

By the time Peter and Katherine arrived at their apartment, Jeff and his children had bathed and dressed Amy in a shroud. Daughter Amelia had done Amy's hair and makeup. Flowers, including her much loved daisies, were placed around the room. Amy's favorite songs played softly in the background. The room's curtains were pulled back, allowing the sun from the new day to shine in. A window was opened to keep the room cool.

As word of Amy's death spread, people arrived in droves. Throughout the day, the apartment was crowded, sometimes standing room only. People told tales, drank toasts, broke bread together, and visited Amy in her beautiful, flower-filled room. Sometimes, they went in groups; others went in alone. Everyone came out teary. Jeff held up fairly well, even as he was hugged hundreds of times. After all, his grief had begun months ago when he knew this day would come. At one point, Jeff and his two children, needing alone time, took a walk and began making plans for the funeral.

At midnight, some twenty-two hours after her death, the hearse came with its body bag stretcher. For Jeff, this was overwhelming. He was overcome with sorrow as he kissed her one last time and pulled the zipper up over her head. He followed the body to the hearse, then disappeared into the night, alone with his grief.

Katherine went home but lay sleepless in bed. Death was a routine part of her professional life. But now it was regularly invading her private life.

She whispered aloud, for the first time, "I hate being old."

CHAPTER 42

Hal had been cleaning Jake's barn all week. New hay and straw had been delivered. Grain was loaded into a covered bin. Jake's old brushes and combs were readied. Vets were contacted. Now, Hal paced back and forth, waiting for the truck with its precious cargo.

Preparations for this day had taken several months. Hal had visited miniature horse farms throughout the northeast and one in Virginia. Two owners wanted to see Oak Place for themselves, uncertain that living in New York City would be a good life for their horse.

When it came time to choose between two horses, the Oak Place Horse Search Committee demanded a field trip. They were more than willing to pay their own way. In the end, Hal had the final say, but everybody agreed with him. Delilah was far and above the horse they all wanted. Her price was a bit high, so Katherine stepped in to negotiate something more reasonable.

"We can guarantee she'll have extraordinary attention and love. She'll be the therapy horse for a thousand-plus people. But we're a nonprofit and we cannot meet your asking price."

Turned out the owner/breeder wanted her horse at Oak Place as much as Oak Place residents wanted Delilah. She halved the price when Katherine proposed the other half be considered an in-kind donation. As an added perk, their breeding farm would be mentioned in articles about the horse. Of course, donations—some large, most small—poured in to help defray costs. The neighborhood fire department passed the hat among its members, collecting $85.

Just before lunch, the truck arrived. Hal had asked that residents and schoolchildren stay away from the immediate vicinity at first so Delilah could familiarize herself with her new home. Still, there was a crowd forming just outside the invisible perimeter. Children stopped playing in the playground as soon as the truck drove up, their teachers holding them back. "Delilah's here! Delilah's here!" they shouted with glee. People were at their windows. Those taking a walk stopped to watch, and every bench was filled.

High rise Queens is a world away from country Connecticut, and two-year-old Delilah, looking out from the truck's safe confines, was hesitant. With some gentle coaxing and a carrot, her owner slowly convinced her to descend the ramp. Then, as if she already sensed she would be the center of attention, she came down the ramp in regal fashion, tail high, head up, and as if on cue, a breeze came out of nowhere and ruffled her mane.

Hal was all smiles as he led her into her new home, which she immediately smelled up and down before testing the new grass by rolling in it. After a short while, she barely paid attention to the hundreds of eyes on her. Chomping on another carrot, Delilah knew she was a star.

She was a beauty, Katherine thought. She was brown, with white halfway up her four legs and on her forehead. She relished being touched by the hands of those few permitted to approach during the first hour. She even leaned against Hal, their bond immediately apparent. Katherine wondered if Hal would give up his studio to sleep with her.

In the ensuing days, Hal took her on one field trip in the morning and one in the afternoon. On day three of her new life, she was at the firehouse getting hugged by firefighters, who, like the children, couldn't keep their hands off her. In love with being touched, Delilah was in horse heaven.

Some minor incidents occurred with the other resident animals. Hester, the miniature poodle, got too close and had her paw stepped on. She howled and startled Delilah, who backed up into a medicine cart, which in turn pinned a nurse to the wall. An initially freaked out Hal calmed when everyone started laughing—except Hester, who, shivering from the trauma, was being cuddled in a resident's arms.

The first days and weeks went smoothly for Delilah. Sunday

afternoons brought many intergenerational families to her small, fenced-in pasture. Signs reappeared asking everyone not to feed her. She even made a field trip to a cancer hospital in midtown Manhattan, where one of the preschoolers was being treated for leukemia. Upon seeing Delilah, the four-year-old child, suffering extreme malaise from the effects of chemo, immediately perked up and smiled. Katherine couldn't accommodate the parents' request for daily visits, but the original Connecticut owner was so touched that she arranged with the hospital to make regular visits with other miniature horses.

❧ ❧ ❧

Hearing the positive stories of Delilah's successful visits through-out Oak Place helped Katherine remain upbeat, especially when less than gratifying issues confronted her.

"My rent check bounced for the last two months," said one tearful assisted living resident. "I don't know where all my money's gone. I had many thousands of dollars. Please don't kick me out! I was dying of loneliness until I came here. Please!" she begged, sobbing. "I can't leave my friends. They're my oxygen. Please!"

"Nobody is kicking you out," replied Katherine. "I promise. Now, take a deep breath and let's figure this out."

Katherine reflected on the resident's words. *Dying of loneliness.* She knew loneliness was like a disease, affecting so many older persons, taking away their will to live.

"Oh, God bless you, Dr. Eich. Can I pay off some of my rent by working here at Oak Place? I retired as a secretary in a doctor's office."

"First things first. Who has access to your accounts?"

"My son. As my power of attorney, he said he had to borrow some money, but would pay it back directly. Then he couldn't, but said he'd be repaying it any day now. What should I do? I cannot believe this."

This was a familiar story. Financial pilfering of a senior's life sav-ings, often by family or supposed friends, was nothing new. Too often, money was taken for drugs or gambling, leaving a senior broke. It could happen to anybody, rich or poor. It had happened to Mickey Rooney, who testified at a Congressional hearing about elder abuse. It's what often kept one Oak Place attorney busy confronting the perpetrators and recouping the money if possible—or at least preventing them from taking additional monies.

"Are you getting any monthly income deposited in your accounts?"

"Yes, social security and my pension, which in the past covered most of my expenses. But my savings are gone! And I needed to take a bit of that monthly to make it. Now, I'll barely be able to scratch by."

"Mrs. Reinhold, would you be willing to talk with our attorney and let her contact your son?"

"I don't want to upset him. He's going through a bad divorce and has a teenager on drugs. His life's out of control. He's my only child. He cries on the phone, telling me he's desperate. Oh, Dr. Eich, what can I do?"

"I'm sorry, Mrs. Reinhold. I know it's hard for you to see the people you love in trouble and suffering. But he shouldn't be taking your money. Oak Place is a nonprofit and we have to meet our expenses. If our residents don't pay their rents, we take a hit. We really do need to speak with your son."

"Okay, when can I see your attorney? I'll not be made to move out of this wonderful place because he's robbed me blind. I'm so sad, but I'm also angry. How could he do this to me, his mother?"

CHAPTER 43

"Can we do lunch today?" said Shirlee over the phone. "I need to talk with you."

"Are you okay?"

"Yeah, yeah, I'm fine. But I need to bounce something off you. How about noon?"

Feeling a bit of apprehension, Katherine accepted, wondering what was going on. *Could this be the conversation I'm dreading,* she thought. *Shirlee can't be ready to retire yet.* She fretted all morning.

As usual, however, the day's events interrupted her thoughts. Mrs. Barclay had died peacefully in her sleep, the fifth death of the week, more than usual. Jim Barclay's wife, Johanna, had called, asking to see Katherine. She was now waiting outside her office, dressed in a Gucci suit and jeweled up to the hilt.

"I'm so sorry for your loss," Katherine said.

"I'd like to donate my mother-in-law's clothes to whoever needs them."

"Thank you, Mrs. Barclay. We'll be able to use them."

"It's not much."

"It's a kind and generous offer."

She stared at the floor as if wanting to say more but not knowing where to start. "Ah," she sputtered, then started crying—or at least pretending to cry. Katherine came from behind her desk to sit next to her. She let her sniffle for a while and offered a tissue, even though there were no tears. Barclay gently dabbed at her eyes, careful not to smear her mascara.

Eventually, after a deep breath, she regained her composure. It was rather dramatic in Katherine's view. "I bet you have many wonderful memories of your mother-in-law. I know I do."

Seemingly having difficulty talking, Barclay managed to say, "She was a great lady, always bringing people together. She made many sacrifices. You know, Jim loved her. It was so hard for him to visit, to witness her curled up and dying. Seems he was angry with everyone around him. I'm sorry he was a problem for you."

"I understand. People express their grief in many ways, and anger is one of them."

"He really is a wonderful man and has been very successful. We have a great house; we travel and live well. Jim takes good care of me. But he's under so much pressure, you know, being CEO of a major company. Sometimes, he brings that home. It's not easy juggling billions of dollars." Katherine bit her tongue at this pointed reminder that she was quite wealthy.

Katherine abhorred materialistic bragging and suspected Johanna herself had suffered from her husband's emotional—if not physical—abuse. "Watching someone you love waste away is never easy," Katherine said, halfheartedly.

"We're going to have a big funeral and invite all our friends and, well, hers too, at least those still alive. I've already ordered the invitations. Jim wants me to cater it at the country club overlooking the water. I wish we could do it waterside at our house, but it's still too cold. We're going to send her off in style. Can you give me the names of any friends she had while she was in assisted living, before she went into the nursing home? I remember her talking about them, but I've forgotten their names and never met them."

Katherine was stoic even though she was disgusted. Did this woman have a clue how pretentious she was? "Let's see. There was Claire Wilson and Norma Barker. Also, Vonnie Levitt, but she passed last year. I'll ask the staff if there were others."

"Do let me know so I can order the right amount of food. Maybe I can send our car for them. On second thought, maybe it should only be her three besties. That's a comfortable number for the limo. I'll need their addresses. This is invitation only. I want to have the right number of tables and chairs."

"And my kids! They have such schedules. It's hard to find the time, especially with my son, who's at Yale. And our daughter has a ski trip that weekend. I'm not sure she'll make it. Oh, so much to do! Today, I'm meeting with both the caterer and string ensemble. Oh, and I must go to the florist, too. You know, pink was her favorite color, so don't you think pink roses for the centerpieces will be lovely?"

Katherine nodded, forcing herself to keep quiet. What she really wanted to say was, "Oh my God, listen to yourself!" For many, death and funerals are opportunities to grieve, reflect, learn. For the Barclays, it seemed to be an opportunity to throw another party.

After Johanna Barclay left, Katherine looked in the bag of clothes she had donated. There, on top, was the infamous silk nightgown, dry cleaning tags attached but still stained from its last wearing. Katherine angrily threw it in the trash can.

⚜ ⚜ ⚜

L unch with Shirlee was as Katherine suspected. She wanted to go to Europe for a month to commemorate David's retirement, a trip partially paid for by his architecture firm after forty years of service. Shirlee assured Katherine her staff could manage without her for a month. Katherine knew that and gave her permission.

Katherine walked back to her office in a sullen mood, imagining the finale of a stimulating professional partnership. With Shirlee there, the present was stable and dependable despite the daily trials and tribulations that surrounded them. Without Shirlee, the future felt emptier, less stable. Change was in the wind; an era was ending.

CHAPTER 44

"You look drop dead gorgeous!" Shirlee said to Jeff after entering the dressing room and gazing at him as he was completing his transformation to Jessica in front of the bright lights of the makeup table.

"Oh, aren't those yellow roses lovely," Jeff said, as Shirlee looked around to see where to place her flowers among the several other arrangements already there. "Jesus! This place looks like a funeral home!"

"Nonsense," said Shirlee. "This is a celebration."

"It's packed out there," added David. "Must be two hundred people—many from Oak Place. Katherine and Peter are saving us seats. Your kids are here too.

"Thanks for the flowers; soooo beautiful," said Jeff, hands trembling ever so slightly, but enough to make the art of applying eye liner, like the intricate lace on a Rembrandt portrait, nearly impossible. "Shit! I look old. This liner is not right on these newfangled fake eye lashes. Where's Amy when you need her?"

"I suspect she's here, laughing that you have to do this yourself. Here, let me help. Just sit back and breathe." Shirlee grabbed the brush and proceeded to even the lines with a steady hand. Jessica closed her eyes and took a few deep breaths. "Okay, where's the mascara?"

Her makeup done, Jessica looked at herself in the mirror. She grimaced as she fought back tears and a couple of drops trickled down her face. "Oh, this isn't going to work. I can't do this!"

Shirlee dabbed the tears gently so as not to smear. "No problem. We've got it under control."

The nightclub in lower Manhattan was brimming with people waiting for Jessica to make her first appearance since Amy's death. Jeff had returned to work at Oak Place and was greeted with much support. He was loved, and the patients that he had cared for so compassionately and competently over the years were not about to abandon him. In his first days back, they had lined up outside his office just to greet him and give him a hug.

Old, widowed ladies had baked him cookies, pans of lasagna, and bread—lots of bread—while talking about the difficult emotional road after losing their partners. One widower said that Amy's death had reactivated the intense grief of losing his own wife some fifteen years ago. "It's like it happened yesterday. I once thought you get over these things, but you never do. I've learned you move on, but my journey has had many peaks and valleys."

While it was sometimes hard to keep talking about Amy, Jeff appreciated the outpouring of kindness. He would leave the office emotionally exhausted, yet strangely at peace. The hard work of grieving was made easier by the abundant expressions of sympathy. After gaining ten pounds consuming the sustenance brought to him, he restarted his exercise regime. After all, Jessica would not allow a bulging tummy under any circumstances.

His friends knew healing had really begun when he started singing again. At first, he attended choir practice at Oak Place. Singing in groups was a good place to reenergize. Soon, he was belting out solos to the delight of anyone who would listen. The drag club where he had sung for decades planned a special comeback. He would perform for forty-five minutes, complete with a costume change.

As Jessica peered out from behind the curtain, she could see the standing room only crowd. She hadn't planned on such a welcome and quickly forgot the first song she was going to sing. The band started playing, people were clapping, shouting, "Jessica! Jessica!" After taking her umpteenth deep breath, Jessica gracefully walked to center stage, smiling, one arm extended in the air, ready to rock 'n' roll. Her rhinestone studded silver crepe dress was sheer about her legs. It wrapped tightly around her trim body and glittered in the lights. Diamond accessories sparkled brilliantly—a mature feminine beauty to behold. People stood and cheered. After a couple minutes, Jessica motioned them to sit down and signaled the band to start: "Celebrate good times, come on! We've got a party goin on." The audience stood up again, cheering loudly.

Later, Jessica changed into her black and white ensemble, left leg revealed by a slit that extended to upper thigh. She performed "Somewhere over the Rainbow." The black and white jewelry round her neck was enough to immobilize a horse, but she hardly noticed the added weight. She gently patted the sweat on her face with a lace handkerchief. The audience was wild as she bowed and left the stage. "More, More, More," they yelled. She came out for a second curtain call. "More!" Then, in rhythmic tandem, "Jessica! Jessica!"

She finally gave the audience a nonverbal cue to sit down, then spoke. "Thank you for all your support these last months. I've been blessed with such loving friendships. You can't imagine what you have meant to me. Amy would thank you also." He signaled the band to play the song he didn't think he would be able to sing, "Bridge Over Troubled Water." He was in tears by the end and so was the audience. A hush came over the room. It didn't seem right to cheer at that moment. Then Jessica reprised "We are Family." After a couple of minutes, she exited the stage, the audience still on their feet.

Jessica had come back center stage, but little did anyone know her grand finale was on the horizon.

CHAPTER 45

Katherine knew who they were before any introductions were made. The resemblance was undeniable. Stella's blue eyes and facial features could be seen in both Seth Noland and his daughter, Melissa. Like Stella, Melissa's hair was curly and thick. Seth had her swooped nose. Any doubts about the hereditary gene pool were quickly short-lived. They were definitely Stella's biological kin.

"Dr. Eich?" asked Seth, nervously wiping his hands on his coat.

"Welcome," said Katherine warmly while squeezing each of their hands. "Call me Katherine. I'm so glad you made this trip. Stella's been up since the wee hours baking her delicious homemade pastries."

"Please, call me Seth. This is my daughter, Melissa. I never thought this day would come. In all my dreams about what my blood parents were like and why they gave me up—I never thought I'd find the answers."

"Dad, you could've had this day years ago if you had listened to me," said Melissa, her immaturity showing behind her own nervousness as she attempted to reverse the parenting roles.

"I know, I know. It takes a daughter bugging you all the time."

"You see, Dr. Eich," said Melissa. "I did this paper in high school about family ancestry. Dad had always told us he was adopted, and I tried to find his roots. But he was never much help."

Seth quickly interjected, "I had very mixed feelings, plus my adopted parents were really insecure about it. I wanted to respect them. Then, life's busyness kept me going in different directions. I got caught up in my education, my work, and my own family. I just kept putting it off. Oh, and don't forget, I was also scared."

"We all need to forgive ourselves for the paths we didn't take," said Katherine. "Thankfully, in your case, the path still exists. Come. Let's not wait around here. There's a lovely lady who's been waiting decades for this day."

As they walked across the Oak Place campus, they passed schoolchildren brushing Delilah. Melissa had a million questions, talking nonstop. Seth manifested his anxiety differently. He was quiet, barely listening to his daughter and Katherine. He held Melissa's hand as if he needed her to steady him. As they rode the elevator to Stella's floor, he began purposeful deep breathing in an effort to calm himself.

In the meantime, Stella was her own nervous wreck. To compose herself, she baked; that is, until she finally realized she'd made three dozen pastries, including blueberry muffins and two batches of cookies. "Hope they're hungry," she said to herself.

After Katherine's secretary called to alert her that they were on their way, she did her own form of deep breathing. Her heart raced and she felt like her whole body was perspiring. She had been up since 6:00 a.m. after a restless sleep. She thought she needed another shower. Still, she looked radiant in a black knit pantsuit with a high neck, white silk blouse. Attached to her jacket was a pearl brooch that Kevin had given her.

The doorbell rang. On each side of the front door, both Stella and Seth took another deep breath. The time had come. After fifty years, they were going to meet again.

Stella had not wanted to cry, but that's exactly what she did. While she couldn't control the tears, she refrained from rushing to hug him for fear it would be too presumptuous. Instead, Seth did that. He walked over to her, looked in her teary eyes and grabbed her tightly, crying himself. Melissa and Katherine couldn't hold back their own tears either. No words were exchanged for almost five minutes.

Finally, Melissa blurted out, "You guys look so much alike!"

"And you're the spitting image of your grandmother," said Katherine.

Stella told Seth how long she had wanted to hug him again, how she cried when, as a newborn, he was taken from her in the hospital.

After a few more minutes, Stella approached Melissa and placed both of her hands on her cheeks. "What a beautiful woman you are! I hope we'll have a lot of time together."

"Don't ask me twice. I want to know everything about you."

"You might be sorry." Stella smiled and winked. "I didn't exactly have a *Leave It to Beaver* life."

"Leave it to who?" asked Melissa with a puzzled expression.

"Oh, I forgot. That was before your time. Let's just say my life was not your typical American dream and apple pie."

"Ah…I get it."

"We have plenty of time to talk. First, let's sit down. I've made fresh coffee. I've also baked my signature pastries. Please don't tell me you're on a diet." Stella didn't consider that they, like her, might be too nervous to eat.

After coffee and pastries were placed on the dining table, everyone helped themselves—and Melissa started asking questions. In fact, she asked four questions before Stella could begin answering one. "Where were you born? Did you go to college? Tell me about Kevin. What happened to him?" She was hardly breathing between questions.

Seth was quiet, staring at his mother and taking in the moment. "Melissa, give her a chance to answer."

"I don't know where to start," said Stella, completely overwhelmed.

"Why did you give Dad up?" asked Melissa. There it was. The hard question. Katherine had expected that to come up later. But twenty-year-olds have a way of cutting to the chase.

"I was a prostitute; Kevin was married," said Stella. She had thought long and hard about how to divulge this truth. But now, facing her kin, the words flowed freely.

Neither Seth nor Melissa expected that answer and their faces showed it. Melissa's eyes opened wide.

Finally, Melissa burst out, "Nooooo! Holy shit! Are you for real?"

"I came from a horrible home and the streets paid well. I worked my way through college laying on my back. Kevin was a client, but we fell in love. I got pregnant early in our relationship and gave your dad up because I didn't want him raised in the life Kevin or I were living. He was back home in South Africa when your dad was born. At first, I didn't tell him about the pregnancy." Stella looked at Seth. "Later, after you, Seth, had already been adopted, I did. Kevin was very disappointed but agreed with my decision. He told me he wished our lives were different and we could have kept you."

"Did he have any other children?" asked Seth.

"No, he was in a pathetic marriage. But let's save that story for another time."

Melissa was silent. Stella, realizing this young lady was out of her league, looked again at Seth. "Kevin and I ended up smuggling millions of dollars' worth of diamonds out of South Africa. After his death in 1990, I was able to convert those diamonds into money for schools and medical clinics for the poor in his homeland. He was murdered for standing up against apartheid. He was a wonderful man who helped me experience real love. We spent some twenty years together, although there were periods of separation when he was overseas. I still miss him.

"I am so sorry, Seth. I didn't feel I could give you a good home. I didn't know how to be a loving mother. Prostitutes don't usually make good soccer moms. Later, I became a Madam and serviced United Nations diplomats. At one time, I had twenty women and two men working for me."

Melissa was still tongue-tied. She looked at her father, who said with a wink, "I bet life would have been interesting if I'd been around."

That broke the ice.

Stella laughed. "You have no idea how interesting! But you were in a better place. Perhaps, had you been born a few years later, things would have been different. Here, try these cinnamon pastries. Kevin taught me how to make these, his grandmother's recipe. I want you to know one more thing. I spent a good deal of time getting young girls, mostly runaways, off the streets and back home or back in school. I rarely hired anyone who was less than thirty, and most were working their way through college."

Seth said, "I won't judge you harshly even if it's hard to understand. I mean, you look like an ex-kindergarten teacher. Forgive me if I seem stunned."

"I did volunteer as a big sister some years back, but I never had a Girl Scout troop."

"How long have you been retired?" Melissa managed to say.

Stella smiled. "A while. I've spent the last few years volunteering for a nonprofit organization that works to curb prostitution and end the sex slave trade. I've helped put more than a few sex traders in jail and reunited many girls with their families. I may have even saved a few lives. For that, I am proud. Now, enough about me. Tell me about you."

Seth and Melissa talked about themselves and the rest of the family. Eventually, the conversation drifted back to Kevin. Stella stared into space intermittently, caressing her brooch as if communicating with Kevin and wishing he was there.

Katherine reluctantly had to take her leave. Most likely, she had determined, they wouldn't abandon Stella because of her past. Their body language, as well as the enthusiastic questions, conveyed their acceptance.

"Before you go, Katherine, I want Seth and Melissa to know something about you." Pointing to Katherine, Stella said, "This lady is the one responsible for this reunion. She gave me the courage to share my story and stood by me every step of the way. Without her, I would've gone to my grave keeping this secret."

Katherine smiled, whispered a thank you, and blew a kiss as she walked out the door. Later, she made a note to herself to thank Gultowski and Walker, who had become empathetic to Stella as their understanding of her story deepened. They deserved to know of Stella and Seth's touching reunion.

CHAPTER 46

Stella's new family spent the weekend getting to know each other, often talking nonstop. Stella still needed periods of rest, but her body cooperated during the emotional reunion weekend. She felt revitalized, even as she shared her diamond smuggling exploits and what she knew of Kevin's murder, which was not much. She found it difficult to say the words *torture* and *bludgeon*.

"Do you know where he's buried?" the ever-inquisitive Melissa tentatively inquired.

"No, I do not. I doubt his family would have paid for a proper burial, perhaps justifying among themselves that the 'shame' he brought to the Finchley name did not warrant a place in the family plot. Then again, perhaps they did do a proper burial to shift focus away from the murder and portray themselves as grieving family. Who knows?"

"Are there people alive who still remember the good he did?" asked Melissa while staring at the photos Stella had placed on an end table.

"I don't know. I've thought about those things but never searched for the answers. I had to keep undercover myself, you know." Stella was shaking slightly from the onslaught of feelings that were being rekindled.

"Could I make some inquiries?" asked Melissa.

Seth interrupted, "Melissa, that might be going too far. You're talking about a man that was murdered. Maybe Stella wants to put this to rest."

Stella admired Melissa's gumption. Even though they had only met, she could see herself in this child. "Actually, I don't see why not. You can start by contacting the Anglican Church where Reverend Timothy Martin was a minister. While he died a while back, somebody there might have some answers."

"Got any addresses?"

"I do."

"Melissa?!" Seth said firmly.

"Dad, I'm just going to write a letter and ask where he's buried. What can that hurt?" Seth knew better than to argue, sensing that she was going to do it with or without his permission. Stella retrieved the notebook she'd given to the FBI, which they had returned.

Gripping the notebook tightly, Stella spoke softly but resolutely. "Melissa. Seth. Listen to me. I am an old woman who has just met my biological family. The last thing I want to do is cause friction. That would break my heart. Wherever Kevin's grave is, I know he's at peace. He died heroically for what he believed in. I honor him by telling his story."

"Stella, you said they wanted to name schools and clinics after him. Is it too late to honor him in that way? Shouldn't people know who he was?"

Even Stella was floored—by a precocious twenty-year-old no less. For the first time in years, she thought of the possibilities. "My dear child, let's take this one step at a time. Maybe first write a letter and see what information we can learn. Seth, would that be okay with you?"

"I suppose. Besides, I know better than to argue with one determined woman, let alone two. And the more I think about it—I mean, he was my biological father. I'd like to know more about him too."

By Sunday noon, Seth and Melissa reluctantly took leave of Stella, with promises to visit again soon. The next day, from her college campus, Melissa sent a letter to the current rector of the late Timothy Martin's church. The first line was, "My grandfather was Kevin Finchley."

❦ ❦ ❦

Several days later, Katherine looked up from her desk to see Stella standing in her doorway. "To what do I owe this visit?"

"You always visit me, and I wanted to see where you live in the daytime."

"Well, have a seat, although I have to be somewhere in fifteen minutes."

"You can bring it in now," Stella shouted to Hal, who appeared carrying a rather large package.

"I did this for you and all you've done for me. A token of my appreciation."

"Stella, you didn't have to, but how nice." Katherine carefully opened the brown wrapping and pulled out an original watercolor of the Oak Place gardens, with two buildings in the background. "Oh, is this special!" The two-by-two-foot painting was beautifully done in intricate detail. The Oak Place rose garden was center stage, with hollyhocks and oriental lilies almost dancing behind them.

"I wanted it to show *life*. Even old people have new beginnings."

"I will treasure this and start by finding a place for it in this office. What a great gift. Thank you, Stella," said Katherine as she walked over to hug her.

Still embracing tightly, Stella said, "I'm so grateful for the day I met you." After she sat down again, she said, "You know, Katherine, Melissa will be going home to D.C. for a break, and since the family will all be together, they've invited me to spend a few days with them. I'm flying out tomorrow."

Katherine's face was beaming. "Who would've thought all this would happen because of a visit from the FBI?"

"Life is good. Too bad Kevin couldn't witness this. Well, I know you have somewhere to go, and I have to buy some gifts for the family. By the way, I've had the photo of Kevin and me copied and framed for Seth. You know, the one of us in front of the marquis? You don't think it's too premature, do you?"

"Not in the least."

"By the way, Melissa says she has a surprise for me. It seems too early for her to hear back from South Africa. But you never know. She was going to send her letter certified, special delivery. They might just view it as a priority since they owe Kevin so much. Maybe they called her?"

CHAPTER 47

Shirlee, Jeff, and Katherine sat in a booth at a neighborhood Italian restaurant. Shirlee greeted Katherine enthusiastically. "Hi, Grandmom!"

"Still getting used to that title. And I love it. Our little Edith is a week old today. Jill is going to be a super-great mother, although she's struggling a bit with breastfeeding."

Katherine and Peter had been called to the hospital late at night and got to hold their granddaughter when she was just an hour old. They were overwhelmed with joy. Katherine, pained at having to fly to Chicago in the morning, whispered to her granddaughter that she would be a big part of her life. Shirlee and Jeff visited within hours after Jill and the baby went home.

After some chit-chat, Shirlee, Jeff, and Katherine got down to business, beginning with Katherine saying, "I think we should do some long-term planning as to our futures at Oak Place. You both know my initial ideas about starting a more formal professional educational/consulting center. I don't know about you, but I view it as my transition from a demanding administrator role to a more reasonable schedule involving minimal time in airports. Instead, people will come to us."

"When do you see this happening?" asked Shirlee.

"For me, soon. Let's face it, Shirlee. We're not getting any younger. And while I by no means want to retire to some Sun City shuffleboard community, I do want to pursue other options before I end up in a rocking chair and forget what day it is. Consider it an encore career, in addition to my role as active grandmother, of course."

Shirlee smiled. "Old sages passing on their legacy. Is it really our turn?"

"I can picture this," said Jeff. "Besides, like you, I'm getting tired of trekking all over the U.S. I want to step off the lecture circuit.

While it's nice being recognized, it's time for the younger generation to deal with the hassles of airport terminals. Besides, on my last flight, there was a screaming baby and a semi-obnoxious mother. My toleration from bygone years has diminished. That sort of put the last nail in my road-show coffin."

"I don't know," said Shirlee. "I'm torn. My energy seems to be shifting quickly from career to extended vacations with my very passionate boyfriend. Europe was so nice. Now, David wants to cruise the Greek Islands."

"Shirlee, last time I was on a boat with you, you barfed the whole time."

"Girlfriend, I'm not talking about a small boat. More *Love Boat* size. Anyway, this professional educational center idea is intriguing, and I'd like to consider being part of it, at least for a while. I have a legacy to pass on too."

"You absolutely do!"

They talked for two hours, hashing through ideas, generating questions, strategizing the plan they would present to the board of directors. Basically, within months, they decided they would firm up their replacements. Within the year, they would begin retiring from their present positions, Shirlee first. The day-to-day running of Oak Place would be in the hands of their replacements, and they would start the professional consultation center, all working part-time, with flexible hours and extended time off.

Shirlee looked at her watch. "Oh dear! I have a class in half an hour. Must run. Talk again soon." She exited hastily.

Jeff and Katherine sat sipping decaf and thinking about their preparations. "Katherine, are you really ready to do this?"

"Yes, I am," said Katherine, rather surprised at the question. "Why do you ask? Do I sound unsure?"

"Not really. Just checking. Huge step for all of us. Quite frankly, I'm a bit scared. We've been through a lot together. Now, here we are talking about our final career curtain call."

"We've known each other most of our lives. And most of that has been pleasantly challenging. We did some great things and are passing on a wonderful legacy. We made it through the storms."

"Yeah," said Jeff. "Even a hurricane, if you recall."

"Oh, I recall. God, would we have fucked up if we had succumbed." Katherine hadn't told Jeff about Peter's suspicions. But she meant what she said. Her feelings for Jeff had subsided over the years, and the daydreams of long ago had ceased. Instead, her feelings for Peter had grown. She was married to a wonderful man. She didn't have to force her love for him. They had a rock-solid union.

"Seems like eons ago."

"At least decades."

"Did you ever tell Peter?"

Katherine hesitated. "Actually, he confronted me not too long ago. Said he had had suspicions. Wanted me to tell the truth about what happened, which I did. It was painful. I had no clue he suspected something."

"I'm sorry, Katherine."

"Amy? Did she know?" asked Katherine.

"I never told her and she never said anything." Jeff looked into Katherine's eyes, "I'm so glad we resolved this and neither of us had to leave Oak Place."

"Me too. When Peter told me he suspected, I didn't realize how very close you and I had come to ruining our lives and the lives of those around us."

"And look what we have instead. Over these many years of trials and tribulations, you've been a fabulous support to me and my family. I consider you one of the dearest friends I've ever had."

"And I feel the same about you." Just then, one of Jeff's friends came over to the table to tell him about an upcoming event. Katherine barely listened, instead pretending to check her cellphone while deep in thought, again thinking back to that troubled time.

Katherine and Peter had had more conversations about the affair that never was. Katherine had leveled with him. "I gave all my energy to Oak Place and got lazy with our marriage. Therapy helped me find balance." Peter had even shared his own feelings of once yearning for another woman at a time when Katherine was working killer hours. He told Katherine those feelings had dissipated rather quickly after he got to know her, saying, "She was really dysfunctional."

"Katherine, where are you?" asked Jeff, interrupting her thoughts. "I have something else to tell you." After a long pause, he said, "Ah, where should I start?"

"Just spit it out. Is something wrong?"

"Jesus, it's not that monumental! Remember that man, Paul, that I've talked with you about?" Katherine nodded.

"Well, over the last few months, we've developed a wonderfully close friendship."

"The sociology professor?"

"Yeah, him. His husband, Keith, died of cancer about two years ago. They had two sons, each by surrogate, who are now grown with their own families."

"You met him through Amy, right?"

"Keith had helped Amy with set designs in several productions, and the four of us socialized on a few occasions. Paul called a while back to see how I was doing after Amy died. Many talks later, we had lunch, then dinner. Lately we're spending a lot of time together. Katherine, his friendship means so much to me. We can talk for hours. He's filled a void in my life that I didn't even know I had."

Katherine smiled, sincerely happy for Jeff. "Nice to hear that. I remember you talking about him." She gave him an inquisitive look. "Ah, ah, is there more? Is there something you're not telling me?"

"Not really," replied Jeff, knowing what she meant. "Just a nice friendship so far. We're talking about traveling together. He also has two grandchildren about the same ages as mine. We've thought about packing them in a van and going camping."

Katherine didn't press the "so far" part. Certainly, she wouldn't be surprised if he were bisexual. She had thought about it before, especially when he transformed to Jessica and played her flawlessly. She knew the vast majority of drag queens were gay, but some were straight, even preforming on RuPaul's *Drag Show*. She remembered asking if Jessica might try out for the show, but she refused, not wanting to call attention to herself or Oak Place. Besides, it was just too much work.

"We're two widowed guys who've found solace in each other. We have a lot in common. I've had guy friends over the years, mostly when I was younger. During my career, it was all work, marriage, and parenting. No time for guy buddies. This one has reminded me how meaningful they can be. We've both been around the block, so to speak. Our life experiences have drawn us together."

"You know, it does seem like women develop close friendships with other women more often than men. Like my friendship with Shirlee."

"You're so right, and I've always admired your friendship with Shirlee. One of the many ways you've been a role model for me. Paul and I are both active and engaged in life, but we still go home at night to loneliness. He and I have talked about that."

"In fact, one of our recent conversations was about whether I should retire Jessica. She's an old lady. I've been mulling it over for some time now."

"You're not going to subject Jessica to age discrimination, are you?"

"No, no, no. I would never do that! But Jessica is tired. She has the right to retire, too."

"Another loss!" Katherine was upset. Jessica had been a part of her life for over thirty years. "I'll miss her. She made me appreciate being a woman."

"Did she really?"

"Oh, yeah. Really. I mean it. She loved her body and being a feminine feminist. She was proud of that. Made me proud of it, too."

"Thanks for sharing that. It'll make a great epitaph: *Jessica: drag queen feminist exemplar.*" They both laughed, then walked back to Oak Place arm in arm, confident and ready to tackle the coming transitions.

CHAPTER 48

During the first months after Stella met Seth and his family, they took turns visiting. Stella often took the short, direct flight from LaGuardia to the Noland's D.C. home, not far from Reagan Airport. Seth's wife, Annie, an English professor, became totally enamored with Stella, fascinated by her gutsy courage.

Family gatherings tended to be centered in the kitchen, with lots of talking while chopping, dicing, or creating sauces and dressings. When Stella needed to sit, she moseyed from the center island, the nucleus of activity, to a nearby chair.

She'd finally gotten to meet Seth's youngest child, Gwen, a junior in high school. At first, Gwen was guarded around Stella, not in a rejecting way, just not quite sure what to make of her. Having a new grandmother was unnerving enough. But a prostitute grandmother was quite remarkable, and Gwen found it difficult to make sense of her feelings about this. Gradually, as she witnessed her mom, dad, and Melissa—when she was home from college—interact with Stella, she relaxed more, although unlike Melissa, it took her a long time to call Stella Grandma. Stella didn't mind. She was still trying to get used to being a mom, let alone a grandmother.

These positive interactions had continued for several months until Seth and his family sat Stella down and asked her to move in with them. "We've known you only a short time, but your impact on us has been profound," Seth had said. "You've changed my life and that of my family. As much as we talk, we've only scratched the surface. Seeing you every few weeks isn't enough. We want you here. I regret that I didn't try to find you sooner. I don't want to regret that I didn't get to know you better. My daughters and wife have come to love you, as have I. We want you to be a permanent part of our lives."

Thoroughly touched, Stella felt she had a family for the first time in her life; a normal one far removed from the abuse she had known as a child and the unconventional life that followed. She was so happy she had a son who accepted her and showed his love for her in so many ways.

But she was hesitant to become a part of their household, which would mean giving up her cherished independence. "I *am* old," she said to Seth. "My body is betraying me. And perhaps, sooner rather than later, I'll develop physical demands like having to have my ass wiped. I'm not sure I want that type of relationship with you. At the same time, I do want to be geographically closer. My world was getting smaller, but you've changed that. People often take their families for granted. Not me. Finding you has been the highest point of my life, a sacred moment. You and your family—my family—are my priority until I die."

Washington, D.C. is an expensive place to live and Seth's house, while comfortable, was small, with just three bedrooms. But it had one big positive: a double-wide attached garage, the receptacle of life's memorabilia and castaways that had not yet made it to the dump or been donated to charity. No cars had ever graced its interior.

For a small portion of Stella's still substantial nest egg, they could convert the garage into a large sleeping and sitting area, along with a bathroom. "If I do this, I want you to hire someone to care for me when the time comes. I will not go down being a burden. Promise me that semblance of dignity. Besides, I have the money to pay for it while still leaving you a nice inheritance."

Seth promised, realizing he agreed with her. Annie's aging parents had needed much caregiving as they succumbed to frailty and serious chronic disease, including her father's Alzheimer's disease. The responsibility had taken a toll on the family, one they accepted readily, but not without stress.

And so it was that Stella and her aged cat, Shay, moved to D.C. to live out her life in the loving arms of her family. When Melissa was home from college, they talked endlessly; Melissa never beating around the bush. "I can't even begin to imagine what it felt like to be sexually abused as a child." As difficult as it was to talk about, Stella spoke honestly, without editing, about the physical and emotional pain.

Melissa was full of questions. "How scared were you when you smuggled all those diamonds? How many men did you sleep with? Was Kevin really the only man you ever loved? Did therapy really save your life? I think I want to be a psychologist." The questions never stopped.

Various family members, together and separately, escorted Stella to lunch in a variety of local restaurants, often talking nonstop. They took Stella to the theater and the opera. Stella bought everyone front row center seats to King Lear.

After turning eighty-five, Stella's health declined, necessitating the hiring of caregivers. She relied heavily on her walker and assistance in slowly shuffling to the bathroom or around the house. Soon, she needed help bathing, dressing, and fixing lunch when everyone was at work during the week. Plus, Seth didn't want to leave her alone.

Despite physical limitations, Stella never lost her cognition. Therefore, she and the family used it to their advantage. They knew there was no time to waste and were learning more about each other in a few months than most families do in a lifetime.

Knowing Stella had no boundaries, Seth asked, "What was a day like in your childhood?"

Stella was brutally honest. "Fingers up my vagina. Belts stinging across my butt and leaving welts. Forever being told I was worthless. Please, tell me about your childhood so I know I did the right thing for you." Their conversations brought tears, laughter, and lots of talk about Kevin. Stella really wanted his legacy told.

Stella rarely left anything out, and Melissa took notes and videotaped her stories. Stella wanted to tell the whole truth about her childhood and visits home, her favored aunt and uncle, details of being on the streets, including the dangers. "In the beginning, I slept with many a man who carried a gun, the significance of which affected me on a very personal level, prompting me to be cautious and compliant, so as not to risk being killed. I was always relieved that nobody knew where I lived. My apartment was my safe house."

One time, after being threatened with a gun, she grabbed her clothes while the man was in the bathroom and made her escape—naked. Running down the stairs, she entered the street partially dressed. He fired at her from a third-floor window but missed. "I ran for cover, while trying to get dressed. I knew he was too drunk to follow me." The gripping details of her life on the street were unquestionably an educational experience for her new family.

"Tell me more about how you helped prostitutes," Melissa said.

"Some of those girls were so scared; many were still children. When I approached them, I knew a pimp might be watching, especially if they kept looking over their shoulder while we talked. I pretended to want a lesbian encounter and asked if they'd like to accompany me back to my hotel. Never theirs, of course, for safety reasons. When we were safe in a hotel, we talked. I paid their fee and told them how they could get off the streets, where to get help, medical treatment, counseling, safe shelter.

"Some, I never saw again. With others, I had two or three encounters. I became close to female counselors from a prostitute rescue organization that worked with the police. When we discovered the name of a pimp, the cops would initiate an undercover sting, which frequently led to an arrest.

"One pimp in particular was horribly brutal and cruel. One of his girls was twelve years old. I rescued her from the streets the first night I encountered her. Within a week, she was in a foster home. The pimp went to jail, but not for long. They never do. And unfortunately, there were always new pimps to take their place, as well as new girls. There's a lot of sadness on the streets. It's pathetic."

❧ ❧ ❧

S tella was most happy when she shared details about Kevin and her life with him. "He loved to read, and we often read the same books so we could discuss them." Stella also spoke about their vacations—from romantic dinners in Paris to remote cabins in the mountains—where they hiked and cooked and laughed. She didn't have to keep telling her new family how much she had loved Kevin. It was plain to see.

"Kevin regularly kissed a scar on my shoulder that was made when my father pushed me onto the hot engine of a lawnmower, puncturing and burning my flesh. 'This scar,' he said, 'is the badge of your courage and what it helped you become.'"

Melissa, who sometimes had trouble hearing her stories, began to cry. "How could he do that to you?" Stella pulled her to her chest, rubbing her back. "You know, both my therapist and Kevin told me all the time that I was a worthwhile person. Eventually I believed them."

When she described in detail her experiences as a smuggler, Seth and the family gripped their chairs. While they already knew the positive ending, it still caused anxiety, like watching a true-story movie with a familiar end that nevertheless leaves you on the edge of your seat. Stella was the only one who could tongue tie the verbose Melissa, leaving her speechless, mouth open.

※ ※ ※

O ne Saturday after Melissa had gone back to college, Stella didn't come out of her room for family breakfast. Seth knocked on her door but got no response. As if fearing what he would find, he was already breathing rapidly when he entered and saw Stella lying peacefully in her bed, dead, rigor mortis setting in, her body already cold. "Oh, Stella! Mom!" he cried as he grabbed her stiff hand, fell to his knees and broke down. Annie and Gwen rushed in and hugged him, rubbing his neck and back. Nobody said a word for almost a half hour. Then, spontaneously, all of them started talking about what it meant to them that Stella had become part of their lives.

"Nooo!" cried Melissa when her father called her. "It's too soon. Are you sure? Call an ambulance! Maybe she's just in a deep sleep."

"No, honey. She's gone, but she looks so peaceful, almost like she's smiling."

"I'm coming home! Don't move her! Please, Dad. I need to see her one more time."

Seth complied. A few hours later, after catching the next flight home, Melissa, consumed with grief, hugged Stella tightly and thanked her once again. Removing her body was heartbreaking for everyone, including Gwen.

Later, Seth called Katherine, at first composed but within seconds unable to talk. "I am eternally grateful for the opportunity to know this remarkable woman and her love story with my dad," he managed to say through tears. "What a gift I've been given."

"What a gift she gave us all," said Katherine, starting to cry herself. "This is one sad day."

"You know, Katherine, most people only get one mother. I got two, different as night and day, both fantastic."

Katherine, though not surprised at Stella's passing, was grief stricken. "I was drawn to her almost immediately. I've encountered a lot of interesting characters in my life, but she tops the list. What a privilege to have known her! I mourn her loss, but I'm comforted knowing we all found each other."

"Since all her friends live in New York," said Seth, "would it be okay if we have a small memorial service at Oak Place? My whole family wants to participate in her eulogy. I'd like to ask you to speak as well."

"I'd be honored."

"One more thing. Along with taking care of my family financially, Stella left Oak Place quite a bit of money as well."

Katherine didn't ask the amount. "How kind and generous."

After she hung up the phone, Katherine smiled and stared at the painting Stella had given her, now hanging prominently in her office. As she remembered the smell of pastry that Stella had so lovingly made, she was calm even as she cried. Like Seth, Katherine felt that knowing Stella had been an honor.

Katherine took a walk through the neighborhood, tears streaming down over the smile on her face. She knew Stella's life had ended in happiness. She had lived a full life, her death was peaceful, she had been surrounded with love and passed on a meaningful legacy. What a great way to die.

❧ ❧ ❧

As if on a mission, Melissa had located, through correspondence with the Anglican Church of Reverend Martin, Kevin Finchley's grave in an obscure cemetery. It was unmarked save a small stone with the number H 67892, but it was registered and verified. Then Seth, like his mother, used his chutzpah to convince the South African authorities that he was Finchley's biological son, producing the original birth certificate, now amended and certified, that Stella Cordrey and Kevin Finchley were his mother and father. South African officials didn't ask—nor did Seth volunteer—anything about his adoption. Except for a couple of nieces and nephews, Finchley's entire immediate family, including his ex-wife, were deceased.

With permission from authorities, Annie and Seth flew to South Africa, exhumed the body, verified the DNA, had him cremated, spread some of his ashes at the grave of Timothy Martin and brought the rest back home. In an act Seth knew would have put a smile on Stella's face, he combined their ashes in a beautiful urn, which he meant to bury, but still rests on his fireplace mantle next to the photo of them hugging at the marquee. On a small plaque firmly attached to the urn is the paraphrase of a famous Shakespeare line: *A man and a woman such as these will never walk this way again.*

WINTER 2020

—

CHAPTER 49

Katherine's office echoed from the emptiness. The last of the pictures and curtains had been taken down, the warmth disappearing like a flickering fire. "Thirty-plus years," she whispered to herself. While confident about her decision to retire and looking forward to a more relaxed life, her stomach still churned when thinking about the magnitude of this transition. Yes, she was tired and yearned for more time with her grandchild. But this was the end of an era—her end to her era. She knew that multitudes of older people had faced this at the pinnacle of their careers, and stepped aside to let the next generation take their place.

She recalled when her daughter, Jill, went to college. Katherine remembered the questions she asked herself. Had she taught Jill everything she needed to know? Did she know not to wash her jeans with bleach?

Today, she sensed that feeling of déjà vu. Would her replacements know what to do? Were they prepared to make the hard decisions? Would they call her if they needed help? They said they would, but would they? She knew she had to let these ruminations go.

Shirlee and Jeff were going through the same process. Jeff rebelled against the stereotype of retirement parties, where the retiree was presented with a gold watch and endless streams of platitudes. Shirlee, on the other hand, loved it—at first. There were parties by staff in all the buildings, parties hosted by residents in the senior living complex, parties by the board of directors. Eventually, all of them—Katherine, Jeff, and Shirlee—tired from the sheer number of events and gifts bestowed upon them. There were engraved thank you plaques, most of which were destined for a back closet with all the other plaques received over the decades.

But their most significant gift was the substantial donation given to them by the Oak Place Foundation to fund the new Professional Consulting Center. They all felt they were retiring to something not from something, a meaningful distinction for Katherine. It would assure the spread of her philosophy before she retired totally; *perhaps after I reach 90,* she thought.

Shirlee didn't last long in her encore career. David had become somewhat frail, plagued by arthritis and intermittent back pain. He wanted to travel before his body's betrayal left him homebound. Shirlee, now in her seventies, wanted to see Kenya, her ancestors' homeland. Her desire to see the successful start of the center was lukewarm. "I just don't have the motivation," she said. "Better move on without me. I don't want to drag you down. I'll help where I can."

David and Shirlee had discussed marriage and rejected it. Their love didn't need a formal sacrament, even though David did buy a beautiful ring for Shirlee's wedding finger. After Shirlee and David moved in together at Oak Place Senior Housing, she helped out much more than Katherine expected, except when travelling or staying at their spacious lake house in Pennsylvania, just across the water from Katherine and Peter's A-frame.

Jeff and Paul continued their now intimate relationship, which included taking advantage of a rare opportunity to buy a duplex near Oak Place, where they each had their own townhouse. They modified the two living spaces by installing an adjoining door between their living rooms and joining the two kitchens into one. Paul's half was professorial, crowded with books and a mahogany rolltop desk. Jeff's was minimalist, except for walls sporting poster size artwork that included a modern, cubist style oil of a performing Jessica. Both men prominently displayed photos of their families and departed spouses.

Jeff spent a fair amount of time at Oak Place consulting in the new center, as well as teaching rotating residents. Paul became a teacher in the Lifelong Learning Center. With a good supply of grandkids from both their families, they continued as doting grandfathers, taking their budding teenagers on trips around the globe.

Jessica performed one more time at Oak Place before Jeff donated all her clothes and jewels to a university theater department, most to be auctioned at a fundraiser. Paul had helped him pack up the possessions of Jessica's life. When the van pulled away with the treasured memorabilia, their arms were tightly wrapped around each other with Jeff's head resting on Paul's shoulder.

Peter began preparing for his retirement, which included a year's sabbatical. Katherine and Peter wanted to spend as much time as they could with their new granddaughter, so they volunteered to babysit twice weekly when Jill went back to work.

Shirlee, Jeff, and Katherine socialized regularly, although their partners allowed only thirty minutes of reminiscing about Oak Place. They complied—sometimes.

⁊⁙ ⁊⁙ ⁊⁙

In a deeply reflective mood, Katherine looked around her office one last time.

Places such as Oak Place, hubs for older persons, might be progressive and liberating, but they're still filled with torturous times as residents die, sometimes in quick succession. Katherine had experienced all the pain and suffering, sitting through hundreds, if not thousands of funerals, some crowded to the rafters, some with very few in attendance.

Some funerals left her crying even if she hadn't known the deceased. Others left her cold because the eulogies failed to capture the spirit and essence of a life; a life Katherine knew deserved a better tribute. She had always hoped that the stories of people's lives, lives such as Stella's or Hal's, could be told and passed on before the casket silenced their voice and dirt covered the grave.

However, amid the sadness, she had also witnessed the upside of aging, which often brought unforeseen joy to the most wrinkled, hunched bodies. Many older people knew that their limitations couldn't erase a lifetime of accumulated wisdom. While death was in the neighborhood of their lives, many were calm and accepting. They pulled their families and friends closer, relishing every moment. They touched more, hugged tighter, embraced longer. If they had a partner, they often made love with their clothes on.

Some wrote their stories or morality tales, cautioning the next generations to not sweat the trivial. They were content if their children were mostly happy, as well as tax paying citizens. Long gone were the bragging platitudes: "Johnny is a lawyer" or "Susie went to Yale." Most no longer kept skeletons in the closet: "My son Harry lost his battle with drugs in 1989" or "I married four times because I was so insecure" or "I regret I didn't follow my dream." The more they talked with each other, the more secrets were revealed. They often found sincere support, ultimately discovering that their life's traumas were not necessarily unique.

They didn't want to die, but most were prepared, complete with funeral planning, advance directives, and prewritten obituaries. They wanted to die in their beds, not an intensive care unit tethered to wires and tubes that might inflate lungs but ravage their dignity. They gently embraced the gifts of each day and were at peace, accepting that the world would go on without them.

Katherine retired knowing that despite the funerals and sadness, Oak Place was a catalyst for creating joy and happiness, making the aging process more tolerable, if not exciting. Residents of Oak Place lived longer and lived better.

❧ ❧ ❧

On the day of her official retirement, Katherine left her office for the last time as a new crop of young interns made their way into the administrative complex. For the first time, overcome with melancholy and barely able to talk, she walked past them without introducing herself. It had occurred to her that they may never know who she was. She took a last glance at the two-by-three-foot watercolor of Jeff, Shirlee, and herself, relaxed and smiling, and now prominently hanging in the waiting area. "The three musketeers," she whispered as she stared at the painting. It was next to the painting of Oak Place that Stella had given her, filled with thick strokes of colorful flowers in bright sunlight.

Peter had been waiting for Katherine in the courtyard, ready to hug her tight. She was mute, biting her lips. They walked away hand-in-hand as he said, "Okay, let's start a new chapter." Even though she knew there were no guarantees, Katherine hoped it would be a long one.

ACKNOWLEDGEMENTS

This book could not have been written without the support and help of my friends and colleagues. I would like to thank the following for their invaluable input during the development of this book: Joni Schroering, Kara Laine Barrett, Rebecca Emery, therapists Lewis and Adrianne Kadushin, Kat Harting, Bill Godfrey, and the late Marilyn Long and Maureen Dorley Smith. Also, for her insights, I thank Ilyana Kadushin, the founder of Stories Love Music, a groundbreaking music therapy approach for persons with dementia and their caregivers.

A special thanks to South African immigrants, Leslie and Ian Finlayson, for sharing their firsthand experience with apartheid and its far-reaching effects.

I would like to thank Page Austin and Joanne Doyle, who started the Association of Lifelong Learning (ALL) in Salisbury for older persons, which has grown from forty participants to more than six hundred. It was a pleasure working with them on this worthy endeavor and seeing firsthand that older persons never want to stop learning, or that retired professors still love to teach.

I also want to give a huge shoutout to MAC, Maintaining Active Citizens, the area agency on aging in Salisbury, MD, for being the incubator of progressive ideas, and whose employees, including the former executive director, Peggy Bradford, demonstrate daily the mission of aging with dignity.

I want to thank my many students at Salisbury University in my psychology of aging classes, who allowed me to experiment with experiential learning as they teamed up with older persons to help them reflect on their lives. Many of those relationships lasted long after the semesters were over.

Here's to the memory of John Prine and his epic song, "Hello in There" (1971), which talks about old people becoming isolated and lonely. I used to play it for my psychology of aging students before they went out into the field to nursing homes and senior centers.

Special thanks to professional editors Madeleine Adams, Susan Sutphen, and Marybeth Fischer for helping me find the rewards in their challenges.

I am grateful to Robin Matlack for pushing and confronting me on certain areas of the book. She made me think and rethink...and rethink again. And to my husband, Charlie, and son, Neil, for doing the same, as well as elevating my confidence to persevere.

Finally, this book is in memory of Katherine and Maria, my grandmothers, whose lives so enriched my own, even before I knew it. And, to my mother, Norma, the unsung strength of my life.

ABOUT THE AUTHOR

For many years, Carolyn Stegman, R.N., Ed.D. taught the psychology of death, dying, and bereavement and the psychology of aging at Salisbury University, while also serving as a consultant for MAC, the area agency on aging. She currently teaches these subjects for the Association of Lifelong Learning (ALL), a continuing education program for older persons. For seven years, she wrote a column in *The Daily Times* on diversity and interpersonal relations, tackling such issues as racism, sexism, and agism. She was commissioned by Maryland's First Lady to write *Women of Achievement in Maryland History,* largely about older women fighting social injustice. She is author of the novel, *A Gold-Mended Life,* which uses, as a metaphor for life, Kintsugi, the ancient Japanese art of mending broken objects and painting the cracks with gold, thus making them stronger and more beautiful than before they were broken.

www.carolynstegman.com

259

Printed in the USA
CPSIA information can be obtained
at www.ICGtesting.com
LVHW020855180724
785533LV00005B/17

9 781628 064032